A Novel

Anita Stansfield

Covenant

Covenant Comunications, Inc.

Published by Covenant Communications, Inc.
American Fork, Utah

Printed in the United States of America
First Printing: January 1997

01 00 99 98 97 96   10 9 8 7 6 5 4 3 2 1
ISBN 1-57734-060-4

Library of Congress Catalog-in-Publication Data

Stansfield, Anita, 1961-
    A Promise of Forever: a novel/Anita Stansfield.
        p. cm.
ISBN 1-57734-060-4
    I. Title.
PS3569.T33354P7   1997
813' .54--dc21   96-49276
                                                     CIP

The day Ellen died, this story was given to me while I was thinking about where she was.

This book is dedicated to all those who love her.

* * * * * *

And a special thank-you to Jacque Green, Chris Saxey, Tyler Hendricks, Chad Sorenson, Karol Christensen, Jacob Decker, Sally Larsen, and Cathirn Sabin.
And your families.
Your faith didn't go unnoticed.

And, with love, to my mother.

Other books by Anita Stansfield:

First Love and Forever

First Love, Second Chances

Now and Forever

By Love and Grace

Author's Note

Through the course of writing this book, I've been asked many questions. And before *you* begin reading it, I would like to answer them. Yes, this book is about cancer. Yes, I had a close friend who died of cancer in the spring of 1994. (My novel *First Love and Forever* was dedicated to her.) But this book is not about her—it was inspired by her. It is fiction. And, yes, I firmly believe that she was occasionally there to help me from the other side of the veil as I wrote it.

My hope is that through this story, readers will come to learn something very special that I learned—quite unexpectedly—through my opportunity to share death with a friend. I ask that you don't approach this story with the attitude that it will be morbid and depressing because it's about disease and death. But rather, it's a story of healing, of starting over, of love that goes beyond this life. Along with these characters, I pray that you will learn—as I did—of all the good and positive things that can emerge from the struggles of this world. And although *A Promise of Forever* is a little different from my previous novels, I think you will realize before you've finished it that I am, always and forever, *a romantic*. Enjoy!

Anita Stansfield

PROLOGUE

Melissa James shifted gears and pushed her BMW to the speed limit along the coastal highway. The setting sun glared annoyingly over the water and through the car window. She turned the radio up intolerably loud, but even that wouldn't muffle the torment.

"What is wrong with me?" she snarled, slamming a fist against the steering wheel.

There had been a time when Melissa believed her life would fall perfectly into place like a child's jigsaw puzzle. She'd filled a successful mission and was earning a college degree doing something she loved. She'd been in love with a wonderful man who shared her beliefs and wanted to marry her. But she had told Sean O'Hara she couldn't be his wife. To this day, it was difficult for her to understand why. She'd simply believed at the time that it wasn't right, and all her prayers and fasting had only convinced her that they were not meant to be together.

Then a day came when Melissa regretted that decision. She'd earned her degree and left Utah to establish her career here in California, where the pay was better. And she quickly discovered there was no available man who compared to Sean O'Hara. Melissa had returned to Utah when her sister's last baby was born, hoping there might be a chance left for her and Sean. But when he'd introduced her to his fiancée, her plan evaporated. And that was the beginning of her downfall.

Looking back, Melissa was amazed at how easy it had been to just let go of everything she'd been taught. But the fulfillment she'd been hoping to find continued to elude her. The emptiness she'd felt when she realized Sean had found a life without her was now magnified tenfold.

Melissa pulled the car off to the side of the road and parked it. She walked down to the beach and watched in dazed silence as the sun went down in bright hues of orange over the ocean's rippling surface. And then she cried.

Melissa lost track of the time as she wandered the water's edge, carrying her sandals, oblivious to the ocean's waves soaking the hem of her skirt. By the time she returned to the car, she knew there was only one choice before her that would bring any peace at all.

The following Sunday, Melissa went to church for the first time in over a year. It was harder than she expected it to be, but nothing compared to the courage it took to meet with her bishop and get right to the point of her problems. Nevertheless, the relief she felt after that first visit gave her the momentum to keep going. Being excommunicated was the most difficult thing Melissa had ever faced. Still, there was peace in knowing that it was not an end, but a beginning. The months of probation were long and hard, and Melissa often wondered how she would ever make it through. Never in her life had she so deeply appreciated the stability of the gospel, and her understanding of the Savior's love. And while having a sister was something she'd not taken for granted, Melissa knew that without Ilene, she never would have made it. Without their long-distance heart-to-heart talks, she felt certain she would have gone insane.

Just when Melissa began to see the light at the end of the tunnel, Ilene called with news that threw her into a whole new downward spiral. It took Melissa several days to even digest the fact that her sister had cancer. Ilene was the only blood family Melissa had; without her, life would have little value. Which made the old wounds come back to taunt her. What was wrong with her, that she couldn't find a suitable husband and settle down to have a family of her own? When she shared her feelings with the bishop, he offered to give her a blessing. It didn't take away the reality that both she and Ilene had some tough roads ahead, but it did give her the fortitude to believe she could make it.

In the blessing, Melissa was reminded that she and her sister were bound eternally by the sealing of their parents. Whatever came of her sister's trials, they would share joy beyond earthly comprehension. Melissa was also told, much to her surprise, that the Lord had someone special in mind for her—a man who would take her to the temple and be sealed to her for eternity. She was told that the experiences of her life up to that point were necessary to prepare her for the mission she'd been foreordained to serve on this earth. The blessing alluded to a work that needed to be done, but which could not be accomplished if she were bound in marriage at this time. She had a feeling that the work was somehow connected to her sister.

Melissa came away feeling incredible peace. She couldn't envision or comprehend what this great mission might be, but she had learned to rely on the Lord and put faith in his ability to foresee what was best for her. In moments of discouragement, she tried to imagine this Prince Charming that God had set aside for her. Ilene often teased her about it, speculating over the phone about what he might be doing now. As always, Melissa's sister had a way of softening the things that seemed most difficult. But in her heart, she knew that her own trivial preoccupation with finding Mister Right could not begin to compare with what Ilene was facing now.

Trying to be positive and have faith, Melissa kept herself busy doing the things she knew were right, and praying always that Ilene would survive her battle with cancer. Without her sister, finding Mister Right didn't have much appeal.

CHAPTER ONE

Salt Lake City, Utah

Bryson found the lump. How ironic, Ilene thought as she stared at the ceiling of the hospital room, that something so terrifying would be discovered during an intimate moment.

"I'm sure it's nothing to worry about." Ilene had laughed it off, hoping to take away the concern that had permanently creased Bryson's forehead since the discovery. "I've always been healthy and I intend to live a good, long time."

But Ilene knew she hadn't fooled Bryson, any more than she had fooled herself. They were both scared; it was as if some kind of silent warning buzzer had sounded in both their heads.

Ilene prepared herself for every possibility. She had imagined dealing with a benign tumor. It would be removed and she could go on with her life. Then, forcing herself to face up to a worse possibility, she had imagined the doctor's declaration that it was malignant, and she decided she could even live with having a breast removed, if that's what it would take to survive. Chemotherapy began to look appealing, if it would only give her another thirty or forty years with Bryson and the kids. But now, she wondered if even that would be enough.

Bryson held her hand when they received the news. The prognosis was sketchy. They knew some things; others were relative to the individual. But one fact stood strong: Ilene Davis had breast cancer.

They would know more after the mastectomy had been completed.

Bryson held Ilene's hand through one more grueling step as they waited for her to be taken into surgery. Ilene had the ceiling memorized; Bryson's focus shifted back and forth from the window, to the wall, to her hand in his, and occasionally to her face. She desperately wanted him to say something, but felt sure that if she were in his position, she wouldn't know what to say, either.

Ilene found her mind wandering through strange memories and disjointed details of her life. She thought of Bryson, the way he'd looked the first time she saw him. How clear her memory was of the feelings he stirred in her, almost immediately, when she'd first caught sight of him across the church gymnasium. Cheering her sister's team on to victory suddenly paled as she became keenly aware of those startling blue eyes. But even more unsettling was the reality that he was equally aware of her. Looking back, Ilene believed their spirits had connected with a familiarity they had once shared in a former life.

Bryson Davis was all male. He had an eager-to-get-on-with-his-life look that was simply irresistible. And from that first moment, Ilene had been well aware of his attraction to her. After they were married and it was appropriate to discuss such things, he'd often told her of the effect she'd had on him, right from the start. Once he'd asked her to marry him, he'd insisted they make it a short engagement; otherwise, he feared his passion might get the better of him and they'd not make it to the temple. But Bryson had always been a gentleman, and even when he'd talked to his wife of her incredible figure and the way just watching her walk could stir him, he'd always done it with respect.

Ilene realized now that she'd taken a certain amount of pride in the figure she'd been blessed with. Even giving birth five times had not taken away the striking contrast of her proportions. In fact, Bryson had told her more than once that he liked the way childbirth had given her a *voluptuous* look that made her all the more attractive.

But now, Ilene faced the reality of having her figure permanently defiled. She knew Bryson would always love her, lopsided or not, but she couldn't deny that something between them would never be the same. While having a breast removed seemed insignificant in light of the reality that her life might be drastically shortened by this disease, she didn't like the idea of spending her remaining time as something less than the woman he had fallen in love with—the one with the incredible figure he'd been so attracted to.

"I'm scared," she finally managed to admit.

"Everything's going to be fine." Bryson smiled, and she wanted to believe him. But something deep inside told her this was the beginning of the end.

The emotional numbness wore off when they came in to take her to surgery. Ilene clutched Bryson's trembling hand as she was wheeled down long hospital halls.

"Okay," the kind orderly said to Bryson as they paused just outside the elevator, "this is where you kiss her and tell her you'll see her later."

Bryson took hold of her other hand, and they exchanged a painful grip that couldn't begin to express the unspoken emotions. "I love you, Ilene," he said, his bright blue eyes brimming with emotion. "I'll always love you."

Ilene nodded, unable to speak. Bryson quickly pressed his lips over hers. His kiss was meek, but filled with a barely masked desperation. He squeezed her hand once more, and she was wheeled away.

Bryson lost track of time as he stood in the hall, watching the doors through which she'd disappeared. He couldn't recall ever being so frightened in his life. Since the day he'd met Ilene, she had been the calming effect that smoothed over his rough edges. She had always kept his world in control, showing just enough of her human qualities to remind him that if she had flaws, perhaps there was a degree of hope that he could catch up with her one day. Even through five pregnancies, Ilene had managed to maintain a collected dignity that left him in awe.

In that moment, his biggest regret was that he hadn't made a point of telling her such things more often. She had occasionally told him he kept his feelings too much to himself. Sitting alone, he could think of a thousand feelings he wanted to express; but once they were together again, as she emerged from the anesthetic, he had little to say. He couldn't help noticing the way her hospital gown draped over her chest, showing drastic evidence of the breast that had been removed. He held her hand and watched her closely, trying to comprehend her pain. He thought of his own fear, and wondered how it might be to see all of this from her point of view. His emotions hovered so close to the surface that he was afraid to speak beyond trivialities for fear of breaking down. He told himself he needed to be strong—for her.

"Are you in much pain?" he asked.

"It's not as bad as I thought it would be," she said. Then she smiled. "It must have been that blessing you gave me. You told me I would be spared much of the discomfort."

"I was just the mouthpiece, babe." He touched her face.

"Did you call your dad?" she asked, and he looked down guiltily. "Bryson," she gently scolded in a familiar tone. She rarely became sharp or angry. "They need to know. If your father finds out something like this has happened without his knowledge, he'll be furious."

"I know," Bryson admitted. His father's determination had kept the family close in spite of his mother's leaving home when Bryson was sixteen. Marie Davis had run off with another man, leaving nothing behind but a note. A divorce had followed, and she was later excommunicated. To this day, Marie made only an occasional appearance in the family, always with some new boyfriend. Bitter and hard, she made it clear that all of the problems in her life were Robert Davis's fault.

But Bryson's father was a man of integrity. The children knew the truth of it. They had all turned out to be successful in spite of their mother's indiscretions. Bryson's three brothers had scattered from their Montana home and were now across the country in various occupations, raising their families in the Church. His sister, Lynette, lived twenty minutes away in Bountiful. She and her husband, Keith, and their four children often visited for holidays. Lynette and Ilene had become gradually closer through the fifteen years since Ilene had married into the family.

Bryson's father remarried just before Bryson left on his mission. Melinda, or *Lindy* as they'd always called her, was a fine woman who made up for much of Robert's troubled marriage to Marie. She always kept in close touch by phone and letters, and never failed to send a package for Christmas and birthdays.

While Bryson held Ilene's hand and thought about his father, he knew he had to call him. They lived in St. George now, where the southern Utah climate was easier on Robert's arthritis.

"I'll call him as soon as I get home," he said. "I promise."

Ilene smiled faintly. "Did you find out how long Lynette is keeping the kids?"

"She said she'd keep them until you get home and feeling better. She figured you'd miss them by then, but she said to tell you she'd be happy to take them again, any time you need a break."

"She's so sweet." Ilene smiled again, but he could tell the medication was making her drowsy.

Bryson came to his feet and kissed her brow. "I think I'll go and let you rest. I'll be back early tomorrow."

Ilene tried to ignore the tube in her arm as she lifted a hand to his face. "I love you, Bryson."

"I love you, too, babe," he whispered and kissed her quickly on the mouth.

Bryson hated the hollow feel of the house as he walked in and groped for the light switch. He turned up the furnace and wondered if it would snow before Halloween this year. Recalling his promise to Ilene, he went straight to the phone in the dining room and called his father. Lindy answered.

"Hello," was all he said before she recognized his voice.

"Bryson," she said with jubilance, "how are you, dear?"

"I'm okay. How are you?"

"We're doing good. Your father had a little cold last week, but he's feeling better now."

"Well, that's good—that he's feeling better, I mean."

When he said nothing more, Lindy asked, "Did you call for a reason, or just to chat?"

By her tone of voice, he knew that she sensed his mood. "Uh . . . maybe you should put Dad on the other phone. There's something I need to tell you, and I'd rather not say it twice." Lindy sounded concerned as she said, "Okay. I'll get him."

"What's up, son?" Robert's voice boomed through the phone.

"Are you there, Lindy?" Bryson asked.

"I'm here," she replied. "Go ahead."

"Well, I've been meaning to call you, but you know how it goes." He took a deep breath and just said it. "Ilene had surgery today."

"She what?" Robert bellowed. "And you didn't tell us?"

"I'm telling you now, Dad. I'm sorry I didn't call before. I've been a little burned out about the whole thing."

"Well, is she all right?" Lindy asked.

"The surgery went well," he reported.

"What kind of surgery?" Robert asked.

"Well, you see, Dad, that's the hard part. She had a mastectomy." He paused when Lindy gasped. "She has breast cancer."

"Oh, Bryson, *no*," Lindy said. He could tell she was crying.

"Is she going to be all right?" Robert asked soberly.

"I don't know, Dad," Bryson said shakily. "She'll be going through some radiation and chemotherapy. It looks like it's going to be a long haul. But I'm sure we'll manage. You know Ilene; she's strong. And the Relief Society is willing to help a great deal. We just wanted to let you know."

"Is there anything we can do?" Lindy asked.

"Not really," Bryson said, already hating this helplessness that he knew would only get worse.

"We'll be praying for her," Lindy said, "and you."

"That's what we need," he replied.

"If there's anything we can do," Robert insisted, "don't you be afraid to ask. Do you hear?"

"Yes, Dad, I hear you. I'm sure we'll manage."

"Do you need any money?" Robert asked.

"Not at the moment."

"How's your new job going?" Lindy asked.

"It's all right. I'm adjusting, I suppose."

"You sound tired, Bryson," Lindy said as only a mother could. "I'm sure you've had a long day."

"Thank you for calling," Robert said. "We'll check back."

"Thanks, Dad."

Long after he hung up the phone, Bryson stared at it, wishing for the first time in many years that his father wasn't so far away.

Through the following days, Bryson spent every minute he could with Ilene, sitting quietly beside her, wondering what to say. He was beginning to hate the silences between them, and hoped it wasn't somehow a foreboding of difficult times to come.

Before Ilene was released from the hospital, the doctor entered her room with his clipboard to find Ilene sitting on the edge of the bed. Bryson sat in a chair next to her, holding her hand.

"We have the results back," the doctor said solemnly as he pulled up a chair to sit close by. "I thought you should know where you stand before you go home, Mrs. Davis." He paused and looked her straight in the eye. "We were able to remove twenty-five lymph nodes. Of those, eighteen were cancerous."

"What does that mean?" Bryson asked sharply.

Ilene wanted to tell him to be kind. This was not the doctor's fault. But Dr. Sherman seemed to understand. He had been recommended by their family doctor as a compassionate man with much experience in the field.

"What it means, Mr. Davis, is that since Ilene has had her right breast removed, if she undergoes the extensive chemotherapy and radiation we discussed, she may have some quality life left. But there is a high possibility, due to the percentage of cancer found in those lymph nodes, that it will eventually attack other areas of the body. The bottom line is that I can't give you any idea what will happen. The fact that Ilene is a thirty-five-year-old woman with active hormones increases the chance that it will reappear. In this case, the firmest advice I can give you now is to hope for the best."

Bryson rubbed a hand over his face as if he could make sense of what had just been said. "Are you trying to tell us that she's going to die?"

Ilene didn't remember exactly how Dr. Sherman answered that question. But she would never forget the way Bryson's hand began to tremble in hers. He had never been one to show his emotions, and visibly he appeared as numb as she felt. That numbness hovered around them through the drive home—as if not talking about it could keep them from feeling it.

Ilene made a fuss over the roses Bryson had left on the coffee table for her, but he noticed that she was still huddled in her coat after she'd been home twenty minutes.

"Are you cold, honey? Do you want me to turn up the heat?"

"No, I'm fine," she said a bit unnaturally as she lay down carefully on the family room couch.

He wondered if she was feeling self-conscious about the change in her appearance, but he didn't know how to ask. He wanted to ask her if the things Dr. Sherman had said were making her as afraid as he felt. But again, the words just wouldn't come.

"Is there anything I can get you?" he asked gently, feeling somehow useless.

"No, thank you."

"Is there anything you want to talk about?" he prodded. She was usually so talkative, and now her silence left him unnerved.

Ilene looked up at him, and he could see his feelings reflected in her eyes. But she said nothing.

"Oh, your sister called this morning before I left. I told her you'd call when you got home." Ilene's expression brightened eagerly. "Do you want me to dial the number for you, or—"

"No, I'll call her from the bedroom," she said as she came carefully to her feet. "Thank you, anyway."

A while later, Bryson went down the hall for the third time to see if Ilene needed anything. He had assured Sister Broadbent, the Relief Society president, that he would be with her all day and see that she was cared for. He had expected to feel more needed. He stopped once again at the door as he heard Ilene still talking. She had talked and cried with her sister for nearly an hour, when she would hardly say a word to him. He supposed it was one of those woman things, and he knew he wasn't prone to being sensitive and easy to talk to. Still, he couldn't help feeling a twinge of jealousy at the close relationship they shared—especially now.

In Bryson's eyes, Ilene and Melissa were as different as two women could be. There was a vague resemblance in their fine facial features, and they both had brown eyes. But Ilene's hair was dark and curly, and she always wore it down around her shoulders. Melissa's was lighter and straight; Bryson had rarely seen it when it wasn't braided or bound into some configuration. Melissa always seemed too skinny to Bryson, but Ilene had a well-rounded figure. And Ilene was quiet and sweet, while Melissa had a sassy little mouth and didn't hesitate to say exactly what she thought. Bryson marveled that the two of them could be so close. To him, they were as different as night and day.

When Ilene finally got off the phone, Bryson peered carefully into the bedroom. He wondered if she was asleep, but she opened her eyes and reached out a hand toward him. Stepping forward to take it, he realized that he probably needed her a lot more than she needed him. He sat on the edge of the bed, and she reached her left arm around him. She seemed hesitant to even move the right one, and he didn't have to wonder why. He gave her a careful embrace and kissed her gently. "Are you okay?" he asked.

"Physically I feel much better than I expected, but . . ." She looked up at him, and big tears pooled in her brown eyes.

"But?" he prodded.

"I guess it's going to take some getting used to."

Bryson knew what she meant, and was quick to say, "Hey, it doesn't matter, Ilene. It doesn't change who you are inside."

"That's what Melissa said." Ilene tried to smile, but she *felt* changed, and it was more difficult to face up to than she had thought it would be.

Bryson chuckled and touched her chin. "Maybe your sister's not so bad, after all."

"She made me promise to tell you to take good care of me."

"Well, you can assure her that I will do my best." He tried not to sound indignant.

"I already did." Not wanting to bring out the tension that Bryson usually exhibited concerning Melissa, Ilene changed the subject. "Bryson, did you remember that Brandon's birthday is the day after tomorrow, and—"

"Oh, boy." He sounded panicked. "Presents. What should I get for him? Should I—"

"Bryson, his presents are in the bottom of the closet. They're all wrapped."

"Of course," he smiled sheepishly. "You always think of every-thing."

"But you'll need to see that Jessica makes a cake. And let Lynette know they're invited, as usual."

"I will," he said. While Bryson watched Ilene's eyes grow distant, his own mind wandered. He wondered what he would ever do without her. Would he be able to get the birthday gifts and see that the homework got done and keep the house clean? The thought almost made him sick to his stomach—not to mention the loneliness he felt at the thought of living without her.

He was actually relieved when she said, "What do you think about what the doctor said?"

"I think we have to hope for the best," he stated, wondering why he felt like a hypocrite.

"And be prepared for the worst," she added.

"Ilene, there is no reason we have to just accept that this is going to kill you."

Her eyes pierced through him with a gentle intensity he believed he would never forget. She set a hand over her heart and said with conviction, "No reason except this feeling I have inside of me, telling me that this will eventually be the end for me. And I must be prepared; I must prepare my family."

"I'm not giving up that easy," Bryson said with an edge of anger.

"Oh, I'm not giving up without a fight, Bryse. I want to be with you as long as possible. But if it's my time to go, no amount of prayer, or faith, or determination is going to change that." She sighed. "I've done little but think about this since we found the lump, Bryse. I've prayed and wrestled with it. But there comes a point where peace can only be found in submitting to God's will— even if it's not what we want."

While Bryson tried to read the deeper meaning in her words, he felt somehow tempted to scream and throw something.

Ilene sighed again and added, "Better this than some accident. At least we have time to prepare."

Bryson wanted to argue. He wanted to tell her she was crazy. But he had never questioned Ilene's ability to feel the Spirit before, and he couldn't do it now. Worst of all, if he honestly acknowledged his deepest feelings, he had to admit that he felt it, too. He just didn't know how to deal with it.

"Did you tell Melissa how you feel?" he asked.

Ilene sighed and turned her head on the pillow. "No, and I'm not going to. Until it comes back, she doesn't need to be burdened with it. She's dealing with her own trials at the moment. For the most part, I think we should keep it to ourselves and just take it as it comes."

After several minutes of anguished silence, Bryson felt a sudden need to be alone. "Are you hungry?" he asked and she nodded. "I'll see what I can scrape together," he added on his way to the door. "Try to get some rest."

Ilene closed her eyes, wishing she could think of something besides feeling like she was somehow less of a woman, and at the same time knowing she was going to die.

Late afternoon, while Ilene was sleeping, Bryson got up to answer the door. It opened before he got there.

"Is anybody here?" Lindy called as she stuck her head in.

"Well, what a surprise," Bryson said, trying to sound happy. While a part of him wanted to lean on his father, he felt somehow uncomfortable having anyone else around when he still hadn't adjusted to all of this himself.

Nevertheless Bryson hugged his stepmother, then his father. "Dad, don't you know it's October? It's too cold for you to be here."

"I think I'll survive a day or two," Robert chortled and took off his coat.

"Is there a . . . reason you came?" Bryson asked.

"Well, I was about to send off Brandon's birthday package," Lindy said, "when I said to Bob, why don't we just go up there and get in on the party, and then we can see how Ilene is coming along." She handed her coat to Robert, who was hanging his in the entry closet. "How is she, Bryson? Is she asleep?"

"She was last I checked, but it's about time for her medication. Have a seat, and I'll see."

Bryson peeked through the bedroom door to find Ilene pulling on her robe. "Where you going?"

"I'm going to the bathroom, and then I'm going to the front room to visit with your parents. There's no question who that booming voice belongs to." She smiled, and he could see that she was glad they'd come. "I'd know your father's voice anywhere."

"Are you up to it?" he asked.

"I'll be just fine if you'll go get me one of those pills."

Bryson met her with a pill and a glass of water when she came out of the bathroom. She took it and thanked him, then she led the way down the hall.

"There's my princess." Robert stood and took Ilene's face into his hands to kiss her cheek. "How are you doing?"

"I'm better now," she said. "I'm always better when you're around. You know I only married Bryse because you were already taken."

Robert laughed and kissed Ilene again, and Bryson chuckled as he observed them. He'd heard Ilene say that a hundred times, but it never failed to make his father laugh.

"It's my turn, Bob." Lindy nudged him away. "Oh, my sweet Ilene," she said. "I've been just worried sick since Bryson called. Why didn't you tell us sooner?"

Ilene glanced at Bryson, then said gently, "We didn't want you to worry."

They sat down to visit and Ilene stayed close to Bryson, holding his hand. Following the usual trivialities of the trip to Salt Lake City and the weather, Lindy asked Ilene, "So, how is your sister? Is she still working for the same decorating firm in L.A.?"

"Yes, she's enjoying it. I just talked to her today. She seems to be doing well."

"I'm glad to hear it. She's such a sweet girl."

"She hasn't gotten married since last week, has she?" Bryson asked Ilene facetiously. She only glared at him, which made him chuckle.

"Do you hear from your stepmother these days?" Lindy asked Ilene.

"Actually, no. I can't remember the last time we talked."

"Well, I'm sure she's doing fine. How long has it been since you lost your father, dear?"

"Nearly six years now," Ilene stated.

Lindy then went into a story of someone in their ward at home who, like Ilene's father, had died of a stroke. Ilene was relieved to change the subject. Her family background was something she'd never been comfortable with.

Ilene had been fifteen when her mother was killed in a car accident. She had missed a canyon turn and gone into a river. She and

Melissa were the only children, until their father remarried a woman with four kids. Their father was a good man, but he worked long hours and the girls spent most of their lives feeling isolated from the other children. Ilene knew their stepmother cared about them, and she hadn't intended to exclude them. But Ilene really couldn't begrudge it when she believed it was the reason she and Melissa were so close. They'd had to be.

Since their father's death, what little connection they had maintained with their other family simply faded into the background. As Bryson's arm came around her shoulders, she felt sure that one of the many things that had drawn them together was the fact that they had both lived through losing a mother. Something reeled inside of her as she realized that her own children would suffer the same loss.

"How is Jessica adjusting to junior high?" Robert asked, startling Ilene from her thoughts.

"She's doing good," Bryson said.

"How old is she now?" Lindy asked.

"Thirteen," Ilene reported.

"It seems like just last month the two of you were married. And now you've got a teenager."

Ilene met Bryson's eyes and didn't miss the sadness there. She wondered how many more anniversaries they might see together. While Bryson's parents continued asking questions about the children, Ilene felt the sadness escalate inside her. Brandon would be ten this week. Would she live to see him ordained a deacon? Greg was eight, and still such a little boy. He was the one she worried about; he'd been born with a chip on his shoulder, and it seemed that she was the only one who could reach him. Amber had just started kindergarten. She was strong-willed and would likely do well, but she was also very dependent on her mother. And Jamie. Little Jamie, her fifth and last. Would she even remember her mother? The thought broke Ilene's heart, and she wanted to just curl up and cry like a baby.

"Are you all right?" Lindy asked, and Ilene wondered if her distress was so obvious. Before she could answer, Lindy observed, "You're worried about the children." Ilene looked up at Bryson.

"Lindy's always been that way," he said. "I'd swear she could read minds."

"It doesn't take a fortune-teller to see that you're upset, Ilene. And since we were talking about the children, I can only assume that's where your thoughts are."

At this, Ilene pressed her forehead into her hand and cried. Lindy came across the room and sat on the other side of Ilene. "It's all right, dear," she said, urging Ilene's head to her shoulder. "You haven't got a mother of your own to turn to. You just go right ahead and cry."

While Ilene cried, Bryson could feel his father surmising that the situation was worse than he had let on. When she had calmed down and apologized with a sniffle, Robert bellowed, "So, what's the truth of it, Bryson? Cancer is a serious thing. What have the doctors told you?"

Bryson met Ilene's swollen eyes. He didn't want to lie to his father, but he didn't know if he could bring himself to say it out loud. She nodded firmly and said, "They have a right to know. We can't do this alone."

"Know what?" Lindy demanded as it became evident that the situation was serious.

"Well . . ." Bryson began, then he cleared his throat. "You see, if she . . ." He hesitated too long and was relieved when Ilene saved him.

"It *is* serious," she stated. "I don't understand the medical side of it, really, but the odds are against me. If the therapy goes well, I will have some quality life left. But I believe it's only a matter of time before the cancer returns."

Robert stared in disbelief while Lindy cried silent tears. Bryson rubbed his eyes with a thumb and forefinger and choked back the emotion rising in his throat. Ilene erupted with fresh tears and cried on Lindy's shoulder.

"I don't want anyone else to know," Ilene said when she had gained a measure of control. "I don't want to live the rest of my life being treated any differently."

"I understand, dear," Lindy said. "It's between us. But I want you to promise to tell us everything."

"That's right," Robert interjected. "No more of this hearing about something after the fact. You call collect every day if you have to. I want to know what's going on."

Bryson nodded, afraid to speak.

Lynette brought the children home just a few minutes before Ilene's visiting teachers arrived with dinner. Ilene appreciated the way everyone behaved as if everything were completely ordinary. That was the way she wanted it.

Robert and Lindy stayed on the sofa sleeper in the den for three nights. Lindy was great to help around the house while Ilene began to get her strength back. Bryson spent some time with his father, and though nothing specific was said about the situation, he felt somehow better knowing that his father knew.

Brandon's birthday party was a great success, and Robert and Lindy returned to St. George on Sunday. Ilene dreaded Monday, knowing that Bryson would go back to work and she would have to start facing life as a changed woman. But she concentrated on spending time with her children and tried not to think about it.

CHAPTER TWO

Bryson sat at the computer terminal in his box of an office and tried to concentrate. He glanced at the calendar. Two months he'd been working here, and he still felt disoriented. He glanced at the clock. Twenty minutes since he'd called Ilene. He wondered how she was doing and wished he could call her again without sounding like a simpering fool. Ilene had been sleeping when he called; Sister Broadbent was with her and assured him that all was well. But he wanted to hear Ilene's voice, as if every evidence that she was living and breathing was somehow miraculous to him and gave him the strength to keep going.

Reminding himself that he would never get home to her if he didn't get his work done, Bryson took a deep breath and resigned himself to concentrating on the information on the screen. It really wasn't such a bad job, but the bitterness of his reason for being here still lingered like a bad taste in his mouth.

After nearly ten years at a job he enjoyed and was good at, Bryson had been laid off without warning. He'd been told it was a necessary cutback, but others with less experience and integrity had been allowed to remain. After three weeks on unemployment and working for the Church welfare system, Bryson had been hired here. Ilene was ecstatic. He would be closer to home, and though the pay was a little less than before, she was sure they could manage. And the benefits more than made up for it.

Bryson had been less than enthusiastic. The work was not nearly so enjoyable as what he had done before, but he reminded himself that he should be grateful to have a job. And, just as he had done many times before, he wondered why he couldn't have Ilene's faith and positive outlook. She had a way of taking life on with a smile that left him in awe. Even now, recovering from a traumatic surgery, knowing what the future held for her, Ilene had quickly managed to deal with the initial shock. She always found a way to smile or come up with something positive to say.

Bryson jolted himself back to the present once again and forced himself to work. Somehow, his thoughts always ran back to Ilene. Almost compulsively he picked up the phone and dialed home. He was disappointed when Sister Broadbent answered, but he tried not to betray it by his tone. "Hello again. This is Bryson. Is Ilene still sleeping?"

"No," she said kindly, "I'll put her on."

Bryson almost held his breath until he heard her speak. "Hello, my love," she said, and he sighed. Her voice alone rejuvenated him.

"How are you, babe?" he asked.

"Still sore, but I think it's getting a little better. Will you be late?"

"I don't think so. Should I pick up something for dinner, or—"

"No, the Relief Society is bringing in a meal again." She laughed softly. "I told them not to bring anything in tomorrow. We've got enough leftovers to feed the whole street."

Bryson became so caught up in the sound of her voice that he forgot to respond.

"Are you there?" she asked.

"Yes, of course." He chuckled. "I'm sorry, I just . . ." Bryson tried to think of some lame excuse, then remembered his resolution to speak his feelings more. "I was only thinking how good it is to hear your voice. You have a beautiful voice, Ilene."

Following a long pause, she replied with emotion, "I love you, Bryse."

"I love you, too, babe. Hang in there. I'm counting down the hours."

She laughed again. "Stop counting hours and get something done."

"You know me too well," he admitted. "I'll see you later."

"*I'll* count the hours," she replied.

For several minutes after she hung up the phone, Ilene stared at the ceiling and tried to get control of her emotions before Sister Broadbent came back into the room. She sensed Bryson's fear, and it tore at her heart—perhaps more than her own fears.

While a part of her felt somehow grateful to *know* that she was going to die, and have the opportunity to prepare, she couldn't help fearing what it would take to reach that point. Her thoughts were either filled with concern for Bryson and the children, or consumed with the reality of what cancer was going to be like firsthand. And though she was recovering well from the surgery, she could hardly tolerate looking at the way she had changed in the mirror. She didn't even want to think about how Bryson might feel to see her this way.

Still, there was a degree of comfort in the way Bryson had become so attentive. He had always been a good man, and her complaints were few. But she couldn't deny how good it felt to hear him say things that he might normally have kept to himself. She knew that it often took a crisis to provoke people to show their true character, and she was grateful to see the gentle, sensitive side of her husband showing through. She only hoped that when the time came, he would be sensitive to the changes in her femininity. It was something she dreaded facing.

A welcome distraction came when Sister Broadbent brought Jamie into the room, declaring with a smile, "She's nearly ready for her nap, but I thought you might like to read her a story first."

"I would love to." Ilene put her good arm around Jamie as the little girl snuggled close to her on the bed. "Thank you, Helen. You've been such a sweetheart. I don't know where you find the time to help me so much."

"It's no problem for the time being, dear," Helen Broadbent assured her. She was a youngish-looking retired widow who took her calling in the Relief Society very seriously, and at the same time seemed to love it. "Of course, there are many willing to give their time. We're making arrangements for others to come in and help as you need it, rather than taking the little ones elsewhere."

"I do prefer having them with me," Ilene said, trying not to sound sad.

"Well," Helen smiled, "one way or another, we'll see that you have what you need."

"Thank you, again," Ilene said, then Helen left her alone with Jamie. Ilene pushed all her anxiety away and just enjoyed sharing these moments with her baby.

* * * * *

Bryson grabbed a sandwich from the snack bar and stayed through lunch. At four-thirty, he was pleased to realize that he was almost finished and could get home early. He was on the final stretch of the day's obligations when Stanley Mortimer burst into his office and nearly scared him out of his shoes.

"News flash!" Stanley bellowed, then laughed at himself. He rarely entered without proclaiming himself newsworthy. "How's it coming, buddy?" he continued. "Are you feeling better?"

"I'm sorry?" Bryson turned in his chair, disoriented.

"You took some sick leave, I hear." The nasal quality of Stanley's voice seemed more pronounced than usual.

"Oh, I explained all that to George. I assumed he would have told you. I was with my wife." He swallowed hard and found it difficult to say, "She had surgery."

Stanley's eyes softened behind his thick glasses. "Is she all right?"

"Oh, yes," Bryson replied, managing a smile. "She's doing fine."

Bryson was relieved when Stanley didn't question him further. He had no desire for the entire company to know that his wife had cancer.

"Here's that report you asked for," Stanley said as he tossed a folder onto the desk. "And this is something you might want to look over."

Bryson took a large envelope from Stanley. "What is it?"

"It's your insurance policies. The insurance is a benefit that began when you started working here. I'm sure they told you that."

Bryson nodded vaguely. He'd hardly given it a second thought, except when he'd copied the number from a card in his wallet onto the hospital forms when Ilene was admitted.

"Anyway," Stanley went on, "since the insurance company is one of our biggest clients, we get a pretty good deal. They automatically give you maximum benefits. Now that you've worked here sixty days, you have the option to cut back, which could put a little more into your take-home pay. Look it over. There's no hurry."

"Thanks," Bryson said absently, feeling almost scared to even look inside the envelope in his hands.

"See you tomorrow," Stanley said and gave a friendly wave as he backed out the door.

Bryson waved back. As odd as Stanley Mortimer was, he was the only one around here that had much of anything friendly to say.

Glancing at the clock, Bryson tossed the envelope aside and hurried to finish his work. He turned off the computer and quickly straightened his desk, tucking the insurance policies in his briefcase. The briefcase was tossed into the passenger seat of the car just before Bryson turned the key in the ignition. He moved to put the car in reverse, but something compelled him to look in the envelope. Stanley had said he'd been given maximum insurance coverage, but what exactly did that mean? Suddenly Bryson felt desperate to know just how much he was going to be in debt for the medical bills that would be steadily accumulating through the coming months.

He slid the papers out and scanned through them, trying to find the vital information. When he finally found it, he had to read it twice to make sure his eyes weren't deceiving him. He was glad he was alone when an unexpected rush of emotion erupted from his throat. There was no denying the evidence of the blessing lying in his hands. The deductible was practically insignificant. There was a low percentage he'd have to pay on office calls, and an even lower one for hospital care. After a certain point, the insurance covered one hundred percent. The maximum he would have to pay in a year was less than the deductible on the policy he'd had through his previous employment.

As Bryson stopped to ponder the timing of his getting this job, he had to wonder if this was the reason. He'd always paid his tithes and offerings, always believed the Lord would see that their needs were met. Was it possible that God had known this was coming, and Bryson's layoff was the only possible route to get the insurance coverage they needed to avoid becoming financially destitute? He no sooner thought it than a warm rush of assurance encompassed him, and Bryson knew it was true. Fighting back the emotion, he pressed his forehead to the steering wheel and uttered a prayer of gratitude. He asked the Lord's forgiveness for being so negative and bitter about these changes, and resolved to approach his work with a better attitude. Again, he wished he could have Ilene's faith. She was such an example to him.

Bryson returned home to find everything in order, and Ilene sitting up in bed with a book. Sister Broadbent made a gracious exit, and Bryson found a quiet moment with Ilene while the kids were occupied with the television. He told her about the insurance and she responded with a teary smile, saying how blessed she was.

Later that evening, when dinner was cleaned up and the kids were asleep, Bryson explored the insurance papers in more detail. He hadn't thought about life insurance for a long time, and hadn't expected to find a policy included. When he saw the amount of coverage in the event of his wife's death, his stomach knotted up. He knew the money would be a blessing and very much needed when the time came, but the thought of receiving such an enormous amount of money as a compensation for losing Ilene made him sick inside. The reality was too much to bear, even though he was grateful to know he would have sufficient means. Bryson stuffed the envelope in the bottom of a desk drawer and went to bed.

As Ilene convalesced and continually felt better, Bryson could almost make himself believe they didn't have to dread the months of chemotherapy. Two weeks after her surgery, Ilene had the drainage tubes removed by the surgeon. They were then referred to another doctor, who set a date to begin the treatments and told them what to expect.

That same evening, Bryson called the children together and told them exactly what the doctor had said. They would have to work together as a family to help their mother through the ill effects of her treatment cycles, and pray that everything would go well. Nothing was said about the possibility of the cancer coming back sometime in the future. They felt it was best to just take that on when it happened.

Bryson called his father and Lindy that night with the same report. They said they would be coming to visit for a few days between Christmas and New Year's Day.

On a snowy evening in late November, Bryson tucked Jamie into bed and found Ilene in the kitchen, washing the last pan from dinner. He watched her a moment and tried to remember the last time he'd made love to her. It wasn't difficult to recall that it was the night before her surgery.

Quietly he eased behind her and pushed an arm around her waist. She jumped as if she was startled.

"Did I scare you?" he teased.

"I knew you were there," she said tensely.

"I never could sneak up on you," he whispered and pressed a kiss to the side of her neck. "How are you feeling?"

"I'm doing okay," she said tonelessly.

Bryson realized he actually felt afraid to approach her in this way, but something told him it had gone too long already. "I've missed you, honey," he said behind her ear, pulling her closer. "It's been so long. Come to bed with me now."

"Bryson." She eased out of his grasp and tried to move away, but he put both hands on the counter and trapped her between his arms.

"What?" he asked when she said nothing more.

She folded her arms unnaturally over her chest and avoided his eyes. Bryson had gotten used to the way her baggy blouses hung differently. She had a prosthetic that she always wore in public, but rarely at home. It was easy to tell that she was uncomfortable even discussing the change with him, and he had given much thought to it, speculating over her reasons. He could understand how it would be difficult for a woman, and he couldn't say the thought hadn't bothered him to some degree. But when he put everything on a scale, carefully balancing things out in his mind, Bryson knew that he loved Ilene with all his heart and soul. She was still a woman, capable of functioning and feeling, and he wasn't about to do or say anything to encourage the way she was obviously letting the situation get to her.

"What?" he repeated when she wouldn't answer him. Still she said nothing, but he didn't miss the way her chin quivered. "Ilene, listen to me. Is there a reason you don't want me to see you?"

"Isn't it obvious?" she retorted.

"No, it's not," he insisted. "You're still Ilene. I haven't been married to you for fifteen years just because you have a gorgeous figure. What's the big deal?"

"I'm different," she said as the tears began to fall.

"No, *you* are still the same."

"I'm *different*," she repeated more firmly.

Bryson lifted her chin with his finger, forcing her to meet his eyes. "I love you, Ilene. What are you afraid of?"

"You always told me that you loved my figure. That you loved that aspect of our marriage because I was so *voluptuous*." She said the word as if it were suddenly vulgar. "Well," she added, almost in spite, "I'm not voluptuous any more."

Bryson pressed a hand down over her hip. "Yes, you are," he said close to her face. She looked up at him dubiously, certain he could never understand.

"Ilene," he said gently, "I realize that men and women perceive sexual things differently, but in the years we've been married you've taught me a lot about what love is really all about, and I know that sex would be little without it. I love you, and you love me, and I'm not going to waste away the time we have left together quibbling over changes that don't mean a blasted thing in the eternal perspective."

Fresh tears filled Ilene's eyes, and he wondered if he had only made things worse. She hesitated a moment then pushed her arms around him, holding him tighter than she had since the surgery. Bryson took a deep breath of relief and bent to kiss her. His relief deepened when she responded and he could feel her inhibitions dissipating. He was really beginning to enjoy it when he heard a small voice say, "Mommy, I need a drink of water."

Bryson looked down at Amber and shook his head. "I already gave you a drink of water, young lady."

"But I need another one, Dad," she said indignantly.

Bryson got the drink and escorted Amber back to bed. Ilene slipped away, and he feared the mood had been broken. He turned out the lights and locked the doors, then went to the bedroom to find her sitting on the bed, wearing a nightgown that she never wore just to sleep in. He locked the door behind him and resisted the urge to just devour her. He sat on the edge of the bed and took her hand into his. She watched him warily as he reached over to kiss her, meekly at first, then he felt her response and his guard slowly slipped away.

Ilene lay back on the pillow and reached over to turn off the lamp on the bedside table. The room was completely dark. Bryson reached over her and turned it back on. He kissed her again and quickly realized that she had missed this as much as he had. Somewhere in the midst of unbuttoning his shirt, she reached over and turned off the lamp. Bryson took off his shirt and turned the lamp on. Ilene looked frustrated but said nothing. She just turned it off again. Bryson immediately turned it back on. "I get the feeling you want it dark in here," he said.

"Whatever gave you that idea?" she asked lightly, but with something close to fear showing in her eyes.

"Ilene," he leaned onto one elbow and looked down at her, "we have been married fifteen years. We have not made love in the dark for twelve."

"Maybe it's time we did. It might be a nice change."

Bryson felt so frustrated that he was tempted to just stand up and walk away. But he knew he couldn't. Instead, he pulled her into his arms and rolled her to the center of the bed where she couldn't reach the lamp.

"I love you," he muttered close to her face. He kissed her long and hard, then said it again. "I love you, and nothing will ever change that. But I can't prove that to you if you won't let me."

Ilene resigned herself to just facing this and getting it over with, certain that he would somehow do or say something to take back his tender words when he saw what the change was really like. But as their passion evolved, she became so caught up in it that she was hardly aware that the moment she had dreaded for so long had come and gone without event. When she finally allowed herself to completely let go of her pride and fear, she found nothing in her husband's arms but pure love and rejuvenation. She chided herself for allowing this to be put off so long, when already she felt a hope and renewal that she knew would help carry her through what lay ahead.

In the peaceful aftermath, Ilene dreamily opened her eyes and found Bryson gazing at her face, a familiar look of passion and adoration sparkling in his eyes. "You are so beautiful," he said with such sincerity that she wanted to cry. As she laid her head on his shoulder, she felt his fingers gently exploring the scarred area where her breast had once been. She looked up at him in question and saw nothing but acceptance. As he silently persisted, apparently intent on acquainting himself with the change, she could almost believe he had the gift of healing in his touch.

"I love you, Bryson," she said. "I am a very lucky woman."

"Nah," he chuckled and kissed her brow, "I am the lucky one."

Ilene thought of the things she had heard other women talking about at a cancer support group meeting she had attended. It seemed a common problem for husbands to have negative reactions following a mastectomy. Perhaps she had taken their comments to heart and had expected the worst. But as Bryson held her closer and kissed her in a way that confirmed the intimacy they had shared, she realized that she should have known better. Despite the little struggles they'd had in their marriage, she knew she was blessed to have such a husband. What lay ahead would not be easy, but she knew she wouldn't have to face it alone.

Ilene often reminded herself of those feelings when she was enduring her treatments and their horrible side effects. She couldn't recall ever feeling this sick through five pregnancies, and there were moments when she thought that dying instantaneously in an accident would have been much easier. But then she would see Bryson's concern for her, and watch her children going about their everyday lives, and she was grateful for this time with them. She knew that once the therapy was done, she would have opportunities to do things with her family that would make all of this worth it. But in the back of her mind, she knew how it would all end . . . and there were things that needed to be taken care of.

"Bryson," she said one evening after the children had gone to bed. He looked up from checking over Greg's math homework and gave her his attention. "Today I was making a list of some things I want to do before . . ." She hesitated and his eyes went wide.

"Before *what?*" he asked. He was almost sure what she meant, but he couldn't quite believe she would treat it so matter-of-factly. He was appalled when she came right out and said it.

"Before I die." Her voice was quiet. She wouldn't look at him.

"And what makes you so sure you will?" he asked with an edge of anger.

She looked at him then, wondering why he had to be so defiant at times. "I've been praying about this, Bryson, and I know in my heart there are things I need to be taking care of."

Bryson leaned back in his chair, but she hated the way his face became hard, almost cold. "Like what?"

"Well," she replied, feeling suddenly flustered, "there are a lot of things. There are scrapbooks and photo albums that need to be caught up. But I don't feel good much of the time, and it's hard just to keep up with the house."

"If there's anything I can do to help with scrapbooks and photo albums, I would be more than happy to do so," he stated, telling himself maybe this wasn't as ominous as she'd first made it sound. "What else?"

"When I finish the treatments, I want to do things with the children. We've been talking for years about taking them to Disneyland, but we haven't done it. I want to go with them. I want to know if there is any way we can afford it."

"Not without going into debt," he said, turning to look at the wall.

"Well, maybe it's worth it." She took a deep breath and added, "With the life insurance, you should easily be able to take care of any debts."

Bryson turned toward her with a sharp glare. "How did you even know we've got life insurance?"

"I looked at the policies. Is there something wrong with that?"

"That life insurance doesn't mean a blasted thing to me," he snarled.

"It should. If my illness had been diagnosed much sooner, you wouldn't have had it. As it is, you'll be able to cover the expenses, get out of debt, and have some to put away for child care and—"

"I can't believe you're saying this." His eyes hardened further. "Do you possibly think that money could ever make up for losing you?"

"I didn't say it would. But at least the financial needs will be taken care of, Bryson. At least I don't have to wonder how you'll make it in that respect."

"You make it sound as if you're going to die next week."

"Not next week, Bryson." Her voice picked up the desperation she felt. "But maybe next year. If I am around longer than that, great, but I'm not going to throw away the blessing of having a chance to prepare my family for this by living in denial."

Bryson swallowed hard and forced himself to subdue his anger. "We can go to Disneyland, if that's what you want. For whatever reason, a family vacation is long overdue, and I believe we should spend more time with the kids. I don't have a problem with that."

"Good." She sighed and mustered the courage to go on to her next concern. "Now, I need to make a will."

Bryson shook his head and chuckled to keep from shouting. "I can't believe this."

"I also need a living will."

"Ilene! I don't understand why this is so important *now*."

"Well, then let me tell you." She leaned toward him, showing a vehemence that rarely penetrated her affable nature. "I have been doing a little research. Let's just say I wanted to know what to expect from all of this. Breast cancer is highly unpredictable, Bryson. The biggest thing I learned about the cancer itself is that I really can't know what to expect. There have been cases similar to mine where it has come back unexpectedly into a vital organ and killed a woman with very little warning."

Bryson pushed a hand through his hair. His lips tightened and his eyes hardened.

"Now, if I die without a will, it could easily complicate things for you and the children, and I don't want you to be dealing with any more stress than you will already have. It's as simple as that.

"To illustrate my point on a living will, let me propose a little scenario that's been going through my mind. Let's say I've got cancer in one of my vital organs, and it suddenly fails while some sweet woman in the ward is here helping me. She calls 911. The paramedics come, and by law they are obligated to revive me unless I have a living will. They call you from the hospital and you go there to find me hooked to life support, then *you* have to make the decision whether or not to let me die."

Bryson squeezed his eyes shut. Ilene reached across the table to take his hand. "Bryson," she said, her voice softer now, "it's up to the Lord when and how I'm supposed to go. I'm not taking the chance of relegating my life to a maze of medical red tape. And I certainly don't want to see you having to deal with something like that. Chances are it wouldn't happen that way, but I'm not willing to risk it."

Bryson made no response. Ilene finally said, "Talk to me, Bryson. Tell me what you're feeling."

Bryson looked into her eyes and wondered how on earth to tell her that just the thought of her dying made his stomach tighten into painful knots. How could he tell her that he truly believed he could not make it without her? What could he possibly say to make her understand that he knew he could have been a better husband and father all these years, and he didn't know if there was time enough to make it up to her?

"Bryson," she urged when he said nothing.

He cleared his throat and looked at the ceiling. "I don't understand how you can just accept all of this so easily."

"Did I say it was easy?"

"No, but you certainly seem to be accepting it, and I'm not sure if I can."

"I'm not sure we have a choice," she said.

Bryson looked at her hard, then stood up abruptly and headed for the door.

"Where are you going?" she asked.

"For a walk. I need to get out."

Ilene sighed and let him go. She knew her dying would be hardest for Bryson, but in her heart she believed that when it was all over he would be a stronger, better man than he already was.

CHAPTER THREE

Soon after Bryson left for work, Ilene managed to get out of bed. She wondered what it might be like to actually feel energetic. Then she ignored the uneasiness that came with wondering if she would ever feel that way again.

Ilene was grateful that Wendy had offered to take the little ones again. Wendy was so much more than a neighbor and a visiting teacher, and Ilene couldn't deny that her extra efforts were appreciated. She simply felt no motivation to be a good mother on the days when this sick feeling hovered so close. Figuring a long bath might rejuvenate her, she started the water and brushed through her hair. She was dismayed to notice the significant amount of hair appearing in her brush. The last couple of days she had noticed it increasing, and she knew well what was happening. But she hadn't said anything to Bryson or to anyone else, perhaps hoping it wouldn't get any worse.

Lying back in the tub, Ilene let her mind wander through the scenes of the novel she'd just finished reading. She'd never been one to indulge in such things, but she had to admit that now it was a blessing. There were times when she only wanted to escape, because she simply couldn't do anything else.

As the water started to cool, Ilene dipped her head back to wet her hair and lather it. She enjoyed the scent of the shampoo and the realization that no children were banging on the door, demanding her attention. Then she realized that something didn't feel right. An audible cry erupted unintentionally when she looked at her hands and found them full of hair. As she carefully tried to rinse out the shampoo, she could feel hair coming out in handfuls. The bath water became thick with it, and she started to sob. Blinded by the tears, she felt her way to pull the drain stopper. Then she turned on the shower to rinse away the wet hair that clung to every part of her except where it belonged. She tried intermittently to grab handfuls of hair from the bath water as it drained, trying to keep it from clogging the pipes, but much of it stuck to the sides of the tub.

When she was finally rinsed off, Ilene sat on the edge of the tub and rubbed a trembling hand over the top of her head. She could only feel scattered tufts of hair remaining, and didn't have the courage to even look in the mirror. Instead, she wrapped herself in a bathrobe, locked both doors to the bedroom, and crawled into bed. She never wanted to leave this room again.

Wendy called mid-afternoon to see how she was doing.

"Are the kids giving you any trouble or—"

"Oh, no," Wendy insisted, "they're fine. I just wondered if you need anything."

"Just some rest," Ilene insisted. "I'm fine."

When Jessica came home from school, Ilene called to her through the bedroom door. "I'm not feeling too good. Would you go get the kids from Wendy's and watch them until Dad gets home?" Jessica went without complaining, and Ilene cried into her pillow.

Bryson came home at the usual time. He wasn't surprised at the disarray of the house or the chaos of the children. Ilene's bad days usually produced such results. But it wasn't the time in her treatment cycle for the general bad days. And he quickly noticed Jessica's distress. "Where's Mom?" he asked right off.

"She's in the bedroom, and she won't come out," Jessica said. "I asked her if she needs anything and she told me no. But I don't think she's eaten anything since breakfast, 'cause there weren't any dirty dishes when I got home."

"Okay, Jess," Bryson said gently. "Thanks for watching the kids. I'll check on her."

Jessica seemed relieved, but he didn't miss the subtle way her lip trembled. Bryson tried the bedroom door and found it locked. He knocked gently. "Honey, are you all right?" There was no response, and he wondered if she was asleep. He knocked again, more loudly. "Ilene, will you please answer me?"

"I'm okay," she snapped. "Just let me rest."

Bryson knew there was something wrong. That tone of voice was highly unusual for Ilene. He also knew he could spring the lock with little effort, but he didn't want to do it unless he felt it was absolutely necessary. If she wanted privacy for some reason, he figured he should respect her wishes.

"Maybe you're okay," he said, "but I'm never very good until I get a kiss. Can I come in?"

There was no response. Bryson decided to try the door from the bathroom, but it was also locked. Sighing in frustration, he glanced around and noticed the shower curtain was closed. She *always* left it open. He quickly pulled it back and gasped. Feeling a little unsteady, he closed the toilet lid and sat down. Then he noticed the wastebasket. It too was full of evidence. He knew now why she didn't want to come out, and he nearly wanted to cry. Idly he picked up a handful of the curly, dark hair and rubbed it between his fingers. He thought of the first time he had seen Ilene, the way her hair had first drawn his attention. She'd always worn it down and full. He didn't have to wonder why losing it would be traumatic, and now he wished they had made more of a point of discussing it before it happened.

Bryson sat in silence for several minutes, wondering what to do. He finally came to the conclusion that he needed a woman's opinion. Closing the bathroom door, he went to the phone.

"Wendy, I need your help."

"I'll be right over, and—"

"No," he said, "I just need to talk to you. Ilene has locked herself in the bedroom, and I think I know why. Apparently she lost most of her hair today when she took a bath; at least that's the way it appears from what I saw in the bathroom."

"Oh, I see."

"If it happened to you, what would you be wishing your husband would do?"

"Well," she hummed, "it's been a long time since I got rid of my husband." She laughed softly, and Bryson knew that Wendy's divorce from an alcoholic husband had been a welcome reprieve. "But obviously, I wouldn't want to be seen like that. I mean, hair is a very feminine thing, don't you think?"

"I suppose."

"Well, I would guess she needs something to wear that will help her feel . . . normal."

"Not a wig. She told me she doesn't want that."

"Okay, then I guess you're going to have to find her some . . . well . . . Bryson, if I could bring my kids over there, then . . . well, why don't you give me some money, and I'll go buy something."

"Would you? Oh, you're a real sweetheart, Wendy. I'd be happy to watch the kids."

As soon as Wendy left, Bryson went back to the bedroom door. At Wendy's suggestion, he didn't say anything about the hair. "Honey, are you hungry? Do you want me to get you something to eat?"

"I'm just tired," she called. He could tell she'd been crying by the strain in her voice.

Bryson tried to remember that this wasn't supposed to be easy. He quietly cleaned the hair out of the bathtub and got what he could out of the wastebasket. It seemed a silly thing, but he tucked it carefully into a little sack and put it away.

Dinner arrived, and he got the children settled with it before he fixed a plate for Ilene and took it into the bathroom.

"Are you awake, babe?"

After a long pause, she called, "Yes."

"I've left you some dinner here on the bathroom counter. I'm going to go eat now. You probably ought to get it before it gets cold."

Another long pause. "Thank you," she said. He went back into the hall, closing the door behind him.

Bryson ate with little enthusiasm, then he assigned each of the children a chore and started loading the dishwasher with Jessica's help. He went to the bathroom and found the dishes on the bathroom counter, but the food was gone. He chuckled to himself and took them to the kitchen.

Wendy came a few minutes later with an interesting assortment of scarves and hats. Bryson looked in the bags and made contemplative noises.

"If there is anything she doesn't like, they're all exchangeable."

"Thank you, Wendy. I owe you one."

"No you don't. Just tell her I love her."

"I will," he said, and took the packages into the bathroom with him.

"Ilene," he called, "can you hear me?"

"Yes."

"Wendy picked some things out for you. They're here in the bathroom." He paused and tried not to get emotional. "She said to tell you she loves you." He paused again and couldn't help the crack in his voice as he added, "I love you, too—no matter what."

Ilene wiped the fresh bout of tears from her face and listened as Bryson went into the hall again and closed the door. Of course he had figured it out. How could he not have noticed the hair she'd left all over the bathroom? And who else would have cleaned it up? She wondered what he'd done with it, then tried to tell herself she didn't care.

She felt a little better now that she'd eaten something, and she couldn't help being curious over what Wendy had picked out. Gingerly, she opened the bathroom door to make certain no one was there. She picked up the sacks and quickly locked the door again. As she pulled out several silk scarves in different colors, some plain, some in elegant prints, Ilene had to admit she felt a little better. She simply hadn't been prepared to lose all of her hair so suddenly. Wendy had also bought four hats in various styles that would go well with the scarves in a number of different combinations. She had to admit Wendy had good taste.

Now that she had a possible solution to her dilemma, Ilene actually found the courage to look in the mirror. She didn't know whether to laugh or cry when she looked at herself, almost completely bald, with only a few straying tufts of hair scattered over her head. She'd never even worn her hair cut short, which made the difference even more pronounced. But she reminded herself to not be vain and learn to live with it. As long as she didn't have to be seen bald, she could at least face her family.

For over an hour, Ilene tried different combinations. She found that tying a scarf around her head and putting the hat over it could actually be quite cute. She tried different earrings and perused the clothes in her closet as she contemplated how to adjust. It would take some getting used to, but perhaps she was one step closer to facing all of this. She certainly wasn't going to spend what little was left of her life behind closed doors—alone.

Bryson had the little ones in bed and the kitchen in some semblance of order when Jessica came in and asked, "Is Mom all right?"

"I think so," he said. He had taken a few minutes at the dinner table to explain the problem to the children, and they all seemed willing to not make a big deal of it. But Jessica's sensitivity was gradually becoming more apparent.

"Do you think she's afraid she'll look ugly without her hair?"

"I don't know how she feels, Jess. But I guess it's got to be hard for her. She's always had long, pretty hair." Bryson smiled. "She's not used to looking cute with short hair like you."

Jessica glanced down, seeming momentarily embarrassed. But he didn't miss her smile. "We'll just have to let her know that she's beautiful no matter what," Bryson added.

"Do you think she would talk to me?"

"You can try," Bryson said. "But don't stay up too much longer. You've got school."

"I know," she said, heading down the hall toward the bedroom.

Ilene was just pulling on a pair of jeans when a knock came at the bedroom door.

"Mom?" Jessica called. "Can I come in?"

"Just a minute, angel," she said.

Ilene took another long look in the mirror and decided her daughter was a good place to start. She took a deep breath and opened the door. Jessica looked up at her and smiled.

"You look cute, Mom. Do you feel better now?"

"I think so," she said and hugged Jessica tightly. "Thank you for your help with the kids today. I don't know what I'd do without you."

"It's okay, Mom," she said.

"But you should be in bed now, shouldn't you?"

"Yes, I just wanted to give you a hug." They embraced again, and Ilene kissed her cheek. "You really look nice, Mom," Jessica said with such sincerity that Ilene had to laugh to keep from crying.

"Thank you, angel. You get some sleep now."

Jessica went off to bed, and Ilene walked quietly down the hall. She found Bryson sitting at the dining table, his back to her, his head in his hands. Ever since they had married, he had accused her of moving around too quietly. For a number of years she had teased him by sneaking up and startling him. He would try to do the same to her, but he never could. Then one day Bryson told her he was determined to not let her get away with it. He figured a man ought to be able to tell when his wife was in the room. Ilene had agreed with him, and after some thought she told him if they were truly one in all things, he should be able to sense her presence.

But she had actually been surprised at the way he'd learned to do it. It took time, but it was rare now that she could stand behind him for more than a few seconds without him realizing she was there. She stood where she was for half a minute and he didn't move, but she knew he was tired and likely had much on his mind. So she concentrated on getting his attention, as if her spirit could reach out and touch his. She had once been told that the strongest form of communication was spirit to spirit. Since that time she had found it to be true, and she believed the human spirit possessed powers beyond what the mind could comprehend.

Another thirty seconds passed before Bryson turned abruptly to see her. "I knew you were there," he said, showing a hint of a smile. She smiled in return but said nothing. "Are you all right?" he asked.

Ilene felt his eyes travel from her bare feet, over her jeans and the baggy, navy-colored sweatshirt, and coming to rest on the pink and navy flowered scarf, topped by a feminine navy-colored cap. She felt self-conscious and somehow afraid as she glanced down and said, "I'm okay."

"You're as beautiful as ever," he said firmly.

Ilene glanced up, searching for sincerity. She was surprised to find it so readily. He clearly meant what he said, and she couldn't hold back the tears.

Bryson rose and put his arms around her. Ilene pressed her face to his shoulder and cried for several minutes before she drew back and wiped at her tears.

"I'm sorry," she laughed softly. "I don't think anyone on earth cries as much as I do."

"It's okay, babe," he said, wiping at her tears with his fingers. "Do you want to sit outside a while? It's nice out."

Ilene nodded. Bryson took her hand and led her to the back porch, where they sat together in the porch swing that hung from chains. She had seen one in a catalog when they were newlyweds, and declared that one day she wanted a house with a swing on the back porch. A year after they'd moved into the house with three young children, Bryson had it delivered for their anniversary. To this day, she often said it was the best gift she'd ever received, and they spent many evenings sitting together when the weather was favorable.

Bryson put his arm around her, and she snuggled close to him. "I guess I didn't handle things very maturely today," she said. "I just didn't expect it to happen all at once like that. I wasn't ready for it."

"It's okay," he said. "I'm just glad Wendy was around."

They sat in silence, and Bryson started the swing moving gently back and forth.

"I love you, Bryson," she said, resting her head against his shoulder.

"I love you, too, babe," he replied.

"I want you to know how much I appreciate your attitude about all of this, Bryse. While I was lying in there feeling sorry for myself, all I could think about was what some of those women at the support group were saying. I couldn't believe some of the cruel and heartless things their husbands had said. I mean . . ." Ilene tried to swallow her emotion, but she knew it was pointless. "I feel so . . . unfeminine."

Bryson looked down at her, surprised.

"It's hard enough dealing with the way I feel about myself. If I had to live with a man who rejected me because—"

"Rejected you?" Bryson sounded appalled. "Why on earth would I *reject* you?"

"I suppose I've had the same fears that every woman has who goes through this. I feel like so much less of a woman, and many women *have* been rejected by their husbands for that reason."

Bryson sighed and shook his head. "Well, you know how men are. They're all just a bunch of insensitive geeks."

Ilene looked up at Bryson and smiled through her tears. "Not all of them."

"I don't know," he said. "I've never been much good at saying the things I ought to say. Looking back over the years, I wonder if you didn't deserve somebody who wasn't so afraid to say what he felt."

Ilene sat forward and turned slightly so she could see his face. "You're a good man, Bryson. You always have been. And I love you."

"I love you, too, Ilene." He touched her face with adoration. "And I know I didn't always treat you as well as I could have. I know I didn't appreciate just how incredible you really are."

Ilene looked down, and the tears came freshly.

"But I'll make it up to you, Ilene. I'm not going to spend the rest of my life with regrets, and I'm not going to spend the rest of *your* life being petty over how much hair you have or the changes in your figure. I love *you*, Ilene."

She looked up at him then, wondering why she should be so blessed. Yes, there were times when she had felt unappreciated, and she had frequently been frustrated because he kept his feelings bottled inside. But she had never questioned that he loved her, and she had never wanted for anything since the day she'd met him. Yet, now, as she was facing the most difficult thing she'd ever dealt with, he was here, letting her know exactly how he felt, telling her exactly what she needed to hear.

When she finally got past the knot in her throat, Ilene put a hand to his face and whispered, "That's the most beautiful thing anyone has ever said to me."

Bryson smiled. "I'm learning, eh?"

"Oh, yes." She smiled back.

Bryson pulled her close to him and squeezed his eyes shut to absorb it more fully. *Just in the nick of time*, he thought to himself, wondering how he was ever going to live without her. He took her face into his hands and bent to kiss her, turning to avoid the brim of her hat. He ran into it anyway, and Ilene laughed as she took it off.

"I've still got a few things to learn yet," he said and pressed his mouth over hers.

Ilene kept the scarf tied around her head while they made love by candlelight. She marveled at the way he touched her and held her as if nothing were any different than it ever had been. For a long while afterward, he held her close and moved his fingers up and down her arm. She tried not to think about the reason his caress felt unfamiliar. This was the time he usually coiled his fingers in her hair. When he didn't move for several minutes she thought he was asleep, until he leaned up onto one elbow and looked down at her. He put a hand to the side of her head and said gently, "Take it off, Ilene."

She shook her head firmly. "I can't. Not yet."

"It doesn't matter," he said.

She bit her lip. "Just . . . give me a little time. I need to get used to it myself first."

Bryson hesitated thoughtfully, then nodded in agreement. "I just don't want you to feel like you have to hide from me." She managed a smile and he added, "Even if I have more hair than you do, you'll always be prettier than me."

He was relieved when she laughed. Then she rolled him onto his back and kissed him in a way that made anything else fade out of his mind.

Two days later, Ilene was still hiding beneath a scarf, and she didn't go out of the house without a hat over it. Her little remaining hair had fallen out, and she told Bryson she could do a fair Yul Brynner imitation. They were able to laugh about it, but she still didn't feel ready to let him see her.

Ilene wore a dressy straw hat with a scarf to church on Sunday. People were considerate and complimentary, but she still felt self-conscious. On Monday afternoon, Jessica called from Mandy's house and asked if she could stay until dinner. Ilene reminded her not to be late, since they would be having family home evening. The family was seated for dinner when Bryson said, "Where is Jessica?"

Ilene stood up to call Mandy's house when Jessica, sporting a hat, ran in the front door and hurried to take her seat. Ilene sat back down, saying, "That was close, young lady. I hope you don't have any homework."

"I already did it," she said.

Bryson was about to ask Jessica to take off her hat at the dinner table, but he glanced at Ilene and said nothing. Instead, he took notice of it as they ate. He'd seen it on her many times before and always thought it was a bit silly. But he'd gotten used to it, and he wondered how Ilene would look in it. It was black fabric and covered most of her head, with a brim that went all the way around, folded back in front and fastened with a big silk sunflower.

"You should loan that hat to your mother sometime," Bryson said. Jessica looked up, visibly panicked.

"Okay," she said after swallowing what was in her mouth. "Maybe we could trade," she added to Ilene.

Ilene smiled. "We should maybe do some hat shopping."

Bryson noticed Jessica shifting uncomfortably. It was something she did when she had to tell them she was getting a bad grade, or that one of her teachers would be calling to say she'd been giggling too much in class again. He was about to ask if she had something she needed to say when she piped up with "Mom, I got my hair cut. Mandy's sister did it. She's going to beauty college, or whatever they call it. I hope you won't be mad at me."

Bryson and Ilene both looked at Jessica, then exchanged a quick glance as they realized the hat covered her hair completely.

"Well, let's have a look at it," Bryson said. "Then we'll decide whether or not to ground you for a year."

"Okay, Dad," she said. "But could we wait till after dinner?"

After the opening prayer for family home evening, Bryson said, "Okay, Jess. I think this would be a good time to unveil your new haircut."

He was concerned when she looked downright afraid. Then she pulled off the hat and he didn't know what to say. Ilene gasped, then remained silent.

"I hope you won't be mad at me," Jessica said, more to her father. Her chin quivered as she added, "I just wanted to have the same hairstyle as Mom."

Bryson glanced at Ilene and wasn't surprised at her tears. Then he looked back to Jessica and smiled. "I think it's beautiful, angel. Be sure to tell Mandy's sister that she's got some real talent."

This made Jessica laugh, then the other children started to laugh. Bryson reached over and took Ilene's hand, relieved to see that she was laughing, too. She held her other hand out toward Jessica, and they hugged each other tightly while Bryson tried to comprehend the sensitivity of a child who, for the sake of her mother, would endure going to junior high without any hair.

"Okay," Ilene announced. "I guess if Jessica can do it, I can do it."

She looked over at Bryson as she pulled off her hat and tossed it. She hesitated a moment, then pushed back her scarf and turned her head dramatically as if she were a model. The children applauded and cheered. Bryson pulled her into his arms and kissed her long and hard on the mouth. This made the children cheer more boisterously. Only Ilene heard him say, "You're still the most beautiful woman in the world."

Ilene remained scarfless through the remainder of the evening, and when the children were all asleep, Bryson took the opportunity to show her that nothing had changed.

The following afternoon, Bryson got a call at work from Jessica's school. Ilene had a doctor's visit and they had obviously been unable to reach her. The principal's secretary informed him that they had a serious concern, and wondered if he could meet with the principal. Bryson left work early and walked in the office to find Jessica sitting glumly with her arms folded. He wanted to ask her what had happened, but he didn't have a chance before Mr. Hopkins invited him to sit down. He sat next to Jessica, and she gripped his hand tightly.

"Mr. Davis," the principal began while his secretary looked on sternly, "we have some growing concerns in the area that cannot be ignored."

"Go on," Bryson said.

Mr. Hopkins then launched into a long and boring oratory on the school's difficulties with gangs, and the incidents that had led up to this problem.

"Is there a reason you're telling me all of this?" Bryson asked, hoping to get on with it.

"Our concern is for Jessica," he stated.

"Has she been associating with these kids you're talking about?" Bryson asked, knowing she hadn't. She wasn't away from home enough to do much of anything he wasn't aware of.

"Not that we have seen. But our concern is about her appearance."

Bryson glanced at Jessica, hiding beneath her hat, and suddenly everything began to make sense. "If you're talking about Jessica's new hairstyle," Bryson said, "I don't think there's anything to be concerned about. She just—"

"Mr. Davis, in case you haven't noticed, your daughter has no hair to style."

"Yes, I've noticed, Mr. Hopkins. But it's—"

"It's a common thing," the principal interrupted, "for these gang members to shave their heads or—"

"Mr. Hopkins," Bryson leaned forward and spoke with an edge to his voice that apparently got the principal's attention, "did you ask Jessica *why* she shaved her head?"

"It's obvious to me. There is only one reason why an impressionable young woman would do such a thing. My concern is that she—"

"If you had any *real* concern, you would ask Jessica the reason before you make her feel as if she's being prosecuted or something." When the principal made no response, Bryson almost shouted, "Go ahead, ask her!"

The principal cleared his throat. "Jessica, is there a reason why you've done this ridiculous thing and—"

"I did it for my mom," she blurted in a tone that almost mimicked her father's.

Mr. Hopkins turned to Bryson, indignantly puzzled, obviously expecting him to clarify this absurdity.

"Jessica's mother has cancer, Mr. Hopkins. She is undergoing extensive chemotherapy, and a few days ago, all of her hair fell out. Do you have any idea what it meant to my wife to have her thirteen-year-old daughter come home with no hair? Do you know how much courage it took Jessica to do something like that, knowing she'd have to be the only bald girl in a junior high the size of this one? Not to mention having to deal with the ridicule of people like you, who won't even stop to consider the possibility that there might be a reason. Mr. Hopkins, my daughter has more courage and integrity than I ever dreamed of having at thirteen. You'd do well to treat her with a little respect—and you can start by apologizing to her for this ridiculous little incident."

Mr. Hopkins fidgeted and cleared his throat. The secretary's expression of scorn had turned to something between pity and embarrassment.

"I apologize, Jessica, for this misunderstanding. I wish your mother all the best."

"Let's go." Bryson came to his feet abruptly and hurried Jessica out the door. Once outside, he muttered under his breath, "What a jerk!"

"Oh, he's not such a bad guy, Dad," she grinned up at him. "But you were *great* in there."

"I was?" He chuckled and hugged her with one arm as they walked to the car.

On the way home, he asked, "Did anyone tease you today?"

"I left my hat on most of the time," she said. "Except in English. Mrs. Johnson won't let us wear hats in class. Some of the kids were jerks about it, but Mrs. Johnson was cool."

"Did she ask you why you'd done it?"

"No, but she gave us an assignment to write an essay, and she suggested that I write about it. I told her I'd be happy to."

Bryson smiled. "Then I guess you've got some homework to do."

"It won't be too hard. I'll just copy down what I wrote in my journal last night."

Bryson was amazed at his daughter's character. He wished he could take some credit for it, but she obviously had Ilene's sensitive spirit, and she was the product of Ilene's careful parenting. Brandon and Greg, on the other hand, were a lot more like him. The following week he was called to the elementary school twice for misbehavior—once for each boy. On the second visit he confessed to the principal, Mrs. Simms, that the boys were going through a struggle.

"Their mother has cancer, you see. Life at home isn't quite what it used to be."

"Oh," Mrs. Simms said kindly, "well, that certainly explains it. Perhaps being aware of that could make a difference."

"I would appreciate anything you can do," Bryson said, "but I'd rather the boys didn't know their teachers are aware of it. I'm afraid they can be a little proud, like their father. I would prefer that it remain confidential, at least for the time being."

"I understand," Mrs. Simms said, and they talked a while about the things they could do to make it easier. She agreed to let Bryson know of anything observed at school that might be a cause for concern, since things naturally tend to come out at school that might not at home.

Driving home, Bryson thought of his two sons and tried to comprehend the reality that their mother was going to die. Something painful erupted inside him as he realized he'd lost his own mother—not to death, but he'd lost her just the same. At this point, the children knew Ilene was sick, and they knew it was serious, but they had no idea just how bad it would get. As Bryson tried to figure how he was going to deal with helping the children through it, along with facing it himself, he felt suddenly so afraid that he started to shake. He sat in the driveway for several minutes, praying silently and trying to get control of these feelings before he went in the house to see how the day had gone in his absence. Ilene would be starting another treatment cycle tomorrow, and he knew she would be uptight. She hated it, and he couldn't blame her. He hated it, too.

CHAPTER FOUR

Melissa had called her sister every day since the cancer was first detected. It was a blessing that her job allowed for the phone calls, and her employer was compassionate about the situation. But Melissa felt helpless.

Though Ilene was more than eight years her senior, the two of them had always been close. But their friendship had deepened during Melissa's seventh-grade year—the same year Ilene had married. Bryse and Ilene's first apartment was walking distance from the junior high, and Melissa had enjoyed visiting her sister after school almost daily while Ilene had suffered through the effects of her first pregnancy.

By all outward evidence, Ilene and Melissa were as different as two women could be. But their spirits bonded as only sisters could. While Ilene was raising children, Melissa had risen up the career ladder; but their sisterhood had not waned. By phone and mail they had kept closely in touch.

Since the discovery of Ilene's illness, Melissa had never found a day of peace. She kept track of every detail of her progress, but a part of her always wanted to be with her sister. She felt torn between two worlds, and every day she wondered if she should just drop everything and go to Utah. She felt a formless desperation—a sense that time was running out.

Melissa felt incomparable relief when Ilene told her the chemotherapy was finished and she was feeling good. She came right out and asked if this would be the end, but Ilene responded with an evasiveness that made Melissa uneasy. She decided then that it was time to visit her sister and find out firsthand what was going on.

* * * * *

"Hello." Bryson answered the phone with a tone of indifference. He was preoccupied with changing a diaper.

"Hello, Bryse," Melissa said cheerfully.

"Oh, hi." His tone didn't change.

"Why are you always so glad to talk to me?" she asked with sarcasm.

"It's nothing personal, Lissa. I'm just busy."

"Too busy to pick me up at the airport tomorrow?"

"You're coming . . . *here?*" he almost gasped.

"Is there a reason why I shouldn't? I'd like to see my sister."

"I'm sure she would be pleased to have your company," he said politely. "How long are you planning to stay?"

"I have a week off. Maybe I could help you out a little."

"I'm managing fine, thank you," he said, glancing around as if to prove himself a hypocrite. He'd have to get the kids busy helping him clean up this mess before Melissa arrived.

"All right, then I'll entertain Ilene. How's she doing, anyway?"

"She's good. Do you want to talk to her?"

"In a minute. You haven't told me if you'll pick me up. It is Saturday. You don't have to work, or anything, do you?"

"I think I can manage. What time?"

"12:18. Delta Airlines, from L.A."

"I'll be there," he said. "Here's Ilene."

Bryson absently handed her the receiver and hurried Jamie off to bed. The next day he asked Wendy to check on Ilene and took the kids with him to the airport. They all bounced up and down and assaulted Melissa with hugs and kisses, except Jamie, who clung to her father. She was too young to remember her Aunt Melissa. Bryson stood with his hands in the pockets of his jeans, watching Melissa pull surprises out of a bag for each of the children. Even Jamie showed an interest when Melissa produced a little doll in a bright pink dress. Since the other children seemed to think this woman was okay, Jamie ventured forward. Melissa then handed Jessica some money and told her to take the children to get some ice cream.

"We'll catch up," Melissa said. "Hold on to Jamie tight, now."

As the children scurried away, Melissa caught Bryson's eyes, wondering why they had become so hard. She looked him over briefly, admiring the way he looked in faded jeans, high-tops, and a forest green sweatshirt. He had definitely improved with age. When Ilene had married Bryson Davis, Melissa had thought of him as something of a nerd. But marriage and fatherhood suited him well; he had matured with dignity. Still, she felt the same tension that had always been there. The differences between her and Ilene had made him somehow dislike her; or perhaps it had simply been the fact that Ilene shared things with her sister that she would never share with a husband. Whatever it was, Bryson and Melissa had a long-time, unspoken agreement to tolerate each other politely.

"It's been a while," she said.

"Since Jamie was born." He looked toward the window. "Funny how time flies."

"How are you, Bryson?"

"I've seen better days. How about yourself?"

"It's good to get away from the same old rut."

"Haven't snagged a husband yet, eh?" he said facetiously.

"Not yet." She smiled, refusing to let him see just how much that fact bothered her. "It's not easy finding someone worthy of me," she stated, lifting an eyebrow comically.

"You mean someone who could put up with you," he retorted.

It was typical of them to banter lightly, but Melissa sensed an unfamiliar bite behind his words that she didn't understand.

"Shall we get my luggage?" she said to change the subject.

They walked side by side for several minutes in silence before Melissa asked, "So, how is Ilene?"

"She's doing good," he stated. "Her hair's growing back." He almost chuckled.

"She told me she has wigs of assorted colors."

"Yeah," he smiled, "she finally resigned herself to it. But she makes a great redhead."

"She's still weak, I presume."

"You talk to her every day. You should know as well as I do."

"She doesn't want to talk about it, Bryse. You live with her. That's why I'm asking you. I want to know where things stand."

"Yes," he admitted, "she's still weak. She's getting out more, even driving a little, but she's not the same woman."

"But she should keep getting better now, right?" Melissa didn't think it was an odd question until Bryson stopped walking, and she was three steps ahead before she figured it out and turned around.

"Who told you that?" he snapped.

"No one's ever told me otherwise," she retorted, feeling an uneasy dread creep up the center of her back. They stared at each other for a full minute while Melissa expected an explanation.

Finally he said, "I can't believe she didn't tell you. Of all people, I thought she would have told *you*." He had a vague memory of Ilene mentioning she didn't want Melissa to know, but now that he'd said this much, he didn't know how to get out of it. But then, Melissa *had* to know. She was Ilene's only blood relative, and she was going to be around for a week. He wasn't about to pretend everything was all right when it wasn't.

"Tell me *what*?" Melissa stepped toward him and looked up into his face. He said nothing. "Tell me what?" she hissed under her breath.

Bryson cleared his throat and reported in a hard voice, "It's in remission, Lissa. There is no way of knowing how long she has before it comes back, and there is no way of knowing where it will show up."

Melissa stared at him in disbelief until the implication set in. She turned abruptly away and pressed a hand over her mouth, squeezing her eyes shut as if she could block out the reality. She understood now, that hardness in his eyes. The woman he loved—her sister—was going to die.

Melissa barely had a chance to digest this realization before the children found them, each enjoying a different color of ice cream. She met a cautious glare in Bryson's eyes and realized the children didn't know how bad it was. His attention shifted as they gathered around, chattering excitedly about the things they wanted to do with Aunt Melissa.

While Melissa's mind was fighting to adjust to the reality that her sister was going to die of cancer, she managed to maintain a smile and remain attentive to the children's chatter through the twenty-minute drive home.

Before they pulled in the driveway, Bryson spouted off a series of orders. "Brandon and Greg, you get Aunt Lissa's luggage and take it to the den. Amber, you take Jamie in to pick up those toys you left out. Jessica, you get lunch started like we talked about. I'll be in to help you in a few minutes."

The kids hurried out of the van, and Melissa smiled toward Bryson. "I'm impressed. You seem to have things running smoothly."

Bryson wasn't amused. "They're just trying to impress you. Give them a day. They know how to buffalo me." He got out and motioned toward the gate. "I think Ilene's in the backyard."

Melissa followed Bryson around the corner of the house, where she could see her sister kneeling by a rose bush, carefully cutting stems. She came slowly to her feet, her countenance glowing as their eyes met across the yard. The sandals and jeans she wore were typical of Ilene, but the baggy blouse couldn't disguise the change in her figure. She wore a wide-brimmed straw hat with a brightly-colored silk scarf beneath it, wrapped around her head and tied at the nape.

"Melissa!" Ilene cried as they embraced.

"Oh, you look great," Melissa said as she drew back. Then they embraced again. They walked arm in arm to the porch swing, where they sat close together and talked and laughed as if nothing were out of the ordinary. Melissa tried to convince herself that Bryson's implication of the seriousness of Ilene's cancer had been exaggerated. But in her heart, she knew it was true. She could feel something different in just being with her sister, but she resolved to not think of it for the moment and just enjoy their time together. They talked and held hands the way they always had, until Bryson came out to announce that lunch was ready.

"Bryson's been so good to me," Ilene said as they followed him into the house and sat down with the children to build their own sandwiches from a variety of cold cuts and cheeses. "He's helped so much with the kids and the house, I don't know what I'd do without him."

Melissa noticed Bryson's apparent embarrassment over the compliment, and she wondered if he was so arrogant that he didn't like being credited with such menial things. But as she observed Ilene and Bryson over the following days, she couldn't deny the changes in him. He still seemed distant, almost cold, but she wondered if that had something to do with her being there. Ilene had hinted that he was more guarded in Melissa's presence. Yet, there was something softer about him. His attitude and behavior toward Ilene were almost reverential at times, though his brashness often came through in little ways that made Melissa angry. But she tried not to judge. Instead, she concentrated on spending time with Ilene, pretending that nothing was wrong, wondering if she would ever have this opportunity again.

Occasionally they took a long drive together, just to be away from the house and the children. They shopped a little, but Ilene didn't have the strength to walk for long. Melissa thoroughly enjoyed every moment of their time together, but she couldn't deny the growing dread she felt as the week drew to a close. She knew in her heart that they had to get the truth in the open, and she prayed fervently that it would come about without upsetting Ilene—or anyone else. She was relieved beyond words when Ilene brought it up.

"Melissa," Ilene said softly while Bryson was getting the children to bed, "there's something I need to tell you—something you need to know."

"Go on," Melissa urged gently.

"It's about the cancer. I . . ."

"Bryson told me," Melissa said when Ilene seemed hesitant to say it.

"Told you what?" She seemed alarmed.

"That it's in remission. That *is* what you wanted to tell me, isn't it? If it's not, it should be."

"Yes," Ilene admitted. "I probably should have told you before, but . . . well, I didn't want you treating me differently. I just wanted things to be the way they always had been between us, Lissa." Tears spilled over Ilene's face. "I suppose I didn't want to face it. But I know it's only a matter of time before it comes back and . . ." She didn't finish.

Melissa pressed the back of her fingers to her mouth, attempting to hold in a degree of the emotion that rushed forward. How could she not cry? Her sister—her best friend, the only person on earth who truly loved her—was going to die. Melissa continued to cry right along with Ilene as she finally came to the raw truth and vented all her deepest feelings. Ilene confessed her fears right from the time the lump had been found, and repeated every step of the way with the details and emotions that Melissa had been spared in their long-distance conversations. She was grateful that Bryson had apparently gone off to the family room to watch T.V., leaving them with much-needed time together.

Ilene couldn't believe the relief she felt as she unburdened herself to her sister. She decided there was simply nothing to replace the friendship and understanding they shared. They talked and cried until there was nothing more to say. Bryson had long since gone to bed, leaving them alone. He'd have to be blind to not figure out what was going on.

"So what do you want me to do, Ilene?" Melissa asked firmly. "You name it, and I'll do it. I'll quit my job and come here to be with you every minute, if that's what—"

"Don't be silly," Ilene insisted. "Such drastic measures are not necessary, I can assure you." Ilene smiled and took Melissa's hand. "It's just so nice to have you here with me now. I only hope we can have . . . more time together."

Their tears welled up again in unison. The reality struck Melissa freshly, and she found herself sobbing on Ilene's shoulder. It was as if she were a child all over again, leaning on her big sister, wondering what she would ever do when her sister was gone. Then the tables turned as Ilene vented her own fears and emotions. She sobbed, at first with anger, and then with sadness. When the tears finally ran down—again—they sat close together, resigning themselves to the inevitability. They talked about the children, and the likelihood of difficulties ahead. And they talked about Bryson.

"He's been so sweet," Ilene said warmly, "but I worry about him. He has a hard time showing his emotions, but I fear if he doesn't . . . well, he's just—"

"In denial?" Melissa guessed.

"Perhaps a little; or maybe he's just trying so hard to cope that he doesn't have time to feel it."

"How has he handled the . . . changes in you?" Melissa asked gently, hoping Ilene would know what she meant.

"Oh," Ilene smiled serenely, "he's been so sweet, so tender—better than I ever imagined." A distant, almost dreamy, look clouded Ilene's eyes. She smiled shyly and said, more to herself, "Bryson is a passionate man."

Melissa tried to absorb this through the long moments Ilene seemed lost in thought. She had difficulty relating the brash, insensitive Bryson Davis she knew to the description Ilene had just given. Sweet. Tender. *Passionate?* Melissa let it go at that and decided it was none of her business. "I'll take your word for it," she said tersely. Then she added, "Is he handling everything okay, Ilene? I mean, if it's going to get worse, do you think he can take the stress? The last thing you need is having him break down on you, and—"

"I'm certain he'll be fine," Ilene insisted. But she didn't seem totally convinced.

"Just promise me you'll call if you need me, Ilene." Melissa looked into her eyes and squeezed her hand. "Please . . . don't allow yourself to be any more miserable than you have to be and leave me ignorant. I want to help you, Ilene. If there's anything—ever—I can do, I want to know about it. Is there anything I can do now, before I go back? Anything at all?"

Ilene contemplated the question for a moment. "Actually . . . there is something I feel should be done, but Bryson . . . well, he's just busy with his job and helping around the house, and . . ."

"What?" Melissa asked. Reading between the lines was easy. What Ilene really meant was *it's something he doesn't want to deal with, so he's ignoring it.*

"I need a will, Lissa," Ilene admitted. "And a living will, too."

Melissa swallowed hard, hating the reality. "Okay," she said. "Tell me what to do, and I'll do it."

"I don't know exactly. I asked Bryson to look into it, but . . ."

Melissa was actually relieved by Ilene's obvious exhaustion as her words faded into a yawn. It was difficult for her to not feel angry with Bryson, but she knew it would be inappropriate to vent her emotion here and now. "Perhaps we should get some sleep, and we'll see to it tomorrow." Ilene agreed and was off to bed with little urging.

The following evening, Melissa was the only one at home when Bryson returned from work. "Where is everybody?" he bellowed, coming into the kitchen where she was peeling potatoes.

"Ilene went to the park with Wendy and all the kids," Melissa reported.

Bryson made an indiscernible noise and turned to leave, but Melissa stopped him. She knew she'd never get another opportunity to talk to him alone. "Listen, Bryse, could I ask you something?"

He took off his tie and hung it over his shoulder. "Sure, what?" he asked dryly.

"Ilene told me last night that she asked you quite a while back to get some legal documents made up, and—"

"I'm well aware of it, Lissa," he interrupted tersely. "It's under control."

Melissa set down the peeler and wiped her hands on a towel. "If it's under control, then why did Ilene ask me to make certain it got done?"

"I don't know, Melissa. But I can assure you it will get done."

"When?" she demanded, feeling like she had to force the issue. Time was something they seemed to have only in limited supply. "Ilene has a right to spend what's left of her life with some peace of mind and security, not wondering if she'll leave a big mess behind."

Bryson said nothing, and she knew he had no argument. Even so, the hardness in his eyes made her certain he was searching for one.

"I have to go home soon, Bryson. I can't be here, but I'm not going to leave my sister up in the air over—"

"I don't understand why you're making such a big deal out of this, Melissa. It's not like she's going to die tomorrow. We have plenty of time to—"

"Do we? Tell me, Bryson, do we honestly have any idea what will happen? Can you put it off just because you don't want to face it?"

"I intend to spend every minute I can *enjoying* life with her, Lissa—not wishing it away."

"Facing up to reality is not wishing her life away, Bryse. There's a difference. If she wants it done, you've got to do it. You don't argue with a dying woman."

"Okay, I'll do it."

"Good. But again I ask: When? I'm not leaving here without some commitment out of you."

"I don't know, but I'll get around to it."

"*When*, Bryson?"

"I don't know!" he shouted.

"Listen," Melissa said in a quiet voice that she hoped would calm him, "my intention was not to add fuel to the fire, Bryse. But Ilene has asked my help, and I have to give it. I have to go back home, but I'm not leaving until I know that you are facing up to reality enough to see that the things that are important to her get done."

While Melissa had hoped to ease his irritation, the anger in his eyes only increased. "No, *you* listen. All I've done for the past several months is face *reality*. You haven't been here. *I* have. So don't stand there and try to tell me what's going on. I'll tell you about reality. Reality is getting up every morning, feeling torn between work and home while Ilene has struggled through week after week of side effects worse than anything she's ever been through in her life. Reality is homework, housework, laundry, dishes, and refereeing five children who can't help but feel the tension. Reality is wondering how I'm going to make it without her, when I can't even make it when she's flat in bed for a week at a time." He took a step toward her and she stepped back, wary of his anger. "The reality here, Melissa, is that my wife is going to die in her prime and leave me with five children, and there isn't a damn thing I can do about it. I will see to the things Ilene wants done. I will do it before we go on vacation next month. In the meantime, I will stay out of the way so you can talk and laugh and cry with Ilene all you want. And when you go back home to your posh little life, I will step back up to the plate and be there with her day in and day out, until she takes her last breath."

Bryson strode down the hall and slammed the bedroom door. Melissa winced, then nearly collapsed onto a chair, setting her elbows on the kitchen table. While she felt an urge to chase him down and throw anger right back at him, she knew it would solve nothing. The bottom line was obvious. As much as she and Bryson disliked each other, they were both in the same boat. They both loved Ilene, and they were both going to lose her.

Melissa pressed her face into her hands and cried. She couldn't deny some relief in knowing that Bryson had promised to take care of Ilene's concerns. For all his brashness, she knew he would keep his word. And there was something vaguely comforting in his apparent determination to care for Ilene. But she had to wonder if he would hold up through the long haul.

Saying good-bye to Ilene at the airport was the hardest thing Melissa had ever done. In her heart she believed she would see her sister again, but she wondered what the circumstances would be when the opportunity came. She cried discreetly all the way home on the plane, then tried to work herself back into a routine, all the while consumed with prayer on behalf of her sister—and her sister's family.

Two weeks later, Ilene called to tell her that Bryson had helped her take care of everything, and she felt much better, knowing it was done. They kept in touch nearly every day, but Melissa hated her own helplessness and wished there was something more she could do.

* * * * *

Bryson had to admit some relief in knowing that everything was taken care of legally. As difficult as it had been, now that it was over, it ceased weighing on his mind like some kind of bad omen.

With everything momentarily under control, the family went to Disneyland, also enjoying many of the sights in the surrounding area. Bryson felt his prayers were being heard as the trip went smoothly and Ilene felt good enough to enjoy it. Most of the time he could almost forget what she'd been through with her treatments—and what she had yet to go through when the cancer inevitably returned.

They took a detour to visit Melissa before returning home. Ilene and the kids enjoyed it, but Bryson was glad to be on the road again. He couldn't define the tension he felt in his sister-in-law's presence, and he didn't particularly want to analyze it. He was just more comfortable when they weren't under the same roof.

Following the vacation, life settled back into a routine that was much as it had been before all of this started. Ilene's hair grew back in soft, thick curls, and it was rare that she showed signs of weakness or strain. While Bryson did his best to live each day normally and not think about what the future might hold, he didn't have to remind himself to be more attentive to his wife and make the most of every moment. They attended the temple together more frequently, and the intimacy they shared in private became something more incredible than he'd ever dreamed possible. In many ways, life was better than it had ever been—an irony he didn't stop to ponder.

CHAPTER FIVE

Ilene felt the pain creep in somewhere in the middle of her back, but deep inside. She'd begun to feel so good that she had almost convinced herself it wouldn't come back, that some miracle would save her. But as the pain became gradually more difficult to ignore, she had to acknowledge what her spirit had known since the moment the lump had been found. Her time on earth was nearly done, and this horrible disease would be the means to take her.

She managed to get through her housework during the days, while she avoided telling Bryson the truth. But once in a while, she would find herself staring at nothing as she speculated on how bad it might get. She'd heard far too many stories of people deteriorating to almost nothing, writhing in pain, helpless and hallucinating from heavy doses of morphine. One afternoon, the fear consumed her so completely that she sat in the middle of the kitchen floor and sobbed. She was grateful the children were in school. Even Amber was in first grade now, and only Jamie was with her during the days. Gratefully, Ilene considered the fact that the less the children were around, the less likely they would be to sense the problem.

But Bryson sensed it. She was both relieved and distressed when he noticed her discomfort and commented with certainty, "It's come back, hasn't it."

Ilene nodded stoically. Bryson watched her for a long moment, as if he could soak up every detail of her to keep in his mind and heart forever. Then, with no warning, he pulled her into his arms with a savage desperation, as if he might never have the chance to do so again.

Bryson had no idea what to expect, but he certainly wasn't prepared for the rapid deterioration of Ilene's life. A month after that first pain crept in, she was confined to a hospital bed that had been added to the family room decor. Meals were being brought in by the Relief Society, and sisters from the ward were coming in to sit with her while Bryson was at work. He often pondered what he might do without their help, and decided he could never manage. He wasn't sure he was managing anyway.

Each day, he both anticipated and dreaded going home. Being away from her, he could almost believe it wasn't really happening; then he would see her, and he just wanted to cry like a baby. But Bryson somehow managed to keep the tears in check with his fear. He was afraid of anything past tomorrow, and believed that if he started to cry he would never be able to stop.

He wanted to spend every minute at home just holding Ilene's hand and talking to her, but instead he was madly rushing about, seeing to her needs in the midst of coaching the children through homework and washing dishes and laundry. The house became steadily more out of control, until it was impossible to find anything without major drama. But through it all, Ilene remained calm and strong in spirit. Bryson's favorite part of the day was after the children had finally gone to sleep. He would sit in the rocking chair at the side of her bed, or sometimes on the edge of the bed with his arm around her frail shoulders. They would hold hands and talk, and sometimes she would cry. He marveled at her faith, and the peace she was gradually beginning to feel as she faced the final days of her life.

Ilene had no trouble with dying. She had accepted it and was comforted with the promise of eternity. She was concerned for her children, but she also knew that God would not be taking her if he didn't have a plan to see them cared for. She firmly believed that she would be able to help her children more from the other side. While Bryson couldn't see the logic in that, he felt no point in arguing. Ilene's only fear was what her body would have to go through in the time she had left. Bryson tried not to think too hard about any of it. He just held her and let her cry, until finally he'd drag his exhausted body back to his own bed—the one he used to share with Ilene.

At moments, the loneliness seemed to close in around him. She was still alive, he reminded himself—still living under the same roof, still eating and breathing and touching their lives with her smile. But in the middle of the night, when he'd wake up alone in their bed, Bryson felt as if she were miles away, completely out of his reach.

The situation worsened steadily. Ilene was in and out of the hospital, undergoing tests and treatments until they both thought they couldn't bear any more. Then they reached a day when the best doctors declared they could do nothing further. "Keep her comfortable," they told Bryson. "It's just a matter of time."

By Thanksgiving, Ilene had cancer in her hip, her spine, her liver, her remaining breast, and several areas of muscle tissue. The Relief Society project had been taken on by the stake, and Bryson marveled at the endless supply of meals and support. But he wondered how long it could go on. And even though a few sisters came in occasionally to help with some cleaning, the deep disorder of a home that had once been in perfect control was only one of many things that made Bryson just want to crawl into that bed and die right beside his wife.

Through it all, Bryson's deepest concern was the children. On several occasions, he and Ilene had taken the time to explain what was happening and allow the children to ask questions. The initial announcement that their mother was going to die brought tears from the older ones, while the others seemed to not comprehend the reality enough to let it disturb them. Through the struggles, Jessica remained quietly cooperative, while a constant melancholy mood hovered about her. Ilene talked to her often, but she seemed hesitant to express her feelings. The boys gradually began misbehaving in ways that were not bad enough to call for drastic measures, but difficult enough to increase the strain on the entire family. Amber vacillated from sweet and helpful to stubborn and obnoxious. And little Jamie was too young to know what was going on. She just cried when she had to be separated from her mother, or when she wanted attention for any reason.

Bryson tried to give each of the children time and affection, but he often felt torn in so many directions that he knew he wasn't doing a very good job of it. His father and Lindy remained supportive from a distance, and they had taken the children to St. George during one of Ilene's hospital stays. Bryson knew they would like to help more, but the children needed to be in school, and his father's arthritis couldn't tolerate the cold weather in northern Utah.

Melissa continued to call every day. Bryson often listened to Ilene's end of the conversation as she lied to her sister and made everything sound much better than it was. And he followed her example—mostly, he decided, for the sake of his pride—and told Melissa they were managing just fine. He wasn't prepared to admit that he needed help from anybody—especially Melissa, in spite of her regular offers.

On a cold evening after the kids had finally settled down, Bryson looked at the calendar and wondered if Ilene would live the nineteen days left until Christmas. At moments he believed she could hang on for many weeks; at others he would expect her to stop breathing any minute. While a part of him wanted her to hang on indefinitely, deep inside he prayed she would be spared the worst of what cancer was capable of doing to her. He looked around at the dirty dishes that had been ignored because of the family home evening project brought over by some neighbors. The kids had enjoyed making Christmas decorations and Bryson appreciated the effort, but the resulting mess was discouraging.

Feeling suddenly unable to function, Bryson pushed his hands into his hair and prayed. This form of conversation in his mind had become commonplace, but he often felt so overwhelmed and distraught that it was difficult to know if his prayers were being heard at all. In the midst of it, the doorbell rang. He glanced at the clock. 9:28 p.m. He almost laughed, wondering if God had sent someone to wash the dishes, or at least to repair the dishwasher. The thought stuck somewhere between his heart and his head when he opened the door to see Melissa, holding two suitcases.

"I took a cab," she explained while he stared at her, wondering if he could handle her along with everything else. "I didn't want you to have to bother coming to get me."

Bryson said nothing, almost fearing that this was supposed to be the answer to his prayers. He wasn't particularly fond of the idea.

"It's cold out here, Bryse. Aren't you going to let me come in?"

"Come in," he said mechanically as he moved aside and took one of her suitcases.

Melissa set down the other suitcase, then pulled off her coat and gloves and tossed them over the top of a chair. She looked around methodically, then almost glared at Bryson. "I thought you said you were doing fine."

"I am," he insisted.

"It looks like a hurricane took a left turn in the dining room."

"I'm not quite the housekeeper Ilene was," he said as if he resented it.

"Where is she?" Melissa asked more softly.

"The family room," he stated. "I think she's asleep."

Melissa descended the steps that divided the dining room from the family room, with only an open rail in between. Bryson followed her, hesitating on the stairs. She turned to look at him in dismay when she saw the hospital bed and all the medical paraphernalia scattered about. The dim glow of a lamp illuminated Ilene's peaked face where she rested against the pillow. It also illuminated Melissa's tears when she turned back to look at Bryson in disbelief.

"Why didn't you *tell* me it was this bad?" she spat at him in a whisper.

"Ilene didn't want me to. You don't argue with a dying woman, Lissa. *You* told me that."

"Just how bad is it? Where exactly does she have cancer now?"

Bryson blew out a long breath and rubbed his eyes. "It would be easier to tell you where she *doesn't* have it. Her digestive system is free of it, so far. Eating is almost her favorite pastime, for which we are extremely grateful. Her mind is functioning fully, though she sleeps a great deal because of the pain medication. The dosage is being increased regularly. Without it, she's . . . well, it's bad."

"What kind of care is she getting?" Melissa asked directly.

"We have a nurse come in every day to check her. Sisters in the ward are helping out while I'm at work. I'm getting pretty good at bathing her. We're still working on other things."

Bryson felt Melissa's eyes bore into him and he almost shivered, as if she could see his very soul. He expected her to somehow ridicule him for the way he was handling all of this—or, more accurately, not handling it. But with a voice softened by empathy she asked, "And how are you, Bryson?"

He only shook his head slowly and went back up the stairs.

Melissa let him go for the moment. She sat carefully by her sister's bed and watched her sleep, losing track of the time that she cried helplessly, grateful that she had these minutes alone to adjust to the shock. Reminding herself that she'd come to help, Melissa wiped her tears and took a deep breath. She felt grateful for the prompting to come to her sister's side as she headed up the stairs toward the kitchen, noting just how bad it really was. She found Bryson washing dishes, very slowly, as if he had no motivation at all.

"You didn't answer my question," she said as she started cleaning off the table, carrying dishes back and forth to the sink.

"I'm doing the best I can, Lissa. That's all I can say."

"Does the house always look this bad?" she asked, trying to sound light. But Bryson glared at her over his shoulder.

"Actually, it's looked worse on occasion."

"Why didn't you call me?" She took the dishrag to wipe off the table and he leaned against the counter, momentarily useless.

"It's no secret that you and I are only on tolerable terms, Melissa. I seriously doubt we could live under the same roof, for any reason."

"Bryson," she tossed the dishrag into the sink and folded her arms, "that's my sister dying in there. If it's going to get worse before it's over, I think you need some help."

"I'll manage."

"How?"

"I don't know," he snapped. "But I will."

"How?" she repeated.

"Where did you get such a sassy little mouth?" he countered.

She ignored him. "This house is filthy, Bryson."

"No," he lifted a finger, "it's a mess, but it is *not* filthy. You will find a great deal of disorder, but you will not find filth." He turned back to the sink. "Unfortunately, I can't take the credit for that. The Relief Society has been coming in once a week to clean. They manage to work around the clutter."

"That's very nice of them," Melissa stated, "but they can't do it forever. What happens when—"

"If you must know," he interrupted, "they don't do it alone. The children and I work with them. They are helping me train the children to clean and do laundry. We are working toward self-sufficiency, in spite of appearances."

Melissa gave a noise of approval. "I'm impressed."

"The Relief Society has been great. I am a bumbling idiot when it comes to such things."

"You need me, don't you," she stated.

"I can manage fine, thank you. I'm sure Ilene will be pleased to see you, but—"

Bryse was interrupted by a weak moan that came from somewhere on the other side of the sink. It wasn't until he had grabbed a towel and hurried down the stairs that Melissa realized there was a monitor sitting on the counter—the kind used in nurseries so a parent could hear the baby crying. As Melissa clearly heard Bryson whispering to Ilene at her bedside, she realized that he would have heard her crying before she'd come upstairs.

While Bryson helped Ilene to the bathroom and back to bed, Melissa finished the dishes. Overhearing the sweet, gentle words he used with Ilene, she found them an interesting contrast to the terse, belligerent tone he used with her.

"Did you get any rest?" he asked gently.

"A little," Ilene replied. Her voice was strained. "But I still feel exhausted."

"It was a hard day . . . and last night wasn't too good, either. You go back to sleep while you can, babe. I have a feeling tomorrow will be an exciting day for you."

"How is that?" she asked.

"Your sister is going to be here."

"Melissa?" Ilene's voice picked up a definite lilt. "She's coming?"

"She'll be sitting right here in this chair, just as soon as you get some rest."

Melissa heard the subtle sounds of a kiss and a whispered exchange of "I love you." She wiped fresh tears away when she realized Bryson was coming up the stairs. He looked around the kitchen in surprise before his eyes came to rest on her.

"Thank you," he said. "It definitely looks better."

"No problem," she replied. "How is she?"

"Pretty tired at the moment. I'm sorry . . . I didn't tell her you were here yet. She's hardly slept, and—"

"It's okay," Melissa assured him. "I can see her tomorrow." She paused then asked, "Why was last night a bad one?"

Bryson glanced guiltily toward the monitor; she'd obviously overheard. He wondered if she realized he'd overheard her crying earlier. He cleared his throat and glanced down. "She gets these muscle spasms that . . . well," he decided to spare her the unnecessary details, "she has a hard time getting comfortable."

"And you were up all night with her."

"Well, it wasn't *all* night."

"How often do you get a good night's sleep, Bryson?"

"What makes you so nosy?" he retorted.

"I'm concerned about you," she snapped. "If you burn out and have a nervous breakdown, then who's going to take care of Ilene—not to mention the kids?"

"I'm going to bed, Melissa." He switched off the kitchen light. "It's getting late." He picked up the monitor and started down the hall. "You can use the same room you did last time, if you can find the bed. That's where we've been storing the clean laundry. Lock the front door, would you?"

Melissa stood as she was for several minutes before she found the motivation to move. She had fully expected coming here to be difficult, but there was no way she could have been prepared for the pain she had felt already. Downstairs was a woman dying. Down the hall was a man falling apart but not willing to admit it. She forced herself to find that bed and get some sleep. She was going to need it.

Melissa awoke to a montage of noise in the distance. She dressed and hurried to the kitchen, only to find total disarray.

"Hurry up," Bryson barked at Jessica, who was choking down cold cereal as fast as she could manage. "If you miss that bus, you're out of luck, young lady." While he was talking, he set a pitcher of orange juice on the table and pulled Jamie out of the cat food.

"If you'd wake me when you're supposed to," Jessica retorted with her mouth full, "I wouldn't have to gag my way through breakfast."

"You've got an alarm clock," Bryson snapped back. "Learn to use it."

"I still need something for show and tell, Dad," Amber scolded in the midst of picking Cheerios out of her bowl of milk with her fingers. "You never listen to me."

"I gave you something for show and tell last night," Bryson said while he put Jamie in the high chair and put some toast and juice in front of her. "If you don't like it, that's your problem, little miss smarty-pants."

"I don't wanna take that. Julie brought her new puppy to show and tell. Can't I take our kitty to—"

"We've already discussed this. No, you may *not* take the cat to show and tell. Now eat your breakfast."

"Good-bye, Dad," Jessica hollered as she grabbed her bag and headed for the door.

"Brush your teeth!" Bryson shouted, but Melissa noticed that Jessica left, pretending she hadn't heard, which would have been impossible.

"Brandon shoved me out of the bathroom," Greg yelled from the hallway and came running into the kitchen with Brandon close behind.

"I was standing there combing my hair, and he pushes his way in there and shoves me out of the way so he can—"

"Hold it!" Bryson took both boys by the backs of their collars and sat them down. "Both of you just settle down. You," he pointed at Greg, "don't need to take fifteen minutes to comb your hair. And you," he pointed at Brandon, "need to wait for your turn in the bathroom. If there's a problem, you come and talk to me about it before you go pushing your way in there. Now eat your breakfast. You've got to leave soon."

Only then did Amber look up and squeal, "Aunt Melissa!"

Bryson sent a brief, hard glance in her direction as the kids scrambled out of their chairs to hug her. "You'll have to get your own breakfast," he snarled. "You've got your choice. Cereal, or toast, or cereal and toast."

"I can get my own breakfast, thank you," she said. "Is there anything I can do to help, or—"

The phone rang and he picked it up quickly, as if it might save him from conversing with her. Melissa sat at the table with the children and tried to keep everything under control while Bryson was obviously distressed with the phone call. She couldn't hear what he was saying, but it was easy to tell his stress level was rising quickly. Keeping her attention on the children, she was surprised to hear him say her name in a kind voice. She turned to see him holding his hand over the mouthpiece on the phone.

"Did you need something?" she asked with an exaggerated smile.

"The woman who was going to help Ilene today can't come, and the Relief Society's having trouble finding a replacement. Do you think you could manage while I'm at work?"

"I'm sure I could manage just fine."

"Thanks," he said with no change of expression, then into the phone, "Listen, Ilene's sister showed up last night. She says she can handle it for today." He paused thoughtfully. "Yes, that would be fine," he said with an expression that indicated he was lying. Whatever it was, it wasn't fine. "Why don't we make that eight o'clock? Give me a chance to get dinner over with. Okay, I'll see you then." Bryson hung up the phone and pushed a tense hand through his hair.

"Is something wrong?" Melissa asked gently.

"No," he snapped, then his voice softened slightly. "I mean . . . I don't know. That was the Relief Society president. She wants to come over and talk to me later." He glanced at his watch. "Good heavens, you kids better get your teeth brushed and—"

"Bryson," she interrupted gently, "go to work. I'll make sure the kids get to school in one piece."

He looked momentarily stunned, then said "Thank you" and hurried down the hall. He came back a few minutes later, wearing a tie and carrying a briefcase. He kissed each of the kids and left without another word to Melissa.

Melissa asked Brandon and Greg questions about when they were supposed to leave and what Jamie would need. They managed to tell her enough that she figured she could get by. She checked on Ilene and found her still sleeping, then she got the children off and dressed Jamie before she heard over the monitor in the kitchen that Ilene was awake.

"Well, good morning," Melissa said from the bottom of the

stairs.

Ilene turned slowly to see her sister. Tears brimmed in her eyes and she held out her hand. "Melissa? Is it really you?"

Melissa took her hand, then bent over the bed to share a careful embrace.

"I can't believe it," Ilene cried. "Bryson told me you would be here, but then I wondered if I had dreamt it." Ilene didn't want to tell her that one of her biggest fears was being subject to hallucinations, and she was grateful to know that this wasn't her imagination. "Oh, I'm so glad you came. I need my sister."

Melissa didn't miss the emotion in Ilene's voice, but she only smiled and said, "Actually, I get to take care of you today. Whoever was scheduled couldn't make it. So, you tell me what to do and I'll do it."

"I just want to talk to you all day," Ilene said almost dreamily. "You can't imagine how much I've missed you."

"Maybe I can," Melissa said, fighting back the emotion she felt rising in her throat.

"But first of all," Ilene moved slowly to sit up, "I'd better get to the bathroom."

Melissa did her best to help Ilene to her feet, but she knew it would take time to get used to what hurt and what didn't. Ilene didn't complain, but Melissa knew she was in pain. Ilene used a walker and insisted that she could manage just fine now that she was on her feet, but Melissa held her breath with every step. While Ilene was in the bathroom, Melissa went to the kitchen and cried, hoping to release enough emotion that she would be able to smile when Ilene got back to bed.

After Ilene had eaten breakfast, they spent the morning talking of trivial things that avoided reality. Melissa couldn't avoid a few tears as she observed Ilene's interaction with Jamie, and the way Jamie had been taught to hug only her mommy's arm, because anything more would be too painful.

Ilene slept through the middle of the day, and Jamie went down for a nap after lunch. Melissa used the time to clean up the kitchen and straighten the remainder of the house. She was looking forward to talking more with Ilene, hoping to get to some of the *real* feelings, but the children started coming in from school soon after Ilene woke up and endured another trek to the bathroom.

Observing the children as Ilene made an effort to talk to each one about school and check on their homework, Melissa noticed the strain Ilene felt, as well as difficult behavior from each of the kids that hadn't been so obvious during her visit last summer. Attempting to ease the stress for Ilene, Melissa spent some time with each of the children, certain this was not easy for them. It wasn't until Bryson came home that she realized how late it was. The house was a mess again, and she had intended to cook some dinner but hadn't even gotten past the intention.

"I'm sorry the house is such a mess," she said, sticking her head in the refrigerator to see what was available.

"Actually," he admitted, "it looks better than most days. What are you doing?"

"I was wondering what I could fix for dinner or—"

"Dinner will be here in about twenty minutes."

Melissa closed the fridge. "Oh, that's nice."

"Yes, it is," he agreed. "Since the ward has had the strain of helping with Ilene and the kids, they took the meal project into other wards in the stake. In one week they had over two hundred women sign up to bring a meal in. People have been great, for the most part. If we can survive eating spaghetti three times a week, we might make it through."

Melissa chuckled, but Bryson didn't even crack a smile. A spaghetti dinner was brought over at six o'clock by a sweet woman whose four children helped carry the food in from the car. Melissa kept control at the table while Bryson fixed Ilene a tray, but he'd barely sat down when he was needed again. Melissa wondered what the children would be doing without her there. She could well imagine the chaos.

Ilene couldn't keep her dinner down, and the vomiting caused spasms in her back. Bryson insisted that Melissa just leave him alone and let him handle it, so she supervised the children through cleaning up the kitchen and doing their homework. At five after eight, the doorbell rang. Jessica answered it and went to get her father. Melissa hovered in the dining room as he greeted the two middle-aged women with a handshake and an apology.

"The evening got hectic, and I confess, I forgot you were coming." He was going to apologize for the mess until he glanced around and realized the front room was relatively tidy.

"Is this a bad time?" Sister Broadbent asked kindly. "Would it be better if—"

"Oh, no." Bryson motioned toward the couch. "Please, sit down. Just give me a minute to make sure Ilene's okay, and then we can talk."

"I'll check on her," Melissa offered, passing through the corner of the front room on her way down the stairs. Bryson cast her a harsh glare out of view of his visitors, and she wondered if she had denied him a moment of escape to gather his wits.

"That was Ilene's sister," Bryson said as he sat on the edge of the chair.

"Oh, is that the same one who came from California last summer to—"

"Yes," he answered, trying not to sound terse.

"Is she staying long, or—"

"No," Bryson interrupted again. "She's just—"

"Ilene is fine," Melissa reported as she came in and sat down. Bryson gave her another hard glare, but she ignored him. It was Ilene's suggestion that she sit in and find out what was going on, but Melissa would have done it, suggestion or not. Her sister was dying, and the situation was difficult. She had a right to know what was happening.

"You must be Melissa," Sister Broadbent said sweetly. "Ilene has talked so much about you. I'm Helen Broadbent, the Relief Society president, and this is one of my counselors, Jane Price."

"It's a pleasure to meet you," Melissa replied. "I understand you've been doing a tremendous job of taking care of my sister's family."

"Not as tremendous as we'd like to," Helen replied with a careful glance toward Bryson. "That's what we need to talk about. You know, Bryson, that when all of this started, I told you I would be completely honest with you, and that Ilene's needs were the most important thing."

"Yes, I know," he said mechanically, already hating this conversation. He knew what was coming. He was well aware of the problem, but he didn't know what to do about it.

"We've really tried to give Ilene the kind of care she needs, Bryson, but it's reached a point where we're having some problems. The truth is, there are very few sisters in the ward who are willing to come into your home and be with Ilene. I've tried to help them see the blessings of service, but many of them are just uncomfortable with the situation. The few from the ward who are willing to be here have enjoyed their time helping her for the most part, and they want to continue helping. You know we branched out into the stake for some help . . . but the women who are willing to come in . . . Ilene doesn't know them and she's not comfortable with the circumstances. After what happened the other day, I've been concerned about Ilene and the—"

"What happened the other day?" Melissa interrupted.

"I'll tell you later," Bryson began to say, but Helen interjected.

"We had a woman here who was more than willing to help, but I think she wasn't prepared for the situation."

Bryson sighed and looked at the floor. Melissa wondered why this made him so uncomfortable.

"Ilene had a bad day and didn't get the help she needed."

Bryson sighed again, and Melissa felt sure there were details he'd like to add. She saw anger in his eyes.

"As I said, Bryson, the main concern is Ilene. We have to do what's best for her, no matter how—"

"If you're trying to tell me that the Relief Society can't help any more, just come out and say it," he insisted.

"Oh, no," Helen looked alarmed and upset. "That's not it at all. I mean—"

"You don't have to tell me it's getting more difficult, Helen. I am well aware of the—"

"I think you should be more polite." Melissa gave Bryson a hard glare that she'd learned from him.

"This has nothing to do with you," Bryson insisted.

"It has *everything* to do with me," Melissa retorted. "Now be quiet and let Sister Broadbent finish."

Helen smiled tensely, but her chin quivered and Melissa felt sure she was going to cry. "I didn't come with the intention of making things worse, I can assure you. I simply wanted to discuss the options and work toward an arrangement that will help Ilene as much as possible."

"I see few options, Helen," Bryson stated. "I either work, or I take care of Ilene. I can't do both at the same time. The insurance doesn't cover any more in-home care than we've already got, and I'm not having her die in some lousy hospital. She hates hospitals."

"I understand, Bryson," Helen said gently. Melissa wondered how many conversations like this they'd had to be on these terms. In spite of the strain, it was evident that they were comfortable with each other. "The bottom line is that one woman cannot take care of Ilene alone as long as she needs to be lifted in and out of bed. There are times when she can manage, but her bad days are going to get worse and more frequent. There are five women, including myself, who are willing to do anything that needs to be done. If I put two on a shift, that's eighteen hours a week that each of us will need to be here. If that is our only option, then we will find a way to do it. That's what the Relief Society is for, Bryson. If something needs to be done, we will find a way. But we need to look at this realistically and consider what is best for Ilene."

A heavy silence followed. Helen wiped at her tears and Jane, who had said nothing, squeezed her hand. Bryson stared at the floor.

Melissa tried to control her emotion enough to speak as she contemplated the decisions that had brought her here. It had seemed so drastic, and she'd wondered many times if she would regret it. But the Spirit had prompted her, and she had known it was right. Now she understood why.

"Helen," Melissa said. "May I call you Helen?"

"Of course, dear." Helen smiled.

"If I am here with Ilene, and you have five women willing to come in, then each of you would only have to come once a week."

Helen looked briefly stunned. Bryson looked as if he wanted to hit Melissa before she had a chance to say anything else.

"But I thought you had to go back to California and—"

"You have a job, Melissa," Bryson interrupted Helen once again.

"You have obligations and—"

"No, I don't," she said with a smile. "I quit my job and put everything into storage before I came here."

"Oh, that's wonderful," Helen said and started to cry again. Jane pulled a tissue out of her purse and handed it to Helen, then she took out another one for herself. "I knew the Lord would make it possible for this to work out somehow."

Bryson got up and left the room. Melissa let him go.

"Is there a problem?" Helen asked quietly.

"Nothing that can't be worked out," Melissa said. "He and I have never gotten along terribly well, but under the circumstances, I'm sure we can overcome our differences."

Melissa talked with Jane and Helen for nearly an hour, going over details of Ilene's needs that Melissa felt compelled to learn. It was easy to see that these women cared a great deal for Ilene and took their callings very seriously. Melissa wondered if she would have been one of those who refused to come because it was uncomfortable. If it wasn't her sister, would she be able to give so much of herself? They talked about Ilene with mutual love and admiration, and were able to work out a schedule before the president and her counselor finally left.

Melissa could see from the top of the stairs that Bryson was with Ilene. She allowed them this time together and put the children to bed, taking a few minutes with each one to talk and make certain they said their prayers. The responsibility she was taking on could be frightening if she thought about it too hard. But Melissa knew the Lord had prompted her to be here, and with his help, she would be able to make a difference in the final weeks of her sister's life.

* * * * *

Bryson told himself he got up and left because he needed to check on Ilene. But he knew if he stayed another minute he'd have lost it.

"What's going on up there?" Ilene asked as he sat down hard in the rocking chair at the side of the bed.

"Helen came to tell us the Relief Society can't handle it

anymore."

"That doesn't sound like Helen."

"Well, she didn't put it that way exactly."

Ilene reached over and put a hand on Bryson's arm. "I'm sorry I'm such a bother," she said.

Bryson turned to look at her and had to choke back the emotion. Why did she have to be so sweet? "You're not a bother, Ilene. I only wish I could be here with you all the time and—"

"But you can't, and there's no use going through all of that again." Bryson sighed and Ilene went on, "So what are we going to do?"

"I guess your sister's getting it all worked out."

"She was wonderful today, Bryse. I can tell her what I need without being embarrassed. She understands me."

"I'm glad she understands somebody," he snarled.

"Why are you always so agitated with her? I don't understand."

"She just embarrassed me in front of Helen and Jane."

"What did she say?" Ilene insisted.

"She told me I should be more polite."

"I tend to agree," Ilene said, and Bryson shot her a hard look. "These ladies are only trying to help, and you're often sharp with them. You *should* be more polite."

"Okay," he admitted, "but she didn't have to say it in front of them and . . ." Bryson stopped when he met the empathy in Ilene's eyes, and the whole thing fell into perspective. Ilene was dying, and he was complaining about something petty and ridiculous. "You're right," he said quietly. "I should be more polite."

"Helen understands what you're going through."

Bryson nodded, but he hated it when people told him they understood. He had yet to find someone who *really* understood. But he knew they meant well, and he tried to keep that in mind.

"So, how is Melissa going to work it all out?" Ilene asked, hating the way she always felt like such a burden. There were moments when she wished she could have been killed instantly in an accident. If it was her time to go, fine. But why all this torment for those she loved?

"She's staying," Bryson stated, but it took Ilene a moment to absorb it.

"How long?" Ilene asked.

"She said she quit her job. I guess you'll have to ask her the rest."

Ilene couldn't explain the peace that came over her at that moment. She wanted to explain it to Bryson, but she knew he wasn't in the mood to appreciate it. Instead, she just took his hand and squeezed it. "I love you, Bryson Davis," she said.

"I love you, too, babe," he said with strength, leaning forward to put his other hand to her face.

"Hold me, Bryson," she whispered. He sat on the edge of the bed and put an arm carefully beneath her shoulders. But it wasn't enough. "No," she said, "*hold* me."

He looked puzzled. "I'm afraid I'll hurt you if I get too close."

"It's okay." She managed a smile and tried to urge him closer. Bryson carefully lifted his legs onto the bed beside her. She laid her head against his shoulder and nuzzled close to his chest, wishing it were possible to know, just once more, what it was like to make love with this man whose passion had always left her in awe. It was the part of their marriage that had always managed to make up for the other little things that came between them. Lifting her face to his, she whispered, "Please kiss me, Bryse."

He smiled, and for a moment she saw the tension leave his eyes. "You don't have to beg me to do that," he said, and pressed his lips over hers.

At the first hint of response, Bryson followed his urge to kiss her harder, wishing he could somehow transfer his life into her and keep her with him. He tried to hold back the long-stifled passion, but as she pressed a gentle hand to the back of his neck, urging him closer, he lost his self-restraint and eased closer. Oh, how he wanted her! He tried to remember how long it had been, and realized he had no sense of time anymore.

It wasn't the physical pain that made Ilene cry, as much as the realization that she was incapable of giving Bryson what she knew he wanted—and needed. She tried to hold back the emotion for his sake, but a sob erupted in the midst of their kiss and he drew back sharply.

"Did I hurt you?" he asked frantically.

Ilene shook her head and touched his face. "No," she lied, "I just wish I could . . ." Emotion cut her words short, but Bryson understood.

"It's all right, Ilene," he said, and he hoped she knew that he meant it. He would endure celibacy for a decade if he thought it could take away even a degree of her suffering. He knew he was arrogant and stubborn, but he loved her with all his heart and soul. And not even death would change that.

CHAPTER SIX

With the children all settled in, Melissa headed down the stairs to see how Ilene was doing. She stopped halfway when she saw Bryson lying on the bed beside her, holding her close. She saw him wipe away her tears with gentle fingers, and the way he pressed a kiss to her brow as if she were precious and fragile. Which, of course, she was.

Melissa turned around and hurried quietly to the front room, where she sat on the couch and put a hand over her mouth to keep from crying aloud. There was something so poignant in all of this. Melissa had often heard of untimely death, and she had thought how tragic and sad it was. But she had never comprehended the reality of the lives affected. The pain she felt in losing her sister was difficult to face. But as much as she loved Ilene and depended on her, she had not been a part of her everyday life for many years. She felt a rush of compassion as she thought of what Bryson must be feeling. She thought of the determination in his voice as he'd told Helen he would not have Ilene die in "some lousy hospital." She thought of him holding his wife and trying to accept the fact that their days together were numbered.

And mixed with all the compassion, Melissa had to indulge in a moment of self-pity. The fact that she was twenty-seven and had never married was a sore point she didn't like to think about. Not that she hadn't had opportunities, but it had never been right and she knew it. But something inside of her ached when she saw the way Bryson held Ilene close and kissed her. Melissa had to admit she was lonely. Perhaps that was the very reason it wasn't so hard to leave her job and her life behind to be a part of this family, at least for the time being. If she could take care of Ilene and help the children adjust, her life would have much more value than if she simply continued decorating the homes of people with too much money for their own good.

Melissa heard Bryson in the kitchen and hurried to dry her tears. "Is she all right?" she asked from the doorway, startling him.

"Yes. She's asleep," he answered dryly, then swallowed two Tylenol. "And that's what I'm going to do while I have a chance."

"Wait," she said as he tried to walk past her. "There's something I want to say."

"I'm listening," he said curtly, and she couldn't help wondering if this was the same man she'd seen holding Ilene a few minutes ago.

"I was sorry to spring it on you that way—about quitting my job, I mean. I prayed about it, and I knew I was supposed to come, that I was needed. I can't begin to understand how you feel, Bryse. But I want you to know that I love her, too. Perhaps we can put our differences aside and work together—for her sake."

Bryson nodded, fearing if he spoke he might cry. She was the first person through all of this who had admitted she didn't understand how he felt. He couldn't deny that he needed her here, and he would be a fool to let pride stand in the way of having his prayers answered. He turned to walk away before his emotion got the better of him. But she stopped him with a hand on his arm.

"And one more thing," she said. "I apologize if what I said embarrassed you . . . about being polite, I mean. I've never dealt with anything like this before."

If Bryson wasn't already on the brink of falling apart, she just had to apologize. He almost wanted a reason to be angry with her, if only for an excuse to release some of this anger that had nowhere to go. But she was being perfectly agreeable, and he had no choice but to accept it willingly. "It's okay, Melissa," he said with a shaky voice. "I've never dealt with anything like this before, either."

Life quickly settled into a routine for Melissa as she tried to work herself into the family's habits and do all she could for Ilene. They had little time to talk with all that had to be done, but occasionally they would find some quiet time together. These were the moments Melissa treasured. She often asked Ilene if there was anything she wanted to have done, but she always answered that everything was taken care of as much as it could be.

Through all of this, Christmas was fast approaching. Melissa helped Bryson and the children bake cookies and decorate the tree, which was put in the family room, rather than the front room as it had been in years past. Bryson said little to Melissa, but he managed to be polite, and she sensed the stress in him decreasing somewhat. She hoped her help was the reason for that, but she didn't dare question it.

With Ilene's suggestions, Melissa managed to slip out occasionally when everything was under control, and do the Christmas shopping for the children. She bought gifts for Bryson from Ilene, and hid everything in her room. Twice she stayed up half the night wrapping presents, feeling the Christmas spirit in a way she hadn't since she was a child. She didn't get much sleep, but she was needed and she managed to keep going.

On the twenty-first, Bryson surprised her by saying more than three consecutive words to her directly. "Listen, Melissa," he said quietly while she was loading clothes into the dryer, "I asked Ilene what I should do about Christmas for the kids, but she said you'd already gotten some things and I should talk to you first."

Melissa wondered what he would have done if she weren't here, but she didn't bother questioning that. She *was* here, and she was grateful to be able to help.

After she turned on the dryer, Melissa motioned for him to follow her. She led him into the den, which had now become her room, and closed the door. She opened the closet and Bryson's eyes went wide. There was barely room for a few of her clothes for all the wrapped gifts piled there.

"Santa's already been here, Bryse," she said. "It's up to you to put it all under the tree on Christmas Eve."

"How did you—"

"I managed," she smiled.

"Where did you get the money?" he asked, having seen no evidence of activity in his bank accounts.

"I had some saved. We'll work it out later."

Bryson said nothing more than a simple "thank you," but Melissa sensed a growing relaxation in him as he seemed determined to enjoy the holiday, knowing it would be his last with Ilene. Perhaps knowing that everything was under control helped him along.

While Bryson fully expected this Christmas to be full of sorrow, he was surprised at the spirit in his home. Perhaps their perspective on life made the real meaning stand out. He knew that was part of it, but he had to admit it had a lot to do with Melissa. She had a way of bringing the world in to Ilene, and taking Ilene's spirit out into the world. While an endless supply of goodies and surprises came in from friends and ward members, Melissa managed to keep similar offerings of the season going out. She and Ilene would discuss those in the neighborhood with certain needs, and through Melissa's hands, Ilene found the means and opportunity to serve through phone calls and letters and gifts to others.

The Monday before Christmas, Melissa announced they were going caroling for family home evening. At first Bryson thought this was an insensitive idea, considering that Ilene was unable to get out of bed. But Melissa took along the video camera and, as they went door to door, neighbors and ward members were filmed sending personal Christmas wishes to Ilene, who laughed and cried as she watched the video. The next day Melissa filmed the children playing in the snow and building a snowman. Ilene watched it three times, and Bryson was thrilled at the joy she found in sharing things with the children that she thought she never would again.

Through all of the Christmas celebrating, Melissa kept the camera running, with Ilene at the center of everything. Bryson had mixed emotions as he contemplated watching this after she was gone. But for the moment, he just enjoyed being with her. They laughed and sang, and the children even got along—most of the time. Bryson took some vacation days, and the spirit of the holidays continued to hover in their home through New Year's Day. But when the children went back to school, the letdown was difficult for all of them.

While Bryson was grateful to see Ilene hanging on this long, when there had been moments he had feared he would lose her hard and fast, he began to wonder how bad it would get if it went on too long. She gradually became weaker, and as the pain became more intense, she was put on a morphine pump that allowed her all the medication she wanted. Addiction was not a concern. He knew she tried to hold back and take only what she absolutely needed, if only so she could stay awake and enjoy what little time she had left. But their time together became rare as she slept a great deal and ate less and less.

When she was coherent, Ilene began to talk about things that made no sense. It was hard for Bryson to deal with, but Melissa quickly set a good example as she simply humored Ilene and did her best to carry on a conversation. Bryson really started getting nervous when Ilene became obsessed with picking things off the sheets that weren't there, and discussing with Melissa the things that were on the ceiling. At first it was Halloween decorations, then ice cubes that she feared would melt and make a terrible mess. Then there were bugs and spiders, creating in Ilene a fear so real that Bryson wanted to scream.

Two weeks into January, Ilene woke the entire house with a shrill whistle that she'd never been capable of in her life. Bryson pulled on his jeans and came running. She was hysterical, insisting that there were snakes everywhere. While Bryson was trying to calm her down and convince her there were none, he was aware of the children hovering close by with terrified expressions. Amber started whimpering and buried herself in Melissa's arms.

"Get the kids out of here!" he snapped at Melissa as he tried to concentrate on Ilene. "It's okay, babe. I swear to you there isn't a snake within miles of here."

"Don't you *dare* try to patronize me!" Ilene actually yelled at him. He was so stunned he couldn't speak. She had *never* yelled at him. "I am not crazy, Bryson Davis. I know a snake when I see it, and they are everywhere. Get them off of me!" she screamed.

Feeling completely desperate and helpless, Bryson turned to the only source of support he knew. "Melissa!" he shouted.

"I'm right here," she said close behind him, startling him. "Don't argue with her," she whispered. "If she wants you to get rid of the snakes, then do it."

"What are you whispering about?" Ilene insisted. "You don't

think I'm crazy, do you, Melissa? Tell him I'm not crazy."

"You're not crazy, Ilene. Bryson just has a little vision problem. Maybe he needs glasses. We'll have to get his eyes checked."

"You do that," Ilene said, still glancing around her frantically as if she were surrounded by slithering creatures. Knowing the children were hovering on the stairs and frightened, Melissa decided she could solve two problems at once. Quietly she sat down with the kids and told them in simple terms what was happening.

"Now," she said, "if your mother believes what she's seeing, then you need to go help her. Do you think you can pretend—for your mother?"

Greg was the first to move forward, eagerly pretending to gather snakes and put them in an imaginary bag. Bryson watched in amazement as the others, even little Jamie, followed his example. They started laughing as they discussed the color of the different snakes and how some were slimier than others. Ilene observed it all and gradually relaxed.

"Aren't they sweet," she said to Bryson. "They are so sweet to get rid of all those nasty snakes for me." Then she added sternly, "You should really get your eyes checked, Bryse."

Bryson chuckled, grateful he could laugh; otherwise he would crumble. Once the snakes had all been taken out to the garbage, Melissa gathered the children around their mother's bed, where they shared a family prayer. Then they all went back to bed without any apparent concerns. Jamie seemed a little distraught, but Melissa took her to bed with her and left Bryson alone with Ilene. He held her hand in silence for a long while, watching her stare at the ceiling, then she turned to him with tears in her eyes and spoke with a sincerity that made him feel as if someone else had been seeing those snakes, but the real Ilene was here now.

"You know, Bryse," she said, "I'm going to die. It won't be much longer now."

"I know, Ilene," he said with a barely steady voice.

"But you mustn't be sad for me. I will be so glad to be free of all this."

"I won't be sad for you, Ilene. I will be sad for me. I don't want to live without you."

"But it won't be for long, Bryson. This lifetime is so short, really, and we'll be together forever."

"I know," he said, pressing a hand to her face.

"Bryson, I want you to get married again, right away. There is someone special for you. She'll help you raise the kids. She'll be a good mother, and a good wife. It's someone you already know, Bryse, and I don't want you to wait very long."

"I can't even think about that now, Ilene. You're the only woman I could ever love."

"You're so sweet," she smiled. "But don't be so sure."

She drifted off to sleep then, and Bryson used more self-control than he'd ever needed before to keep from crying. He knew if he started, his emotions would take over and he'd never be able to function.

The next morning, Bryson went to work exhausted and scared. It simply wasn't a good day to be notified that the company would be laying off several employees, and he was a prime candidate. He practically stormed into George Reese's office, demanding to know why.

"It's just one of those things, Mr. Davis," his supervisor explained. "I have little control over the situation."

"But you decide who gets it in this department, and I'm telling you, if I am laid off right now, it will be devastating to my family. It simply cannot happen."

"You're not the only man in this department with a family to support," George said kindly. "I understand this kind of thing can be difficult, but—"

"No," Bryson said, "you *don't* understand." He suddenly felt so angry he couldn't even think straight. "How can you possibly understand what kinds of lives your employees are leading when they go home at night? You sit behind your desk and look at your statistics, and you don't have any idea in hell what you're doing to people's lives. I'm telling you, if I lose this job, what little my children have left will be gone."

Their eyes met for a long, tense moment. Bryson could see this man was not affected by his speech, and he was so close to losing *all* of his pride that he simply turned and walked out. He returned to his office, feeling a fear so intense it was almost painful. Quietly he closed the door and knelt beside his desk chair, praying with every fiber of his being that he would not lose his job. They were barely making it on his income now. There were medical bills and debts. If he lost his job, he'd lose his insurance. And the life insurance. How could he possibly pay all the bills and afford day care if he had no life insurance?

With his dilemma laid out before the Lord, Bryson fumbled through his work and went home, wishing he could just die right along with Ilene, and put the pain of the world behind him. But as soon as he saw the children, he knew he had to stay. They needed him, and they needed him to be sane and strong and whole. He couldn't break down now. He had to have faith that they would make it. In his mind he did his best to turn it over to the Lord. Surely he would not take Ilene if he didn't have a way for them to make it without her.

Melissa noticed Bryson's somber mood, but there was too much going on to question it. After dinner he sat by Ilene's side, staring at the wall, holding her hand, toying with her wedding rings. Melissa was helping Brandon with his homework when the doorbell rang and she went to answer it.

"Mrs. Davis?" a middle-aged man she'd never seen before said with a stern smile.

"Uh . . . no. I'm Mrs. Davis's sister. May I help you?"

"I was wondering if Bryson is at home. He and I work together, and I wanted to talk to him about something."

"Come in," Melissa motioned him inside and closed the door. "Have a seat. I'll get him."

Melissa went quietly down the stairs and whispered behind his ear. "Bryse, there's a man here to see you. He says he works with you and wants to talk to you."

Bryson's eyes widened in fear as he stood slowly and turned around. Would they actually come to his home to tell him he didn't have a job? The thought made him angry even before he went up the stairs to find George Reese sitting in his front room, looking around nonchalantly.

"This is certainly a surprise," Bryson said, making no effort to hide the edge in his voice.

"Well," George leaned forward, "you suggested that I see the way my employees live, so I thought I'd start here." He looked around again. "You have a nice home here, Bryson."

"Yes, it is," he said. "I'd like to keep it that way."

"I understand that Gibbs is just trying to buy a home. He'd have a hard time if he lost his job."

"Gibbs is a newlywed with no children," Bryson stated, hating the way he felt like he was bartering for his life. "His wife has a good job. They would manage."

"I met your wife's sister," George said. "Pretty girl. Does she live here?"

"For the time being."

"Are you supporting her, then?"

"For the time being. Is this part of my job requirement? To report the status of my household? Couldn't I just tell you I need my job and keep it without losing my pride completely?"

"Is that what this is about? Pride? I never took you for a proud man, Davis. I've always admired your work. But I think there's something you're not telling me. Honesty is an important thing with my employees, and if there is a reason you need this job that badly, I'd like to know about it. I can keep a confidence, but I can't base a decision on something I know nothing about. In the meantime, I'd like to meet your wife. Is she at home?"

"Yes, she's home," Bryson said. He wondered in that moment why he had never wanted the people he worked with to know the truth. Whatever reason it might have been, it simply had no merit anymore.

"Come downstairs." Bryson motioned with his arm, and George Reese followed. George was only a few steps behind when Bryson stopped at the foot of the stairs. "Is Ilene asleep?" he asked Melissa, who was sitting in the rocker at the side of the bed, reading Jamie a story. Jessica and Brandon were sprawled on the floor, playing *Sorry*. Amber was coloring, with crayons scattered everywhere. Greg was on the couch, working on his nightly reading assignment.

"I'm afraid she is," Melissa answered quietly. She cast a questioning glance toward the visitor, wondering what was going on, then she turned her attention back to the storybook in her hands.

Bryson turned and leaned against the stair railing. George stopped beside him and took in the picture of the family room, its central focus the bed that looked more likely to be in a white, sterile room.

"I'm afraid she's asleep, Mr. Reese," he said quietly. "She sleeps most of the time, actually. When she is awake, she is rarely herself anyway." George shot him a questioning glance. "I don't know why I didn't want anyone at work to know the truth," Bryson admitted. "Maybe it was because I didn't want the pity. Or perhaps I didn't want any reminders of the reality during the hours I was just trying to forget about it in order to make a living. Maybe it *was* pride. I don't know. But maybe I was wrong.

"The truth is," Bryson sighed and turned to look at Ilene, "my wife is dying of cancer. It was discovered a month or so after you hired me. She had surgery. She went through extensive chemotherapy and radiation, then we enjoyed several months of remission. Now she has evidence of cancer in most of her major organs, and also in her bones. At this point, she could die any day. Her morphine dosages are so high that she hallucinates frequently. I was up last night for a couple of hours, trying to convince her there weren't snakes crawling all over her bed.

"Now, I'm not telling you all of this to get you to feel sorry for me. If you want to feel sorry for someone, feel sorry for Ilene. She's not afraid to die, but she's not very happy about what her body has to go through before it will happen. Feel sorry for my kids. Without Ilene, they don't have much, because I make a poor excuse for a mother. Ilene has told me that I'm a proud man, and maybe I am. But I'm not too proud to admit that I need my job, George. Your hiring me was an answer to prayers before I even knew I needed them. The insurance coverage has saved us, but if it's terminated before all of this is over, we could be in real trouble. The life insurance will possibly keep me from going under if I need to start paying for day care for the younger ones. If I lose those benefits and have no employment, even for a few weeks, I will likely be left with one option—bankruptcy. And I would undoubtedly lose my home in the process.

"You said it's a nice house. You're right. We were very fortunate to get it. We've had it long enough that we actually have some equity, and the payments are manageable. At the going rate, our mortgage payment is equivalent to the rent for a two-bedroom apartment. I have tried very hard to comprehend what it will be like for my children when their mother is finally gone. It's difficult to face. But I don't even want to think about what it would be like for my children to lose their mother and then have to move away from the friends and neighbors that help give them a sense of security. I can't comprehend raising my five children in a two-bedroom apartment, and in so much debt that I couldn't afford to give them anything that might remotely compensate for what they are facing right now. Jessica is thirteen. She cries every night in bed. She doesn't think I know, but I do. The others have various outlets for their pain, much of which is bad behavior at school.

"I wouldn't question that my work may well have been less than up to par the last few months, Mr. Reese. I average four hours of sleep at night. I spend every minute I'm not working either seeing to my wife's needs, or helping my children deal with schoolwork and life.

"You wanted me to be honest. Now you have it. If it takes information to make an educated decision, you certainly should have enough of that. If you want to visit Gibbs first, feel free."

George Reese looked again toward where Ilene lay, then he turned and went back up the stairs. Bryson followed.

"You've certainly given me a lot to think about, Bryson," he said soberly. "And I'm not going to give you pity in return, but I do want you to know that it's nice to meet a man who has his priorities in the right place."

George reached out a hand and Bryson shook it firmly. "Thank you for coming," he said as he opened the door and George left.

Bryson leaned against the door and blew out a long breath.

"What was that all about?" Melissa asked, startling him.

"Why do you always sneak up on me like that? Is it a family trait or something?"

Melissa shrugged her shoulders and chuckled. Then she met his eyes with a clear indication that she expected an answer. Bryson knew she deserved one. "I found out today that they're going to lay off several employees. My department is required to lose at least one. It was between me and some nerd named Gibbs, who wears suits only the mafia could afford."

"So, why the visit?" Melissa sat on the edge of the couch.

Bryson pushed a hand through his hair. "I got angry and stormed into his office and told him he had no idea what he was doing, that he couldn't make a decision without knowing what was *really* going on in people's lives. I really didn't expect him to come."

"Maybe the Lord had something to do with that."

A subtle smile crept into Bryson's countenance. "Well, I did pray."

The next morning, Bryson looked up from his desk to see Larry Gibbs stroll into his office. "What can I do for you?" Bryson asked absently, paying more attention to the computer screen.

"You know the layoff was between you and me," he stated.

"Yes, I know," Bryson said sourly. He could almost hear it coming. For what other reason would Gibbs come in here than to brag it up over keeping his job?

"Well, congratulations, Davis," Gibbs said with an edge to his voice. "My days here are numbered. I don't know what kind of story you gave old Reese last night, but it worked."

Bryson leaned back in his chair and looked up at Gibbs. While a part of him was tempted to throw back some of the same belligerence, he reminded himself that this was an answer to his prayers.

"Thank you for being the one to tell me, Gibbs," Bryson said in a kind voice. "I wish you the best of luck."

"Yeah, I'm going to need it," Gibbs said and huffed out of the room.

Bryson squeezed his eyes shut in a brief prayer of gratitude, then he focused on his work. He wasn't about to give Reese any excuse to wish he'd done it the other way around.

It was almost quitting time before he was informed that George Reese wanted to see him in his office. Bryson went right away, trying to ignore the pounding of his heart.

"I've made a decision," Reese announced right off.

"Yes, I know. Gibbs told me this morning."

Reese's eyes went wide. "Well, that wasn't very nice of him, now was it?"

"Unless he was lying to me, I understand you're going to let me stay."

"It's true."

"Thank you. I won't let you down."

"No," Reese said with something almost warm in his eyes, "I don't believe you will. But there is one stipulation. I gave Gibbs his two-weeks' notice. I want you to take the next two weeks off."

"Off?" Bryson leaned forward skeptically.

"It's obvious there isn't enough work to keep both of you terribly busy, so while he's working, I'd like you to be at home with your family."

"I'm not sure I can afford to—"

"With pay, of course."

Bryson chuckled tensely. "This is sounding a little too good to be true."

"Bryson," George leaned his forearms onto his desk and looked at him directly, "I've become a little crusty around the edges through the years I've been in the business world. But on the way home from your house last night, a thought occurred to me that made me stop and look at myself. I believe I felt a little like Scrooge after he had the chance to look at Bob Cratchit's life."

Bryson couldn't help but chuckle. "I don't think it's as bad as all that."

"In technicalities, no. But sometimes I think we get so caught up in climbing the financial ladder, we forget about people. I talked to my wife about it. Bless her heart; she's a good woman. And we came to the decision to do this. I will personally cover your wages for two weeks, Bryson. I'll hardly miss the money. And I will not accept any protests. Please allow an old man to do something worthwhile for the first time in years."

Bryson took a deep breath and swallowed his emotion. He extended a hand across the desk and George rose to take it in a firm grip.

"Thank you, Mr. Reese. I can assure you the time will be deeply appreciated."

George nodded, and Bryson turned to leave after a tense moment of silence.

"Oh, Bryson," George stopped him and he turned back, "are you LDS, by chance?"

Bryson lifted his chin and found great pleasure in saying, "Yes, sir. I am."

"I thought so." George smiled. "My wife joined the Church a number of years ago. So far, she's not been able to make me come to my senses. But I want you to know I admire what you stand for."

"Thank you," Bryson said, finding it more and more difficult to keep his voice steady.

"And Bryson, please let me know."

It took Bryson a moment to figure out what he meant, and then he could only nod and leave as quickly as possible. He was able to subdue the emotion by working quickly to finish up the necessary work and putting everything in order enough to leave it for two weeks. Driving home, he realized it was later than he'd thought, and he wished he'd called to let Melissa know. Then the reality of all he'd been blessed with today struck him, and he finished the drive with an audible prayer, expressing his gratitude for his many blessings, in spite of the obvious struggles.

"Is anything wrong?" Melissa asked when Bryson came through the door nearly an hour late.

"No. Is Ilene—"

"She's asleep. She's mostly rested today."

"The kids?"

"They're at Wendy's, watching a video."

Bryson sighed and tossed his jacket over a chair.

"Did you find out anything—about your job, I mean?" Melissa was almost afraid to ask, but she knew it would be heavy on his mind.

"Yes," Bryson gave a hint of a smile, "I found out that prayers really are answered. Not only do I keep my job, but Reese is giving me two weeks off, with pay, to be with Ilene."

Melissa didn't realize how worried she had been until the relief spilled out in a bout of tears. "Oh, I'm sorry." She turned away. "The last thing you need is to listen to me cry."

"It's okay, Lissa." He handed her the box of tissues from the end table. "Maybe you could cry enough for both of us."

Melissa met his eyes as she took the box. For the first time since she'd arrived, she felt a real kinship with him. "Thank you," she said. "Maybe you ought to cry a little yourself, Bryse. This is not easy for you."

Bryson chuckled in order to avoid sobbing. "If I start to cry, Lissa, I will never be able to stop. And then I'd be more useless around here than I already am."

"I think that's the most genuine thing I've ever heard you say."

"Yes, well," he chuckled again, rubbing a hand over his eyes, "don't be too shocked. I have a feeling the worst is yet to come."

Melissa felt the emotion rushing forward again and headed toward the kitchen. "I'll heat your dinner," she barely managed to say.

"Melissa," he said and she turned back, "I know I haven't been easy to deal with, but . . . I want you to know how much I appreciate all you've done for us. We never could have made it without you."

"Well," she smiled and sniffled while a fresh stream of tears dampened her face, "it's nice to be appreciated. But if you must know, I don't feel like I'm doing anybody any favors by being here. I'm *supposed* to be here, Bryse. She's my sister, and I would die in her place if I could. Sometimes I think it would be better for everyone if that were the case. After all, I don't have a husband and children to leave behind."

"That's a good reason to go on living, Melissa. I have a feeling that when this is all over, you'll probably meet someone incredible and be darn glad that you're alive."

"Do you think so?" Melissa tried to smile. It was the last thing she cared about at the moment.

"It's just a speculation, but I admit that I've been grateful you were in the position to be here. Maybe God had something to do with that."

"I'm sure he did," she replied, and went to put Bryson's dinner in the microwave while he sat by Ilene's side. When she went to tell him it was hot, he was talking quietly to Ilene and stroking his fingers over her face. She was still fast asleep.

Through the next few days, Ilene's condition worsened so drastically that Melissa wondered what she would have done without Bryson. With him at home, they utilized the Relief Society by having the children taken out of the home as much as possible. Bryson felt sure it was not a positive experience for them to see their mother this way. Where she had done little but sleep for days, now she rarely slept at all. Bryson and Melissa alternated sitting at her bedside and sleeping. Bryson had just taken over, and Melissa had barely made it to the couch before she collapsed into an exhausted sleep. Ilene drifted in and out of a restless sleep, then she came wide awake and turned to look at Bryson. Their eyes met, and she lifted a hand toward his face. She was too weak to complete the gesture, but Bryson took her hand and pressed it to his cheek.

"Oh, my love," she said, though her words were strained, "this is hard for you." It wasn't a question.

Bryson nodded and kissed the palm of her hand.

"I'm so sorry," she added. Tears ran from the corners of her eyes into the hair at her temples. Bryson was in awe. Even now, with all the pain she was enduring, she was concerned for him. "I wish you didn't have to go through this, Bryse."

"I love you, Ilene. I would far prefer that I could take the pain myself."

An emotional smile subtly touched her lips. She closed her eyes, and for a minute he thought she was asleep. Then, without warning, her eyes flew open in apparent fear. "Bryson," she sobbed, "what's that on the ceiling?"

He looked up, already knowing nothing was there. "I don't know," he said. "What does it look like?"

She rambled something he could barely discern about bugs and spiders. He reassured her that he would not let them hurt her, and was surprised when she accepted it. Then, just as quickly, she squeezed her eyes shut and fresh tears seeped out. Her head moved back and forth on the pillow as she whimpered and cried over and over, "Oh, it hurts. It hurts."

Bryson whispered words of reassurance and kept a soothing touch moving over her face. He pumped more medication and prayed she would be free of her misery. She gradually relaxed, though only for a short time. As he watched her, a new realization sank deep into his heart. He *wanted* her to die. Her suffering had simply gone on long enough, and as much as he feared that final separation, he wanted with all his heart and soul to know that she was free of the pain and restriction of her deteriorating body.

The following morning, with little sleep behind him, Bryson asked Melissa if she could manage alone for a few hours.

"I'm sure I can. Why?"

"I'd like to go to the temple," he stated.

Ilene had apparently been asleep until she turned to look at him. "Yes, go," she said. "Think about me, Bryse. We'll be together again, you know. We have forever."

Bryson's breathing became sharp and his chin quivered, but he managed to blink back the tears. "I don't think I've ever gone without you, since I came home from my mission."

Ilene replied with a peaceful smile, then closed her eyes. "Take all the time you need," Melissa said. "We'll be fine."

Bryson squeezed Ilene's hand and pressed a kiss to her brow, then he went to his room to change. He'd only been gone a minute when Ilene said, "Why does he never cry?"

Through much of the session, Bryson's mind was absorbed in prayer. He sat in the celestial room longer than he ever had, just staring upward, trying to comprehend the spectrum of life and death. He realized, as he absorbed his surroundings, that the feeling here was somehow familiar. Then it occurred to him that sitting with Ilene had filled him with the same tranquility. He wasn't surprised to think that Ilene was so close to heaven that she would be surrounded by this kind of celestial peace. But he had a difficult time comprehending himself worthy to be part of such a thing.

As Bryson continued to pray in his mind that Ilene would be spared any more suffering, the thought came clearly to his mind that it was up to him to let her go. Instantly he knew what needed to be done, but he also knew that doing it would be one of the hardest things that had ever been required of him. Still, he went home feeling peace over Ilene's forthcoming death. He knew in his heart it was her time to go, and he believed that somehow he had known before he ever came to this earth that he would only have her for a short time. But they *would* have forever. If anything could give him faith to endure to the end, it was the prospect of being with Ilene again, to see her strong and whole.

CHAPTER SEVEN

Driving home from the temple, Bryson's emotion erupted. Like a volcano that had rumbled and threatened for months, it began in the pit of his chest, tightening with a painful grip that soon had no other outlet but to explode through his throat. It took every ounce of his self-discipline to keep the car on the road as the tears ran in torrents and he sobbed like a child.

Once in the driveway, he lost track of the time he sat in the car, just trying to release enough of this pain to be able to walk into the house and deal with whatever might be waiting.

Melissa looked up from where she sat to see Bryson on the stairs. It wasn't difficult to recognize the signs of emotion. He'd been crying, good and hard. And it was about time.

"How is she?" he asked wearily, sitting close beside Ilene.

"She's been pretty much out of it," Melissa said quietly.

Bryson nodded and took Ilene's hand into his. Tears streamed over his face, and Melissa couldn't help crying as she watched him. He pressed Ilene's fingers to his lips and cried without restraint. Melissa had an urge to just put her arms around him, but instead she went upstairs to shed her own tears in privacy, leaving Bryson to share these moments with Ilene.

Observing her sister's incoherency, Melissa wondered if the end was near. Ilene remained mostly unconscious through the night, and the following day the nurse confirmed that it couldn't be much longer. While the nurse was with Ilene, Bryson asked Melissa if she would pick up the children from the various friends and ward members where they had been staying, and bring them home. She didn't have time to question his motives before he went quietly to his bedroom and closed the door.

Bryson wondered how he would ever find the strength to get through this as he fell to his knees and sobbed in anguished prayer. Never had he felt so humble, so afraid. But as he prayed, he realized that he had never felt the Spirit so close to him. He knew beyond any doubt that the Savior would carry him through this—and the children, too. He could almost feel heavenly arms around him as he petitioned for the help he needed in doing what he had to do. By the time Melissa returned with the children, he felt ready to face them.

"Mary just left," Melissa reported. The nurse had come to their home so many times she was almost like a part of the family. "She said to call any time, day or night, if we need her."

Bryson nodded, and they joined the children in the family room while Ilene remained in apparent sleep. He asked Melissa if she would say a prayer, and when that was done, he cleared his throat and said softly, "The time is getting close, and . . ."

When he faltered, Greg asked, "You mean Mom's really going to die?"

Bryson swallowed hard, praying that he could face this without blubbering like a baby. Then in his mind, he felt a certain calm in the sudden thought that it was important for his children to see him cry. They needed to know this was hard, and that he wasn't afraid to let it show.

"Yes, Greg," he said as fresh tears rolled over his face, "she's going to die very soon." Following a long silence and a variety of sniffles in the room, Bryson found the fortitude to continue. "She's been sick for a long time, but now she can go back to live with Heavenly Father, and she won't be sick anymore."

"But . . . Dad," Brandon said with a seriousness that was not typical of him, "can't you give her a priesthood blessing and make her well again?"

Greg and Amber made noises to indicate that they had the same question. Bryson turned unwillingly to Melissa, hoping for some kind of support. Though she was obviously as baffled as he about how to answer such a question, he found some comfort in knowing that he was not alone.

"I have given your mother many priesthood blessings through her illness," Bryson began. "And there have been many times that I have wanted more than anything to just say the words that would make her get well. But I know that's not how the priesthood works, Brandon. The power of the priesthood must go along with the will of our Heavenly Father. It's your mother's time to go back home, and nothing can change that. I know we'll all miss her, but she has been in so much pain, and so miserable, and it would be selfish of us to ask her to stay when she could be free of all that."

Bryson allowed them a moment to absorb the meaning of his words, hoping that they would. He wiped a sleeve over his face and took a deep breath. "I wanted you all together so that we could pray as a family to have your mother go in peace and be free of all her pain. After we do that, I'm going to give her a blessing. I've called Aunt Lynette. She and Uncle Keith are on their way over. After you have a chance to say whatever you want to say to your mother, they'll take you home with them so you can stay there until it's over."

"How can we talk to her if she's asleep?" Amber asked, gazing forlornly at her mother.

"I believe her spirit can hear you," Melissa said quietly, and Bryson felt grateful that he didn't have to answer *all* the questions.

Glancing around the room at the children's faces, Bryson felt the sobriety of the occasion hit him all over again. They all bore varied expressions of sadness, but there was something almost hard in Jessica's eyes. He felt prompted to ask, "Is something bothering you, Jess?"

She looked up at him guiltily, then he saw courage gather in her eyes before she blurted, "You sound like you just . . . *want* her to die."

Bryson prayed silently for help and knew he had to be completely honest. She was too perceptive to accept anything less. Even if it took time for her to understand, he had to tell her the truth. "Yes," he admitted with fresh tears, "I do want her to die, Jess. I don't want to be without her. I love her with all my heart. That's why I don't want to see her suffer anymore."

He had no idea whether Jessica accepted his explanation or not.

The silence became unbearable, and he was grateful when Melissa went to her knees and urged the children to do the same. They held hands as a family while Bryson prayed aloud. A few minutes after they had finished, Keith and Lynette arrived.

Bryson couldn't recall ever being so afraid in his life as he laid his hands on Ilene's head and gave her a blessing to release her. But he felt the Spirit with him, and that same comfort warmed him fully. The children each said good-bye to their mother while Bryson looked on and cried. He hugged them all tightly, then they left with Keith and Lynette.

The house became eerily quiet. Bryson sat close to Ilene, wondering how much longer it would be, wishing he could be free of this horrible dread. As much as he wanted it, the finality frightened him. Then he reminded himself that this was not the end. He'd never been so grateful for the knowledge of eternal marriage.

Bryson called his father and talked to him and Lindy on the phone for nearly an hour. While he poured out his emotion and tried to comprehend the reality of what he was facing, Bryson felt a renewed gratitude for his family.

Mary checked in early the next morning, promising to return in the late afternoon. Bryson opted to miss church, fearing that Ilene would leave in his absence. But the day dragged interminably as he and Melissa took turns sitting at her side and trying to rest. Their feeling of helplessness was enhanced by the deathly silence hovering around them.

Mary returned around five to report that Ilene's vitals indicated the end was getting close. She made a phone call and said she would stay. Time lost all meaning as they sat together into the night, praying and waiting. Bryson had heard that the actual death could often be traumatic, even violent with the final struggle to breathe or fight off the pain. While Ilene seemed tranquil now, he wondered what it would be like. He prayed that her death would be a fitting closure to the life she had lived.

"You know," Mary spoke softly to Bryson and Melissa, "Ilene is a special woman. I've seen many patients go through this. But I don't think I've ever felt such . . . well, how do I explain? It seems that the closer a person gets to death, the more they become their true self.

Maybe it's partly the morphine; perhaps it frees a person from all inhibition. In any case, many people become bitter and angry as they go through these final stages. But Ilene has always been so sweet and kind—at least when I've been with her."

"That's true," Melissa agreed, watching her sister closely. "In spite of everything, she's hardly complained at all. And she's never stopped being thoughtful and concerned for others. She's an example to me."

Bryson wanted to agree. He wanted to tell them how she'd always been that way. But he was so overcome with emotion that he didn't dare speak. He somehow believed that words would only cheapen the feelings swelling inside him. He marveled that a man like himself had been so blessed to share his life with a woman as good as Ilene.

The room was barely absorbing the first light of dawn when Mary told them it couldn't be much longer now. "Stay close to her," she encouraged. "Tell her what you want to say. Comfort her as much as possible. Despite being unconscious, she may well be able to hear you."

Melissa met Bryson's eyes and saw a silent plea for her to go first. He held Ilene's left hand while Melissa took her right. It took little for the tears to start as she spoke softly to her sister of all that made her special. She talked of trivial memories and of the things Ilene had done to leave an impression on Melissa that affected her life. She promised to make sure the children were cared for, and assured her that Bryson was a good man. He was a good father to them.

Melissa finished with a cracked, "I love you, Ilene. We will be together again. I know we will. Save a place for me, just like you used to at the matinee, while I was busy buying popcorn." She sobbed and wiped frantically at the endless stream of tears. "I love you, Ilene."

That very instant, Ilene's eyes came open. While Melissa believed Ilene's spirit had not been completely with them for days, there was no doubting now that it was. As they made eye contact, Melissa could feel that same silent understanding they had always shared.

"I love you, Ilene," she repeated. Ilene's eyes blinked and showed a subtle sparkle. Melissa glanced over at Bryson. "She's here," Melissa whispered. As if to investigate Melissa's comment, Ilene turned her head, her eyes vaguely focused on Bryson.

Seeing his emotion, Melissa offered quietly, "Do you want to be alone, or—"

"No. Please stay," he said. Then he leaned closer to Ilene. His brow furrowed as he looked into her eyes and knew what Melissa had said was true. Ilene was with them. And she understood what was happening. Mist filled Bryson's eyes. He squeezed them shut, and the tears trickled down his face.

For a moment he didn't know what to say. He uttered a silent prayer that he would be able to make the words come before the opportunity was lost. As soon as he started to speak, his thoughts flowed freely. He told her how she had changed his life, and how blessed he was to have been given these years with her. He apologized for taking her for granted, and swore he would live worthy to be with her again. When he saw tears leak from the corners of her eyes, Bryson lost all control.

"I love you," he sobbed. "I love you more than life, Ilene. Promise you'll always be there when I need you. I can't do it alone. Dear God," he cried, "how am I going to live without you? I love you so much."

Bryson didn't realize his tears were falling onto her face until she barely managed to lift a trembling hand to her cheek, as if to acknowledge that she felt them. Then she turned her hand as if she wanted to touch his face, but couldn't. Bryson took her frail fingers into his and pressed them to his cheek. There was no denying the serenity that came into her eyes. And with it, Bryson could almost literally see a light. The glow of faith and courage she'd always had. It was there. It was real. And it gave Bryson the fortitude to know he *could* make it, because he would never be completely alone.

"I love you, Ilene. You light the path for me, and I will follow it. I promise."

Her lips moved as if she meant to speak, but he could hear nothing. He shook his head to indicate he didn't understand, then he held his ear directly over her lips. In a breath of a whisper she distinctly said, "Forever."

Bryson turned quickly to meet her eyes, as if to convince himself she'd said it. Tranquility emanated from her entire countenance. "Forever," he repeated. She showed a hint of a smile, then her eyes shifted slightly and her focus moved behind him. Bryson and Melissa turned to look that direction at the same moment. They saw nothing and immediately turned back to Ilene. Her focus was intent. Bryson felt her grip tighten on his hand, then it relaxed. He wondered for a moment if she would die with her eyes open, and the thought left him briefly panicked. But she closed her eyes. Her head fell slightly to one side. She took a strained breath. And Bryson knew she was gone.

Melissa pressed a hand to her mouth to keep from crying out as she watched Bryson pull Ilene into his arms. He pressed his face to hers and sobbed, rocking her back and forth, uttering over and over that he loved her.

Bryson had no idea how long he held Ilene and cried. He knew she was gone. He knew it was for himself that he held her, relishing this final opportunity to hold her body next to his in a way he hadn't been able to for months, knowing it would only cause her pain.

"Bryson." Melissa's voice was as gentle as the hand she put on his shoulder. She said nothing more, but he knew it was time to let Ilene rest in peace. He carefully laid her back on the bed, noting the way her arms lay limp at her sides. While he was trying to comprehend the reality that Ilene was gone, Melissa's hand took hold of his, full of strength, warm with life. Instinctively he returned the tenacity of her grip. He could see nothing through the burning tears, but he heard Melissa weeping and knew she shared his grief. Blindly he turned toward her and found his face against her shoulder, where he wept helplessly, finding a degree of comfort in the realization that she was doing the same.

After the initial shock subsided, the reality settled in. Bryson and Melissa sat side by side on the family room couch, too stunned to speak. Long after Ilene's body had been taken away, neither of them found the will to even move.

"Are you okay?" Melissa finally asked, startling Bryson from deep thought. He only shrugged his shoulders. "I thought I was prepared," Melissa spoke again, if only to ease the silence. "I was praying for her to go, so why do I feel this way?" She started to cry again. Bryson handed her a tissue and squeezed her hand. "In many ways, I think she's been gone for a long time, but . . ." She couldn't finish.

"I suppose the reality of death is a pretty humbling thing,"

Bryson finally spoke, his voice hoarse and strained.

"She's at peace now, Bryse. She's not hurting anymore."

"I know," he choked. "I know."

Following another long bout of tears, Bryson cleared his throat and said, "So, what now?"

"I think we should bring the children home."

"Yes," he agreed, "but not until we get that bed out of here."

Hearing the torment in his voice, Melissa took a deep breath and gathered her wits. She would have plenty of time to cry. Right now, Ilene's family needed her. She encouraged Bryson to go pick up the children and tell them how it had happened, father to children. While he was gone, Melissa took over, arranging with the medical supply company to have all of the rented paraphernalia removed from the house. She worked vigorously to clean up the family room and rearrange the furniture just enough to make the absence a little less keen. When she was finished, Melissa sat down and looked at the room and cried again. It felt the same way Ilene's body had looked—devoid of spirit and life.

Bryson returned with the children and spent the day just sitting with them, talking to them, crying with them. He avoided the family room. He and Melissa each made several calls to let family, friends, and ward members know that Ilene had passed away. He was relieved when Lindy said they would be coming up the following day to help with the children. Bryson sensed varying degrees of emotion from the kids, but he hardly knew how to help them when he could barely comprehend it himself.

After the children were finally sleeping, Melissa expected to feel exhausted. They'd been awake most of last night, and the day had been draining. But she felt no desire for sleep. She was numb and somehow stunned. She mechanically went through the process of cleaning up the kitchen, grateful as always that the Relief Society had brought in dinner. When there was nothing more to do, she wandered aimlessly to the family room, all too aware of its emptiness, when she was so accustomed to having the purpose of caring for Ilene.

She had thought Bryson had gone to bed, but he was sitting on the edge of the couch, his elbows on his knees, his chin in his hands, staring at the wall where the head of the bed had been. Melissa sat beside him without breaking the silence. Several minutes passed before Bryson said quietly, "You know how it feels after you take out the Christmas tree, and the room looks so clean and spacious? You're glad to see the tree go because the needles were falling off and Christmas was long over anyway. But you can't help feeling a little emptiness because you know the holidays are over. Do you know that feeling, Melissa?"

"Yes, I know the feeling, Bryson," she replied quietly, fresh tears spilling as if they came from an endless source. "And I can see the analogy."

"But Christmas always comes again, you know," he went on. "And life goes on." Bryson's voice broke and he covered his eyes with his hand. Tears ran from beneath it until he wiped at them halfheartedly. "I can't comprehend life going on without her, but I know it will. It has to. Oh!" He stifled a sob and pushed both hands into his hair. "I don't have any trouble understanding why she had to go. I don't feel bitter or angry. And I know she is at peace, that she is happier now. But dear heaven above, I don't understand how I'm supposed to live without missing her!"

Bryson cried into his hands for several minutes while Melissa watched him and cried, too. He wiped his face with his shirt sleeve and cleared his throat. "I've always been grateful to be a Mormon, Lissa. I've never questioned the truths of this gospel. But I've never been so grateful for those truths as I am right now. If I thought her existence had ended, if I believed I would never see her again, I don't think I could make it." He chuckled and sobbed at the same time. "I'm not sure I'm going to make it anyway."

"You'll make it," Melissa said resolutely. "I think you're a lot stronger than you realize."

"I think that women were blessed with most of the strength in this world. Men are nothing but a bunch of helpless fools. If we didn't have the priesthood, we'd have nothing."

"I wouldn't say that," Melissa replied warmly. "All things considered, I think you've handled this with courage and dignity. I wonder if most men could do as well."

Bryson shook his head dubiously, certain she was patronizing him. He felt like he was on the verge of a nervous breakdown. It was only thoughts of the children that made him determined to keep his head clear and keep going.

"You know," he said, "as hard as all of this has been, I have to admit something that I must say surprised me."

"What's that?" she asked gently.

Bryson looked directly into her eyes as he said, "I didn't realize death could be such an incredibly spiritual experience. I've never felt so close to heaven in my life."

Melissa briefly squeezed Bryson's hand. "I know exactly what you mean, Bryse. It's amazing."

Bryson wondered more and more what he would ever have done without Melissa. She did most of the talking as they made arrangements with the mortuary. She arranged the funeral, always asking his approval. She ordered flowers, prepared Ilene's temple clothing, and talked calmly with every concerned relative or friend who called or came by. Bryson knew Melissa was struggling with her emotion as much as he, but somehow she managed to maintain self-control.

Bryson dreaded the evening of the viewing—not only the reality of seeing his sweet Ilene in a casket, but the thought of having to accept the condolences of anyone who might come to pay their respects. He wondered how he would hold up, and did little but pray in the hours leading up to it.

When Bryson finally emerged from the bedroom, dressed and ready to go, feeling barely calm, he felt almost guilty to recall that he had five children, and he'd hardly given them a second thought. But Melissa had them gathered in the front room, in new suits and dresses that she'd bought for them the day before. They all looked so nice that he almost felt like they should be going to a wedding or something.

After Bryson recovered from his surprise, he hugged each child in turn, telling them how much he loved them, and how good they'd been through all of this. When that was done, he turned to face Melissa and could see tears brimming in her eyes. Impulsively he put his arms around her and hugged her tightly, finding some comfort in the way she hugged him back. He drew back and met her eyes, saying gently, "Thank you, Melissa, for everything. You're the best little sister a guy could ever want."

Melissa managed a smile and wished she could tell him how much his acceptance meant to her. He'd long since stopped showing any animosity toward her, but it was a big step for him to admit that he could accept and appreciate what they'd been through.

"I'm glad to be here, Bryse," she replied. "Really, I am." She wanted to add that she had gained a whole new respect for him through these weeks. But she didn't know how to say it without embarrassing him. Instead, she suggested they have a family prayer before they left for the mortuary.

Seeing Ilene wasn't as difficult as Bryson had expected it to be. She looked so beautiful, so at peace, that it somehow gave him comfort. The children asked questions and they all cried a little, but by the time visitors began to arrive, Bryson felt calm and in control. He noticed that Melissa was quiet and reserved, holding back and watching out for the children. He felt concerned for her, but didn't know how to ask if she was all right without threatening his own unsteady emotions.

The evening was tiring, but Bryson couldn't begrudge the endless throng of love and support from loved ones and acquaintances. Ilene's stepmother came, along with a couple of her children. He noticed Melissa spending quite a long time visiting with them, and he wondered how they perceived all of this.

When it was finally over, Bryson crawled into bed and cried himself into exhaustion. It was the only way he could manage to sleep, knowing his wife's funeral would be tomorrow.

* * * * *

Larry Gibbs sat at his desk, preoccupied with the reality that he was losing his job. His wife had suggested it was more the losing of his pride that he was having trouble with. She wasn't concerned about him finding work, or the slight delay in building a home. So why was it eating at him? Maybe it was the fact that it had been between him and Bryson Davis.

Davis was the quiet one around here. He came and went like some kind of ghost, and simply had no personality at all. When he did speak, his words were often terse and barely polite. Stanley Mortimer was the only one who really liked Davis. The guy simply rubbed Larry wrong. And he didn't like the idea of losing his job to someone he didn't even like.

While Larry sat and stewed about it, he got angry enough that he decided to talk to Reese one more time. Maybe he could convince him he'd made a mistake. Then he could save his job *and* his pride.

Larry knocked at Reese's office door and heard him call, "Come in."

Larry entered, but he stood there for several moments while Reese stared at the wall, apparently lost in thought.

"Oh, hello, Larry," he said, finally rousing himself into the present.

"Listen, Reese, I know we've talked about this before, but I'm really having a hard time with this layoff. I know it's cutbacks and all, but I'm not sure you made the right choice. I mean, Davis is a nice guy and all, but—"

"I'm glad you brought this up," Reese said, leaning forward in his chair. "I must admit this decision has weighed heavily on me, but not for the reasons you might suspect. I wonder if you would mind going somewhere with me this morning. Maybe we'd have a chance to talk about it."

"All right." Gibbs straightened his lapels and fought back a smug smile. "Where are we going?"

"A viewing."

"A viewing?"

"You know, it's the customary thing prior to a funeral."

"I know what a viewing is, but—"

"I've got to be going if I want to make it. I just thought you might come along for company. Might be a diversion for you."

Gibbs went along without question, hoping just to score some points with the boss. He avoided discussing the job situation, hoping Reese would bring it up, and instead indulged the old man with pointless small talk. He was expecting to go to a mortuary, but Reese drove his car into a church parking lot. A hearse and limo were parked out front.

Gibbs hated things like this, but if it would help him keep his job, he'd do just about anything. They went inside and got in a long line. Gibbs hated lines, and he couldn't imagine standing in one this long to see somebody dead he didn't even know. But the time went quickly as Reese started talking about his beliefs in the business world. Gibbs absorbed some of it, but a lot of it sounded like philosophical nonsense. He even said something silly about Scrooge and Bob Cratchit. It made little sense to Gibbs. He just wanted to keep his job. The thought of having to send out resumes and go through interviews was downright nauseating.

They were rounding the corner of the room, almost to the casket, when Gibbs caught a glimpse of someone familiar through the crowd. It took him a minute to place the face, while he was wondering why this many people would flock to a viewing. When the person's identity struck him, Larry felt a sick knot form in his stomach. He suddenly didn't want to be here. He didn't know who was in that casket, but the man standing beside it was Bryson Davis.

"Hey," Gibbs said quietly, "this isn't fair. Why didn't you tell me this had something to do with Davis?"

"I didn't figure you'd come."

"You're right about that."

"Well, it probably wasn't fair, Gibbs. But I felt much the same way when I visited Bryson's home and realized his wife was dying of cancer. They have five children, you know. If nothing else, this might make it easier for you to face losing your job."

Gibbs said nothing as they came closer and he had a good view of Bryson's wife. Larry thought of his own wife, and something tugged at his insides.

Bryson wasn't completely surprised to see George Reese in line, but he couldn't figure why Larry Gibbs was with him. Reese held out a hand and Bryson accepted it eagerly.

"Thank you for coming," Bryson said in a barely steady voice that had become permanent.

"We can't stay for the funeral," George apologized, "but I wanted you to know that I was thinking about you."

"Thank you," Bryson said again.

George handed him an envelope. "I want you to have this," he said. "It might help you through."

Bryson tried to give it back. "You've already done so much."

"Please," George said, then his eyes shifted to Ilene's serene face. Bryson reluctantly shoved the envelope inside his jacket as George added, "She's a beautiful woman, Bryson."

"Yes, she always was," Bryson managed.

"You remember Gibbs," George said, urging Larry forward.

"Of course." Bryson tried to smile as he shook Larry's hand. "Thank you for coming."

Larry barely nodded and choked out a meek, "I was sorry to hear."

Larry was just hoping they would move along and get out of here when he heard the whimper of a small child, and Bryson reached down to pick up a little girl who looked much like the woman in the casket.

"This must be your youngest," George said with a smile.

"This is Jamie," Bryson said proudly.

"That's a beautiful dress you have on, Jamie," George said in a grandfatherly voice.

"Mommy go to heaven," Jamie said. Bryson gave an emotional smile and hugged the child tightly.

In the car, Larry had to admit he was glad Reese had brought him here. It *did* make it easier to lose his job. He could see now why Reese had chosen Davis, and he felt like a fool for making such a big deal over the whole thing.

"Loss is a hard thing, Gibbs," Reese said gently. "Whether it's a job or a loved one, it can be difficult to face and get over. But if we never lost anything, we would never learn to cope with life. Sometimes loss can make us better human beings, if we don't let it get the better of us."

"I wouldn't keep that job now if you gave it to me on a silver platter, George. In the days I have left, I promise not to question your judgment again."

There was a tense moment of silence before they laughed together. Then they each contemplated what it might feel like to be Bryson Davis today.

CHAPTER EIGHT

Following the family prayer, Bryson realized he was shaking. This was the moment he'd been dreading. With reverence he pressed his fingers to Ilene's face one last time, then he touched his lips meekly to hers, oblivious to the cold feel of her skin, heedless of the family members surrounding him. He wiped futilely at his tears while Melissa arranged the veil over Ilene's face, then he picked up Jamie and felt the other children clinging to him as the casket was closed. Jessica became nearly hysterical, sobbing helplessly. Bryson tried to set Jamie down and reach for her, but he relaxed when she buried herself in Melissa's arms and they cried together.

Bryson felt as if he were somehow on the outside looking at himself as Ilene's casket was wheeled into the chapel and he followed it. As he sat down and situated Jamie on his lap, he looked down the bench at his children and found the irony nearly unbearable. How many sacrament meetings had he sat through in this room with Ilene by his side? He concentrated on the beautiful casket in front of him and tried to think of Ilene's radiant spirit somewhere close by, rather than her body lying inside. He studied the spray of flowers over the top of it, grateful for Melissa's good taste. She *was* a professional decorator, he thought. But he never would have guessed she'd choose something so perfect. The huge white calla lilies, interspersed with red roses and baby's breath, seemed so perfect—a poignant combination of death, birth, and love.

The funeral was beautiful and helped reinforce everything Bryson knew, but needed to hear. His gratitude ran deep for the eternal prin-

ciples of the gospel and the blessings of the temple. He *knew* that he
and Ilene would be together again, and at the moment, nothing else
mattered.

Jamie slept in Bryson's arms through the brief ride to the cemetery. No one said a word, not even the children. The interior of the
limousine seemed eerily quiet as it followed the hearse to Ilene's final
resting place. Occasionally Bryson would catch Melissa's eye,
absorbing an unspoken comfort that he couldn't put words to.

A clear, blue sky made the day colder than usual as the pallbearers
carried the casket through the snow to the open grave. Jamie
continued to sleep against Bryson's shoulder, oblivious to the impact
this event would have on her life. Following the dedication of the
grave, friends and family gradually filtered away, but Bryson felt hesitant to leave. The children cried and hovered close to him, as if they
shared his reluctance to leave the tangible remains of Ilene here in the
cold. He was grateful for Melissa's insistence that they break away
and return to the limousine. He felt numb, and wondered again what
he would have done without her. In the limo, she comforted the children and handed him some tissues from her purse as a new batch of
tears surfaced.

Bryson managed to gain control of his emotion before they
returned to the church building for the luncheon. He reminded
himself that he had a life to live, and he had children to care for. One
way or another, he had to put this behind him and move forward. He
had to.

* * * * *

The morning after the funeral, Bryson woke up with a sense of
panic. First he had to look at the calendar to figure how many days
before he had to get back to work. The next question that popped
into his head sent him bounding down the hall. He found Melissa in
the kitchen, frying bacon. They'd had nothing but cold cereal for so
long that he'd almost forgotten what bacon smelled like.

"You look awful," she said, glancing over her shoulder.

"I was going to get a shower, but . . ."

"But you smelled bacon and couldn't wait."

"Well, it smells great, but actually, I . . ."

Melissa turned to face him. "Is something wrong?"

"No, I just . . . was wondering if . . . well, now that it's all over and . . . well, the kids are having a hard time with this . . . and if you left, I'm afraid it would . . . well . . ."

"If you're trying to ask me to stay, the answer is easy. I was already planning on it. If you're trying to ask me to go, the answer is easy. I won't. At least, not yet. I'm in no hurry to get anywhere. I figured the kids could use a little time to adjust."

Bryson sighed audibly. "Yes, I agree. Thank you." Bryson glanced down at himself. "I think I'll go take a quick shower before breakfast."

"Good idea. Oh, Bryson." He turned back. "People might talk."

He furrowed his brow, feeling half asleep as he tried to comprehend what she was getting at. "About what?"

"Now that she's gone," Melissa clarified, "some might think it's not appropriate for me to stay here."

"What do you think?" Bryson asked, appalled. If people had any idea how he and Melissa were doing well just to tolerate each other, there would be no reason for concern.

"I don't care what people think, Bryse. I never have. But this is your ward, your neighborhood. You're the one who has to live with what people think and say."

"Let them talk," he said. "If you don't have a problem with it, I certainly don't."

"That's all I wanted to know," she said and turned back to the bacon.

Through the day, Melissa tried to encourage normality for the children—as well as herself. She sent them to school in spite of protests, and while they were gone she found several cleaning projects to keep her occupied while Bryson took care of Jamie. When the children returned, she sent them off to play with friends and cooked a nice dinner. She enjoyed cooking, and found some pleasure in telling Sister Broadbent they wouldn't be needing any more meals. She could handle the kitchen just fine now that Ilene didn't need her anymore.

The evening went relatively well. It seemed that the children's ability to deal with losing their mother was directly proportionate to their ages. Jamie was doing perfectly fine. Jessica was moody and cried frequently. The ones in between showed varying degrees of grief. Bryson was quiet and polite, but twice during dinner he put his hands over his eyes and she knew he was crying.

"That was nice, Melissa," he said when he'd finished eating. "Thank you."

Bryson helped the kids with their homework and got them to bed while Melissa did up the dishes. When the house was quiet, she found Bryson sitting in the family room, watching T.V. She stopped on the stairs when she realized it was the video they'd made last Christmas. Melissa watched it for a few minutes and wiped away some stray tears, then she watched Bryson and tried to comprehend what he must be feeling. She left him to his solitude, locked the doors, and went to bed. When she got up after midnight to get a drink of water, he was still sitting in the same place, apparently playing the video over and over. Melissa went back to bed and cried, for herself, for the children. And for Bryson, too.

* * * * *

Life settled into a pattern more quickly than Melissa expected. She wondered if perhaps they had all done so much mourning prior to Ilene's death that it was easier now to put it behind them and move on. Of course there were moments when the reality hit, and she would just cry. She knew Bryson likely did the same, though she rarely saw evidence of it. He became increasingly quiet and distant, though he spent quality time with each of the children, and she knew he was doing his best to help them through.

On the surface, everything seemed fine. But Melissa sensed an underlying tension in the home that made her wonder if feelings were being buried instead of acknowledged. She attempted to talk to each of the children, hoping to urge their feelings out, but she got little response. She expressed her concerns to Bryson, and he agreed. But neither of them had any answers. Ilene's loss was acute and still too close for comfort. For the moment, it seemed that there was little to be done but allow time to help heal the wounds. Meanwhile,

Melissa prayed fervently, and even fasted, that she would find ways to help this family deal with Ilene's death before it was time for her to move on.

* * * * *

The phone rang while Melissa was setting dinner on the table and the children were running down the hall to wash up. Bryson answered it, talked quietly for only a minute, then hung up. Melissa stopped with a basket of rolls in her hands when she noticed the concern in his expression.

"Is something wrong?"

"I don't know. The bishop wants to see us."

"Us?" Melissa questioned, the pitch of her voice rising.

"That's what he said. We'd better hurry and eat. I told him we'd be there in forty-five minutes."

They were barely seated in Bishop Hodges' office when Bryson said, "So, what's this about, Bishop? Is something wrong?"

"Well," he replied, "since you seem eager to get to the point, I'll do the same. There are some people in the ward who have expressed concern about your present living situation."

Bryson sighed in disgust. Melissa rubbed a hand quickly over her face. Bryson's first impulse was to get angry, but he met Melissa's eyes briefly and knew he had nothing to be defensive about. Her calmness soothed him, and he listened quietly to what the bishop had to say.

"I'm not by any means implying that I suspect anything is out of order, Bryson. I simply must follow through and make certain everything is all right."

"I can assure you everything is fine," Melissa stated. "Before Ilene died, she requested that I stay as long as possible and help the children through the adjustment. Bryson and I have both prayed about it and feel good about the situation. He has been nothing but a perfect gentleman. Well," she gave him a sidelong grin, "he's a little ornery sometimes, but I can keep him in line."

The bishop chuckled and the tension let up a bit. "I'm sure that the two of you are doing the best you can under the circumstances. My only concern is how the children might perceive the situation.

Do you feel they clearly understand the boundaries of your relationship?"

"I'd like you to clarify that, Bishop," Bryson said, trying not to sound terse.

"If the children see Melissa doing the tasks around the house that Ilene once did, and the two of you working together to help them grow and learn, is it possible they could assume that the two of you share the same relationship that you shared with Ilene? After being married for so many years, being alone can't be easy."

There was no tangible reason why Bryson felt the sudden rush of emotion, but tears burned into his eyes before he was prepared enough to hold them back. He put a hand over his face and was hoping no one would notice, but Bishop Hodges quickly said, "I'm sorry, Bryson. My intention was not to upset you."

Bryson wanted to tell him it was all right, but he was trying to swallow the knot in his throat. Like so many times before, he was grateful for the way Melissa spoke up and handled it so well.

"Bishop, I sleep in a bedroom in the basement. Bryson sleeps where he always has, upstairs. I often read stories to the children in my room, or play games with them there. They sit on my bed with me and watch television once in a while. They help me with the laundry and household chores. Bryson is like a brother to me. They are very well aware that I share no relationship with him beyond that."

Bryson finally found his voice. "Bishop, at this point in my life it is difficult to comprehend anything beyond tomorrow. But there is one thing I can guarantee. I promised Ilene that I would be with her again, and there is only one way I can do that. Whatever I do with my life, Bishop, I will honor the covenants I made that will make it possible for us to be together again. No amount of loneliness could shake my conviction on that. I spend my time alone trying to do the things that will keep me close to the Spirit for that very reason. I've never spent so much time studying the scriptures in my entire life. There are moments when I wonder how I'm going to make it, but so far I'm managing. I know one thing, though—I never would have managed without Melissa. I'm sure a time will come when she'll need to move on, but I'm not going to take away what she shares with the children because of some gossipmongers who have nothing else to worry about."

The bishop was silent a moment, then he said firmly, "Well, I appreciate your being honest with me, and I hope you won't be upset by this. If nothing else, I can assure anyone who has concerns that I am convinced everything is in order. And, just so you know, in my opinion, I feel the situation is good, for the time being. After all, it's only been a few weeks. Melissa has been a blessing to the ward, as much as to your family."

They talked for several minutes about Bryson's job and each of the children. On the way home, Melissa asked quietly, "Does it make you uncomfortable to have me living with you?"

"Heavens, no!" he insisted. "In spite of your sassy little mouth," he chuckled, "I am grateful to have you around. And I don't care what anybody might say. It's between you and me and the Lord." When Melissa didn't respond, he asked, "What about you?"

"I agree," she replied, and they drove home in silence.

The next day, Bryson came home from work to find Melissa scolding Greg and Brandon severely.

"What's up?" he asked sternly.

Melissa took a step back and folded her arms. "Go ahead," she said to the boys, "tell your father what you did."

Following a long, tense silence, Bryson said, "Well? I'm waiting."

"We didn't go to school," Brandon finally said.

"Were you sick?" Bryson asked, glancing at Melissa.

"Let me add," Melissa said, "they left for school like normal, but Mrs. Sylmer saw them playing in the park and called to tell me. They just *didn't go* to school. Then when I asked them about it, they lied."

Bryson sighed and pushed a hand through his hair. The boys stared at the floor sheepishly. Melissa added softly, "Now that you're home, I'll let you handle it."

At moments like this, it was difficult for Melissa to know where she should stand. She felt more like a baby-sitter or a housekeeper as she reminded herself that it was none of her business how Bryson disciplined his children. But rather than acting in ignorance, she brought it up once the kids were in bed.

"I hope I didn't act out of line today with the boys," she said to

Bryson, sitting down on the other end of the couch. "I'm not sure where I should stand."

"You handled it just fine," he stated blandly. "I appreciate your being there when I can't be."

"Is something wrong?" she asked at the risk of prying.

"I'm just not sure I can raise them alone, Melissa. And I'm not going out there to find a wife just so someone can be here with the kids. Even *if* I do get married again, it'll be a good long time." He turned to look at her, admitting humbly, "I just don't know if I can do it. How do I handle such a problem? What makes them want to do something like cutting school?"

"My guess is that it has something to do with losing their mother."

Bryson chuckled dubiously. "I'm sorry, but I don't get the connection."

"Well, I don't understand it, really, but I've heard that trauma can come out in all kinds of bad behavior."

"But how do we deal with something like this, Melissa? I don't even know where to begin."

"We can pray," she stated.

"I have been," he replied.

"So have I. I'm sure things will get better."

Bryson didn't seem convinced. She left him alone and went to bed, wishing she could do more.

Bryson lost track of the time that he sat alone in the family room, staring at the wall where Ilene's hospital bed had been not so long ago. His mind wandered down paths that he'd explored a lot lately. Memories of the past and concerns for the future mingled together until his head ached. And tears inevitably came. He thought of all the months he'd refused to cry while Ilene had struggled through treatments and difficulties. Now he couldn't stop.

Most of the time, Bryson managed to do what he needed to do and not be consumed with the loss in his life. But there were moments that occasionally caught him, and he felt near despair. He tried to think of Ilene where she was now and somehow draw peace from the vision. Then his mind wandered back to the kids and their struggles, and he almost wished he could just die, too.

Then, with no warning, Bryson was struck by a sensation that made him sit up straight, suddenly alert to his surroundings. He knew this feeling well, but it had been so long since he'd experienced it that he needed a moment to recognize it. This was how he used to feel when he knew that Ilene was standing behind him. His immediate urge was to turn and say, "I knew you were there." He'd done it hundreds of times in their marriage. But he knew she wasn't, and turning would only make him painfully aware of the reality. Instead he closed his eyes, concentrating on the feeling, relishing it, encouraging it. He was actually surprised when it deepened. And warm tears confirmed it. Ilene was in the room with him, and he knew it with every fiber of his being.

"I know you're there," he said quietly, and a moment later he felt her arms come around him from behind. He'd always believed that such things could happen, but he was amazed at the reality of it. He could almost hear her whispering words of comfort in his ear. Though he couldn't discern what they were exactly, he somehow knew she was speaking to him—spirit to spirit—and he understood. Everything would be all right. When God had taken Ilene home, he had promised her that her children would be cared for, and they would grow up strong and fine. This loneliness he felt was only temporary. Yes, everything would be all right.

The sensation of Ilene's nearness was brief, but it left an impression that Bryson knew would carry him through. The evidence that her spirit lived on gave him the hope he needed to keep going. He went to bed and slept better than he had in weeks. His heart was full of gratitude for the mercy of a Heavenly Father who had allowed him just one more moment with his sweet Ilene.

* * * * *

A month past Ilene's death, Melissa's biggest concern was still the children. Bryson seemed to be adjusting well for the most part. And she had to admit that in spite of the loss, she felt a peace that carried her through the moments of missing her sister. But Jessica continued to be moody and depressed, and the boys were misbehaving terribly at times. Amber seemed to be doing all right, but there were moments when she cried because she missed her mommy. Those were moments when Melissa cried, too.

One day, Melissa was pondering deeply on what could be done to help the children when she went out to get the mail. Something tore at her a little as she read the handwriting on a card: *Bryson and Ilene Davis*. There was a return address in Provo with no name, and she wondered who might not have been aware of Ilene's death. Melissa debated whether or not to open it, then decided it couldn't hurt. She tossed the rest of the mail aside and tore the envelope, pulling out a card that was obviously a birth announcement. At the bottom it said: *Please let Melissa know.* She couldn't help smiling, despite a twinge of sadness.

When Bryson came home, she showed it to him. "I went ahead and opened it. It's from Sean O'Hara. He and his wife have a new baby girl."

"Oh, that's nice," Bryson said absently. Melissa became lost in thought and was surprised when he added an unusually perceptive question. "Are you okay?"

"Sure, why?"

"You look . . . sad."

Melissa could almost feel him putting the pieces together, and she wanted to run downstairs and hide from embarrassment.

"Do I detect some . . . regret, perhaps?" he asked. Melissa looked down and cleared her throat tensely. "I'm sorry," he added. "It's probably none of my business, but . . ."

"It's okay," she said when he didn't finish. "Since my sister isn't around to talk to, I guess you're the next best thing." Bryson chuckled softly and she went on. "I suppose I do feel a little sad. I mean . . . there was a time when I really thought Sean and I would be married. I loved him. He loved me. But I knew it wasn't right to marry him. I began to wonder once if I'd made the wrong choice, but he was engaged by then. I can't really regret my choices when I know in my heart that he and I simply weren't meant to be together, but . . ." Melissa swallowed her emotion. Bryson was the man who'd once cruelly teased her about not being able to find a husband, and now here she was, telling him her deepest feelings on such a sensitive subject. He had changed, but still, she had no desire to cry about it in front of him. "Well," she went on, "I'm very happy for Sean. I know he's where he's supposed to be. But there are moments when I wonder if there's *anyone* out there for me."

"Well," Bryson finally broke a tense silence, "if it's any consolation, I'm grateful you've been able to be here. You've got your whole life ahead of you, Lissa."

Melissa smiled. She stood and patted Bryson on the shoulder, adding on her way to the kitchen, "I think I'll send them a gift for the baby—from all of us, if that's okay."

"I think that's a good idea," he replied, and Melissa tried not to think about it.

Two days later she was still thinking about it, but when she finally stopped to analyze where her feelings were coming from, she felt much better. She truly *was* happy for Sean. She didn't have a problem with that. What she'd been blind to was the simple fact that Sean O'Hara was the answer to her prayers. Or at least she hoped so.

It wasn't difficult to find his number. He was listed in the Provo phone book as a professional family counselor. She called and a machine answered. She almost hung up before the beep, but instead she just stated her purpose. "Hi, Sean. This is Melissa James. Congratulations on that new baby. We have a gift for her. And there's something I'd like to talk to you about—professionally. Please call me." She repeated the number and hung up the phone. Less than an hour later, he called back.

"Melissa?" he said as soon as she picked up the phone.

"Sean. Hello."

"I got your message." His voice sounded so familiar, and she suddenly felt more at ease. He was an old friend and she knew he would help her. "How are you?"

"I'm doing good," she answered, "considering. How's that baby?"

"Oh, she's beautiful." The joy in his voice was apparent.

"And your wife?"

"Tara's doing good." He paused and asked, "You're doing good, *considering* what, Melissa?"

"Well," she hesitated, wishing the tears didn't have to show up at moments like this, "to put it bluntly, Ilene died last month."

There was a long pause before Sean said with emotion, "I can't believe it. What happened?"

"It was cancer," she stated. "I moved in with them before Christmas, trying to help. And I'm not in any big hurry to move out. The kids need me and I enjoy being here with them, but . . . well, some of them are struggling with this, Sean. I'm just not sure how to handle it. When I got your announcement, I . . . well, I was hoping you might be an answer to my prayers." She laughed softly, wanting to ease the tension. "How much do you charge for a group session, Dr. O'Hara?"

"Well," he chuckled, "I'm not a doctor . . . yet. But for you, fifty cents."

"The money's not a problem, Sean. I just want someone I know and trust to handle this right."

"I'd be more than happy to do what I can, Lissa. But my price is fifty cents an hour. Take it or leave it."

"I'll take it," she laughed.

"When would be a good time?" he asked. "Do you want the whole family involved, or—"

"I don't know. What do you think?"

"Well, it might be good to talk to you and Bryson first of all, since you're the adults dealing with the situation. And then we could decide when to meet with the children."

"Okay, but I'll have to see when Bryson is available. Actually, I haven't even talked to him about this. I hope he's agreeable. I'm just . . ."

Melissa was embarrassed when she faltered into tears. But Sean's voice was compassionate. "It's okay, Lissa. Death is a difficult thing to deal with, in any circumstances. I'm flexible. If Bryson isn't ready, then we'll work with the children the best we can. If he's willing, we'll find a time. I've got some evenings open. Why don't you talk to him and call me back."

"I will, Sean. Thank you." She paused and added, "I'm really happy about the baby. I mean it. You and Tara make a beautiful couple. I'm happy for you."

"Thanks, Lissa. That means a lot coming from you."

Melissa was relieved when he didn't ask if she'd met anyone yet. He said he'd be expecting to hear from her, but she dreaded bringing up the subject with Bryson. She prayed and tried to approach it gently, and she was actually surprised at how receptive he was. She called Sean the next morning and made an appointment for the following evening.

The drive to Provo was long and silent, but Melissa didn't feel as uncomfortable as she might have expected. In fact, it surprised her that she had actually become quite at ease in Bryson's presence. But then, they'd been through a great deal together.

It was good to see Sean, and her happiness on his behalf deepened as he opened their gift and showed them pictures of his new daughter, all the while beaming with pride. Once the greetings were completed, Sean looked Bryson in the eye and said, "I was sorry to hear, Bryse. I still can hardly believe it."

"Yeah," Bryson chuckled tensely, "there are moments when I still have trouble believing it myself."

Sean ushered them into a comfortable room with soft chairs and a pleasant decor. It was nothing like the office Melissa might have expected.

"So," Sean leaned back and crossed an ankle over his knee, "where do you want to start?"

Melissa glanced briefly at Bryson and knew it was up to her. "Well, as I told you, the problem is with the children. There's been a lot of moodiness and bad behavior that we just can't seem to get on top of. We've tried to talk with them and get them to vent their feelings, but apparently we're not doing it right."

"There are a number of possibilities why people don't want to talk about such things," Sean said. "You're likely not doing anything *wrong*. More likely, they're not acknowledging that the problems are related to losing their mother, because the real feelings are subconscious. Or, they sense that the two of you are hurting for the same reasons, and they don't want to add to your burden. Surprisingly, one of the strongest emotions related to death is anger, and—"

"Anger?" Bryson countered. "I can imagine my children feeling loneliness, or grief, or just plain sad. But *anger?*"

"It sounds strange, I know." Sean smiled easily. "But the truth is, anger is the first stage of mourning. Many people have trouble getting past it, because it seems logically unacceptable to express anger in relation to death. In Ilene's case, who is there to be angry with? She wasn't killed by a drunk driver, or murdered. There is no one tangible to put the blame on. Sometimes it finds a scapegoat for some absurd reason. But more often, there's this abstract anger floating around the house that doesn't get aired out."

Sean paused as if he were allowing the information to be absorbed. Then he looked at Melissa and asked, "Did you feel any kind of anger concerning Ilene's death?"

She thought about this for a minute. "I felt angry when I first realized she was going to die. But it didn't take long to get past it."

"Being a mature, emotionally healthy adult," Sean explained, "you were able to reason it out and get past it. You moved beyond that stage of mourning her death before she even died. But did the kids?" He waited a moment, then added, "My point is this. If the two of you understand that the most likely problem is anger, then you will be prepared to allow them to vent it. The best thing I can do for your children, Bryson, is give them permission to be angry. Sometimes it takes an objective, unbiased third party to help things along. But *you* need to be ready for it. You need to be willing to allow them to say *anything* they feel they need to say. Once we get some momentum going, this is not the place for teaching, or judgment, or discipline. We can talk things through and help them understand, but not until they have a chance to say *exactly* what they're feeling, and know they won't be criticized or chastened for it. Am I making any sense?"

"I'm relieved to say that you are," Bryson admitted. "I wasn't sure I'd be able to understand any of this. Ilene was always so good at handling the kids that . . . well . . ." He didn't finish.

A moment later Sean said, "Forgive me if I'm pushing too fast, Bryse, but may I ask how you're doing with all of this?"

Bryson pressed a hand over his face and swallowed hard. He'd expected such an inquiry, and thought he was ready to talk about it. But he shouldn't have been surprised by the tears that came along with it.

"We can talk about this privately if you would prefer," Sean said, and Melissa gave him an approving nod.

"It's okay," Bryson admitted, taking a deep breath. "Melissa's seen me cry far too much for me to get embarrassed now."

Melissa met Sean's eyes and realized he was attempting to convey something to her. Trying to pick up on the obvious, she came to her feet, saying, "All the same, I think I'm in need of the ladies' room." Sean's subtle smile let her know she'd gotten it right. Bryson was trying to be gracious, but Sean could likely get further without her there. She didn't have a problem with that. Bryson's deepest feelings were none of her business, anyway.

Melissa made a gracious exit and found the rest room, if only to make her story good. She then went to the small waiting room and found a couple of magazines to keep her distracted. Over an hour later, Sean and Bryson emerged, laughing and talking comfortably, apparently at ease.

"I'll be coming to the house a week from Saturday," Sean announced to Melissa. "We decided we might do better on home turf, as long as we can take the phone off the hook. And Bryse said you could probably leave the little one with a neighbor; I doubt this would pertain to her."

"That sounds good," Melissa agreed and shook Sean's hand. "Thank you, Sean."

"Yes, thank you," Bryson added, shaking his hand as well. "We appreciate your time."

"Give him a dollar, Bryse," Melissa whispered and nudged him in the ribs.

"Oh, yes," Bryson chuckled and slapped a dollar bill into Sean's hand. "Keep the change."

On the way home, Bryson said nothing until they reached the Point of the Mountain when Melissa asked, "How did it go?" When he hesitated, she added, "You don't have to tell me if you don't want to. I just wondered if it was worth your time."

"Yes." he gave a faint smile. "I think it helped. Maybe I'm not doing as bad as I thought."

"Actually, I think you've handled all this pretty well."

"Thanks to you," he admitted, then he laughed and started to talk about Ilene in a peaceful, reminiscent way that warmed Melissa. They both shed a few tears, but she believed they were healing.

Bryson stopped at a 7-Eleven near the house and bought some ice cream and cookies. They got home to find the children all sleeping, and they sat at the kitchen table for another hour, eating and sharing thoughts and feelings about the common bond in their lives: Ilene and the children she'd left behind.

* * * * *

Melissa got up from the dinner table to get the ketchup out of the fridge. The doorbell rang and Bryson slid his chair back to get up, but Melissa stopped him. "I'll get it. I'm already up."

Melissa pulled the door open to see an overly thin, hard-looking woman in her middle fifties, she guessed. They studied each other through a moment of silence, then the woman asked curtly, "Well, who are you?" Before Melissa could come up with an appropriate response for the circumstances, the woman added, "Where's Ilene?"

Melissa had even more trouble trying to answer that one. She was relieved when Bryson came to the door to investigate, but she wasn't expecting him to say, "Hello, Mother. I thought I heard your delightful voice." Melissa stepped back, trying to cover her surprise as Bryson motioned his mother inside and closed the door.

"Hello, Bryson," Marie said with a false sweetness, then her gaze turned to Melissa. "Where's Ilene?"

"This is Ilene's sister, Melissa," Bryson stated, wishing there was some polite way to tell his mother what had happened since her last appearance.

"It's nice to meet you, Melissa," Marie said as if she were lying.

"Melissa, this is my mother, Marie . . . Sorry, I can't recall the last name."

"No matter," Marie said as if her numerous unsuccessful marriages were irrelevant. "So, where's Ilene?" She glared at Bryson.

"We were just sitting down to eat, Mother. Why don't you join us, and we'll talk about it later."

Marie became distracted by the children, who greeted her politely but with little enthusiasm. Melissa set an extra place at the table and Marie sat down, helping herself to dinner, commenting on how the children had changed since she'd last seen them. Bryson wanted to tell her that if she'd come by more than once every three or four years, it would help. She made no comment about Jamie, but Bryson knew his mother had never seen her before. Ilene had been pregnant on his mother's last visit. He suggested that the children tell their grandmother about their friends and what they were doing at school. This kept him from having to talk to her through most of the meal.

"So," Marie said once the children had finished eating and gone off to play, "where's Ilene? She didn't leave you, did she?"

"No, Mother, she didn't leave me," he stated while Melissa started taking dishes to the sink. She was having a hard time tolerating this woman. But then, it was evident that Bryson was, too. "Although you probably think she should have. You told her that a time or two, I recall. Didn't you tell her I was an arrogant, insensitive idiot like my father?"

Marie shook her head as if this was all very amusing. "You men are all alike."

"Perhaps we are," Bryson said, "but fortunately, all women are not alike."

"Where's Ilene?" Marie asked again. "You're trying to avoid telling me, which means something's gone wrong." She glanced toward Melissa as if she'd like to suspect some foul play going on between them.

"Ilene is dead," Bryson stated as if he'd told her to pass the salt. For the first time in his life, he found his mother momentarily speechless. Before she had a chance to demand the details, he added, "She died of breast cancer in January. Fifteen months before that, she had a mastectomy. The rest isn't worth repeating." Marie glanced again toward Melissa, and he added, "Melissa has been here since December, helping with the children."

Marie's painted-on eyebrows arched skeptically. She might as well have come right out and asked if he was sleeping with her. For Melissa's sake, he was glad she didn't.

"Well, I just can't believe it," Marie said as Bryson got up to help Melissa clear the table. Marie remained seated. "Cancer doesn't have to kill people, Bryson."

"What's that supposed to mean?" He stopped with a couple of glasses in his hands.

"Well, if it's caught early enough, it can be cured."

"Yes, Mother." He turned his back and set the glasses on the counter. "I know that."

"So, why did Ilene have to die if—"

"Apparently it wasn't caught early enough," he snapped, leaning his hands against the counter, hardly daring to face his mother for fear of erupting. She always did this to him, and he *hated* it. But why now? Why couldn't she have come next year, when his pain was not so raw? He was surprised to feel a calming hand on his arm, and looked up to see Melissa close by.

Melissa moved back toward the table, apparently to pick up more dishes, but she stopped and looked Marie in the eye. "Are you implying that Bryson is somehow at fault for my sister's death?"

Marie looked so taken off guard that Bryson wished he had a camera. "Well, I suppose there isn't anything he could have done about it. It's just too bad it couldn't have been caught sooner. Ilene was such a sweet girl. I don't know why rotten luck just seems to follow some people, and others just sail through life. I mean, look at me. I've just had one lousy thing after another, ever since the day I—"

"Mother," Bryson interrupted, perhaps spurred on by Melissa's display of courage, "why does the conversation always come back around to your *hard luck?* Don't you have anything better to do with your life than come around every few years to remind us of your hard luck?"

"Well, of all the insensitive things to say to your own mother," she snarled. "You'd think I could at least get a little sympathy or—"

"Do you hear what you just said?" Melissa interrupted. Marie's garish face gaped in silence. Wondering if she was acting out of line, Melissa turned briefly toward Bryson, a silent question in her eyes. Bryson nodded with full approval, and she turned back toward Marie. She pressed her hands flat on the table and leaned forward, looking her straight in the eye. "Excuse me, but your son just lost his wife to cancer. How dare you come into his home, making accusations and assumptions, passing judgments and begging for sympathy? You have no idea what has taken place here in the last several months, or you wouldn't have the nerve to walk in here and say what you just said."

Melissa pointed a finger and leaned forward a little further. "My sister was a strong, courageous woman who died with dignity and faith. Her cancer was not some punishment or disgrace. It was just one of those things that happened. But she took it on and won. She won because she was able to lie on her deathbed and show concern for everyone but herself. Cancer didn't kill her integrity, or her kindness. And she never once asked for sympathy.

"It's been hard for all of us, but blessings have come, and Bryson will tell you he has much to be grateful for. He's a good man who took good care of his wife through the worst of times. He understands that luck has nothing to do with the reality of life. Everybody has problems. Everybody struggles. But we can either choose to let those struggles do us in, or we can fight to overcome them and make the most of them. If you choose to wallow in your hard luck, fine. But don't come into my sister's home and gripe, because frankly, I don't think anybody wants to hear about it."

Bryson didn't know whether to laugh or cry as Melissa took a step back and his mother continued to gape in silence. She'd just said things he'd been wanting to say for years—everything Marie needed to hear. Ilene had always been so sweet and patronizing with his mother. Bryson had learned to not let her bully him, but he'd never been able to cross certain boundaries with his frustrations. Seeing Melissa's willingness to stand up for what she felt strongly about, he felt a new respect for her. And he realized that she had just stood up for him, too. Not knowing what to say, he summed it up with a simple, "Thank you, Melissa. I couldn't have said it better myself." He turned and started filling the sink with hot water before his mother could find a comeback. "You're welcome to stay the night on the couch, Mom," he added. "Please don't smoke in the house."

Marie quietly went off to find the children while Melissa helped Bryson with the dishes. "Are you okay?" she asked when they were alone.

"No . . . but then, I'm never okay when my mother is around."

"Ilene told me about the situation, but I think she buffered it a little."

"Ilene had a way of looking at everything in a better light." Bryson briefly pressed his fingers between his eyes, willing back the emotion that had been threatening ever since his mother had demanded to know where Ilene was. "But I'll be all right," he added. "She never stays long. Besides," he managed a genuine chuckle, "I have your sassy little mouth here to protect me."

Marie said nothing beyond necessary exchanges through the remainder of the evening. She spent the night on the couch, and Bryson wondered, as always, if his home wasn't just an alternative to a motel room. He knew she would have liked to grumble about the den being in use, but she probably didn't dare.

Melissa was washing the breakfast dishes when Marie finally emerged from the family room, yawning and stretching. "Where is everybody?" she asked.

"Bryson's gone to work. The kids are all at school, except Jamie. She's playing in her room."

"She's a cute little thing," Marie said through a loud yawn.

"Yes, she is," Melissa agreed.

"I don't suppose you have any coffee."

"No, we don't." Melissa didn't apologize. "But there's some bacon and hash browns in the fridge. You can stick them in the microwave if you like."

"Thanks, but I think I should be going."

She hurried off to the bathroom, and Melissa wondered why she seemed so eager to leave. While she finished up the dishes and started a load of laundry, she contemplated the reality that this was Bryson's mother. She marveled that he had grown up as well as he had. But then, his father was a good man with many strengths.

Melissa was folding clothes on the family room floor when Marie appeared, ready to leave. "I'm off," she announced. "Tell Bryse and the children good-bye for me."

"Are you sure you don't want to stay and tell them yourself?" Melissa offered, if only to be gracious. Still, she wondered what spending a day with this woman might reveal.

"Nah," Marie shrugged, "they won't miss me." Melissa stopped for a moment and looked up at her. "Take good care of Bryse, now. He's a fine boy, in spite of me."

"I think he'd like to hear you say that," Melissa suggested.

Marie tipped her head thoughtfully. "Well, I'll think about that . . . and everything else you said, too. You might have a point."

Long after Marie left, Melissa found herself thinking about Bryson's relationship with his mother—or rather, the lack of it. She wondered what kind of impact her leaving home when he was sixteen must have had on his life. Melissa had lost her own mother in a different way, and she could well understand the struggles he must have had—struggles that could only be made more difficult by losing his wife. Her compassion for Bryson Davis wedged a little deeper inside, and she hoped he would not be too upset by his mother's brief visit.

CHAPTER NINE

Bryson went to the kitchen to find Melissa, and realized she'd already gone to bed. Knowing he couldn't sleep if he didn't get something off his mind, he went downstairs and knocked at her door. She opened it wearing flowered thermal leggings and a huge T-shirt. But he was more distracted by her hair. In all the time they'd lived under the same roof, he couldn't recall seeing her hair when it wasn't pulled back, braided, or twisted into a bun. But now it was hanging down around her shoulders, and the overall effect somehow reminded him of Ilene.

"Did you need something?" she asked, and he realized he must have been staring at her.

"I'm sorry." He glanced down and cleared his throat. "You look . . . different with your hair down." Feeling suddenly stupid for mentioning it at all, he added, "It looks nice."

"Thank you," she responded, wondering if he would get to his purpose for coming to her room. It was a rare occurrence.

"Ilene always wore her hair down," he stated, perhaps hoping to explain his unusual behavior.

Melissa said nothing as she realized that his stammering was likely from being reminded of Ilene. Their father had always said they looked more alike when Melissa wore her hair down. "Did you need something?" she asked, if only to relieve him from apparent discomfort.

"Uh . . . yes, I . . ." Bryson cleared his throat, trying to find his original train of thought. "I was wondering if you're busy tomorrow.

There's something I'd like your help with, and I have the next couple of days off since they're doing some painting in the office."

"I don't have anything specific planned," she said, "other than the usual. What did you have in mind?"

Bryson glanced at the floor, then he cleared his throat again. "Well, I need to go through some of Ilene's things." He hesitated, and Melissa understood now why he seemed so uncomfortable. This was a difficult step for him. "For a while I didn't want to; I wanted to see her things around. But . . . well, it's getting so I can't take it. Every time I open the closet, or the medicine chest, or . . ." He faltered with emotion and was relieved when Melissa saved him from saying any more.

"I'd be happy to help you," she said. "We can start as soon as the kids get off to school."

Bryson nodded and left without another word. As soon as the breakfast dishes were finished and the kids were gone, Melissa found Bryson with Jamie in her room, dressing a doll.

"Where do you want to start?" she asked.

"The bedroom," he stated, and she could tell he didn't want to do this. He left Jamie to play and followed Melissa to his closet, where she opened the door and sighed. She knew she could either get emotional, or she could get busy enough to avoid thinking about it. The latter seemed the best option for both of them.

"Okay," she said with an authoritative voice, "if it doesn't have sentimental value, we send it to Deseret Industries. I'll start pulling things out; if you want something saved, speak up."

Bryson was relieved when Melissa took charge and kept talking enough about the kids and trivial things to keep his mind off the reality of what they were doing and why. He only interrupted once to say, "If there's anything you want to keep, just say so."

"Well," Melissa said with warmth, "she had some beautiful clothes, but unfortunately I couldn't fill them out if I wanted to."

Without thinking, Bryson replied, "You always were too skinny." Melissa looked up in surprise, and he realized what he'd just said. He was relieved when she laughed.

They continued to work quickly, but a few minutes later she said, "You know, Bryse, that was really rude. I can't believe you said that."

He relaxed when her smile made it evident she was mostly teasing. "How many years have you been thinking behind my back that I was too skinny?"

"Ever since I met you," he admitted.

"Well," she said, "I always thought you were a *nerd*."

"A *nerd?*" he laughed. "I was always a little out of it, but I never considered myself a nerd. I mean, I didn't have thick glasses and wear pocket protectors, you know. And I never wore polyester."

Melissa laughed. "That's true. I admit I was wrong. You were more like . . . a borderline dweeb."

Bryson tried to look offended, but he couldn't help laughing. "Well, if you aren't the sassiest little thing. But then, you always were. If I was a dweeb, you were a brat."

They continued to talk and laugh until most of Ilene's clothes and shoes were bagged up and Bryson took them straight to the van so they could go to D.I. a little later. There was only one dress that he wanted to save, for reasons he didn't explain. Melissa folded it and set it aside before she got on a chair to start cleaning off the closet shelf. Bryson came back in the room just as she was pulling down a number of hats and scarves. Her hands were suddenly too full, and Bryson's eyes followed the few that fell to the floor. "Send them away," he stated almost coldly. Melissa said nothing, but she felt touched by these remnants of Ilene. They somehow signified all she had suffered, and Melissa wanted to keep them. She quietly took them to her room, thinking she would find a good box and store them away.

Melissa returned to the bedroom to find the contents of several drawers dumped on the bed. She took a deep breath, and tried to distract Bryson from his seeming helplessness by sorting and talking. The job became more difficult as they got to more personal belongings—keepsakes, jewelry, and unfinished projects. Bryson's momentum slowed considerably as he fingered her things longingly and couldn't seem to make up his mind what to do with many of them.

"Do you think I'm being too hasty with this?" he asked quietly. "Should I wait, and—"

"I think we should finish what we've started and not feel guilty over it, Bryse. Ilene's earthly belongings are not going to make any difference to her spirit. She would want all of us—especially you—to go on living and not wallow in the past. You don't need her things in the dresser for her to know that you love her."

"Thanks," he said. "I think I needed to hear that."

"But," she added, "maybe we've done enough for one day. We've finished the bedroom except these few things. Why don't you take a load to D.I., and I'll put this stuff back for now."

Bryson nodded gratefully and hurried to the van, where he cried through most of the drive. But the next day he felt more motivated, and they were able to finish. He appreciated Melissa's willingness and insight. She made logical suggestions but allowed him to make the decisions. Everything kept for sentimental reasons was put neatly into Ilene's cedar chest, much of it to be given to her children when they were older. Melissa saved a few things for herself, and kept out a few odd things that she suggested Bryson give to the children now. He did so when they got home from school, and they seemed to enjoy having something of their mother's.

After the children had gone to bed, Melissa went to the family room where Bryson was sitting, and handed him a shoe box.

"What is this?"

"Something she asked me to keep until the time was right. I think that might be now."

Bryson hesitantly opened the box to see that it contained several cassette tapes. "What is this?" he asked, feeling somehow afraid.

"She made a tape for each of the children, Bryse. These are copies. I put the originals in your safe deposit box at the bank. There's a tape for you, too."

Bryson swallowed hard. "You mean she . . ."

Melissa sat down and put a hand on his arm. "She wanted to be able to tell her children all the things they should hear from their own mother."

Though Bryson had nearly worn out the video that showed Ilene alive, laughing and talking, he felt somehow disconcerted to realize he was holding the means to hear her voice. While he couldn't deny what a wonderful gift this was to him and the children, he was almost afraid to listen to the tape marked simply: *To Bryson.*

"Anyway," Melissa said, realizing he wasn't going to say anything, "I'll let you handle it from here. You can give them to the kids whenever you think it's appropriate. I'm going to bed now."

"Good night," he said as she walked away. "And thank you . . . for everything."

"I'm glad to help," she said and left him alone.

It took Bryson two days to get the courage to listen to that tape. He put it in the cassette player as he went to bed and turned out the lights. How could he not cry to hear Ilene's sweet voice, telling him how much she loved him, reminding him of the things they'd done together, the memories they'd shared? She spoke of her concern that he was being left with so much to worry about, but more than once she said that she knew God would not take her without providing a way. She spoke of eternity, and the peace she felt to know they would be together again.

When her words ended and the tape continued to run in silence, Bryson felt emotionally and physically exhausted. But he couldn't deny that he was one step closer to healing. Her faith and strength gave him courage and a desire to live the way she would want him to. Hoping the tapes would have the same effect on the children, he decided to pass them along soon. Then, recalling that Sean would be coming to talk with them on Saturday, he thought it might be best to wait until after that.

The following day after work, Bryson stopped at the cemetery. He laid a single rose over the top of Ilene's grave, then stuffed his hands deep into his pockets and stared at her name, engraved deeply in unweathered granite. He'd come here so many times that he'd lost track, but he could see that his need to be here was gradually becoming less intense. There was little peace or comfort to be derived from a cold piece of stone. But he had five children, all a part of Ilene, living and breathing, who needed him. And he had the gospel—the knowledge that life was eternal and marriage forever.

Bryson looked toward the sky and tried to swallow his emotion. He thought of the hopes and dreams he'd shared with Ilene as they'd fallen in love and begun their life together. He never would have imagined himself a widower in his late thirties. Determined to not get discouraged, he forced his thoughts in positive directions. In spite of it all, he had much to be grateful for. It didn't take much thought to come up with a long list of good things in his life. He turned and walked back to the car, recounting them in his mind. In the car he said aloud, "I love you, Ilene." Then he chuckled softly, almost certain she'd heard him.

* * * * *

Sean arrived a few minutes early on Saturday, and Melissa hurried to take Jamie over to Wendy's. She returned to find him interacting casually with Brandon and Greg, asking them questions about school and hobbies. By the time they were all seated together in the family room, with the front door locked and the phone off the hook, everyone seemed relaxed and comfortable. Except Jessica.

Melissa wondered how on earth such a subject could be approached without tension, but Sean made it seem easy when he simply said, "I understand you guys lost your mom a while back. That's not an easy thing to go through, even for grown-ups. Your Aunt Melissa and I used to be good friends a long time ago, and she asked me if I'd come and talk to you a little bit. Maybe if we all talk about how we feel, it might help. What do you think?"

"I guess so," Brandon finally volunteered on behalf of his siblings.

"Did your mom die, too?" Amber asked Sean, and Melissa suddenly felt nervous, recalling the sensitive situation with Sean's family. She had no idea where it stood after all these years, and wondered how he'd respond.

"Yes, Amber, my mom died. I was all grown up when it happened, but it was still really hard. I cried a lot, and sometimes I still miss her."

Bryson listened carefully as Sean kept talking about his own feelings, interspersing them with questions directed at the individual children. They each in turn began to talk more and more, and the questions gradually became more probing. Brandon was the first to cry, and the first to admit to the real truth of his feelings. Bryson hadn't doubted Sean when he'd told him the anger theory, but he was amazed at how literally it came through with his children. Once the ice was broken, the tears spilled freely and emotions flowed. They were angry with their mother for leaving, even though they knew it wasn't her fault. And they were angry with God for taking her. Bryson just watched and listened, as did Melissa, crying silent tears at the reality of their pain.

Sean guided the children by asking simple questions about their mother's death that helped put the situation in perspective. "Death just happens, and it's often nobody's fault," he explained. He told them it was okay to be angry, as long as they understood why and learned how to deal with it. He asked them what they could do to be more open with their feelings and not let it affect their school work and their relationships with others. Melissa marveled at his skill, not to mention a special gift he seemed to have of compassion and intuition.

Two hours later, all of the children except Jessica had made significant progress. Following a few moments of silence, Sean turned to her. "You haven't said much, Jessica. What do you think of all this?"

She gave a surprisingly mature response. "I've learned a lot by listening. I think it will help me, too."

"That's good," Sean said, "but isn't there anything you'd like to say? Perhaps there's something about this that's troubled you but hasn't come up yet—something you'd like to talk about while the family is together."

Bryson felt Jessica's eyes shift to him, and he knew that whatever she was hesitant to talk about was somehow related to him. Fearing that she would insist on keeping it to herself, he uttered a silent prayer that she would get it out and get it over with, while they had Sean to help them buffer it and offer some sound advice. He was relieved when Jessica turned to Sean, making it evident that she intended to speak.

"I . . . I keep thinking about just before Mom died, and . . . how Dad said he *wanted* her to die." Jessica's tears erupted with her words. Bryson pressed a hand over his mouth to keep himself from trying to explain. A quick glance from Sean reminded him of what they'd discussed earlier. Jessica needed to be able to express her feelings without restraint.

"I didn't understand," Jessica cried, "how he could *want* her to leave us, and then he gave her a blessing and asked Heavenly Father to *take* her."

Bryson suddenly wanted to slither into a hole and die. Hot tears burned into his eyes, and he kept his hand over his mouth to keep from sobbing. He didn't know how Melissa's hand got into his, but he took hold of it eagerly, squeezing so hard he feared he'd hurt her.

"I . . . I wanted Dad to bless her so she could . . . so she could . . . live." Jessica's emotion became more intense. "But . . . she . . . she died . . . and Dad . . . Dad . . . wanted her to die."

When it became evident that she'd said what she wanted to, Sean asked gently, "Jessica, did you ask your father why he said what he did? Did you ask him why he gave her that blessing?"

Jessica shook her head firmly, looking frustrated but unable to respond because of her emotion.

"Do you want to ask him now?" Sean questioned.

Jessica shook her head again, and Bryson panicked. He had to have a chance to explain to her. He just *had* to. He couldn't let her believe that he'd wanted Ilene to die.

Sean leaned back in his chair and sent a barely detectable glance toward Bryson and Melissa, indicating the need to be patient. After a few minutes, Jessica got control of her emotion and took a deep breath. It was evident that she had something else to say.

"At first it really bothered me," Jessica said, seeming to avoid her father's gaze, "but then I could see how Dad missed Mom, and I prayed about it, 'cause Melissa told me I should pray if I had trouble with anything. And Mom used to tell me that, too. Then one night when I was lying in bed, and I was crying, I started to think about it and I felt different. I understood that Dad wanted her to die because she was so sick, and she would never get better."

Bryson wanted to collapse from relief. Instead he just offered a silent prayer of gratitude, and relished the gentle squeeze of Melissa's hand that told him she understood.

"I realized that I was glad Mom had died so she wouldn't have to be afraid or in pain anymore. But sometimes . . ." Her voice faltered again. ". . . Sometimes I feel . . . guilty for wanting her to be dead, because I . . . I miss her . . . so much, and . . ."

When Jessica's tears erupted again, Bryson was relieved to see

Sean motion subtly for him to take over. He hurried across the room and sat close to Jessica, putting his arm around her. She pressed her face to his shoulder and cried.

"It's okay, Jess," he whispered, "sometimes I feel the same way."

"I love you, Dad," she cried and held on to him tighter.

"I love you, too, Jessica—more than I could ever tell you."

Melissa observed the scene, crying silent tears. She met Sean's eyes briefly and he offered a serene smile, full of compassion and understanding. She marveled at what they had accomplished through this time together, and silently thanked God for giving her a friend like Sean.

When the emotion had subsided once again, Sean asked Jessica some questions to help her put things in perspective and make a plan for dealing with the inevitable doubts and grief she would feel occasionally in the future. He summarized again with each family member, including Bryson and Melissa, giving them an opportunity to say anything they felt they needed to. When they were finished, he clapped his hands together and said, "Lunch is on me—at that pizza joint with all the toys. Let's go. I'm starved."

The children were out to the van in no time. Once they'd had their fill of pizza and were playing, with Jessica keeping an eye on Jamie, Sean took the opportunity to verify some things with Bryson and Melissa.

"You know," he said, "they're actually handling it pretty well as far as I can see. Everything that came out was normal and expected, and they seemed to accept my advice eagerly. Of course, that doesn't mean you won't continue to have struggles. Life is tough for kids in the best of circumstances, but losing a parent is traumatic and it takes time. For yourselves, as well as for the children."

"Thank you, Sean," Bryson said firmly. "You can't know how much we appreciate it."

"It's my pleasure," he smiled. "I don't see any reason at this point to schedule more time, but if something comes up, feel free to call."

"Maybe this isn't a good time to ask," Melissa said, "but I couldn't help wondering about . . . well, you said that your mother passed away. Has anything changed with your father, or . . . ?" She hesitated, knowing from the years they'd dated that Sean's being disowned by his Catholic father when he'd joined the Church was a sensitive subject.

"Actually," he smiled and Melissa felt some relief, "I was able to see my mother again before she died, and about a year later, my father came to my graduation when I got my master's degree." Sean chuckled. "He's still stubborn and ornery, but we keep in touch."

"Oh, that's wonderful," Melissa said with strength. "You must be thrilled."

"Yes," he nodded firmly, "I most certainly am. I have everything a man could ever want."

That evening, Bryson gathered the children around and told them some of his feelings concerning Ilene's death that he felt they should hear. He then gave them their tapes, except for Jamie's, which he put away with his own until she was older. He explained that they should only listen to them when they felt a real need, otherwise they would lose their special quality. They read together from the Book of Mormon, then shared family prayer and the children went to bed.

Bryson wrote a quick letter of thanks to Sean and included a check for a hundred dollars. It seemed a small price to pay for the progress they'd made today as a family, and he knew Sean could use the money, even if he was too gracious to admit it in person.

A week later, Bryson realized that Sean had been right in saying they would continue to have struggles. But for the most part, he felt like he understood them now, and was able to deal with behavior problems more realistically by communicating and following through with appropriate consequences. Melissa was supportive, but deferred to him as long as he was around. He appreciated her attitude, except for the moments when he would have preferred to have someone else deal with the problems.

Jessica was the only one he had trouble understanding. He felt like they'd come a long way, and there were moments when he believed they were close and able to communicate. But there were other times when it took self-restraint not to spank her. When she came home significantly late for the third day in a row, he had to remind himself to stay calm.

"Where have you been?" he asked solemnly before she could sneak off to her room.

"I was at Mandy's," she retorted in a tone of voice that tempted him to forget his self-restraint.

"You were told to be home at a certain time, and that was over an hour ago. Is there a reason you can't come home when you're expected to?"

"Oh, get real, Dad. I don't know *anyone* who has to be home that early."

"I don't care who has to be home when. You're *my* daughter, and *you* are going to come home when you're supposed to. If there's a reason you have to be late, you can find a phone and use it, otherwise—"

"Dad," she said as if he were some kind of imbecile, "there are lots of places that don't have phones, and I'm not going to—"

Bryson took hold of her arm so abruptly she gasped. "Now, you listen to me, young lady. You will not use that tone of voice with me, or with anyone else for that matter. And you will come home when you're told. If you can't obey a simple rule, then maybe some privileges need to be cut back. You either keep the rules, or you will be grounded to that room so fast your head will spin. Do I make myself clear?"

Bryson expected her to back down and admit defeat. Instead, she shook free of his grasp and looked over his shoulder. He didn't know Melissa was sitting there until Jessica said, "Aunt Melissa, will you tell him that's not fair? I just want to hang out with my friends a little, and . . ."

She stopped when Melissa put her hands up in a gesture to indicate she would not get involved. Jessica sighed dramatically and sulked off to her room. Bryson turned to glare at Melissa.

"Don't look at me like that," she said. "I was sitting here before the argument started."

"Well, you could have said something," he grumbled.

"I'm not getting involved," she stated.

"You *are* involved," he insisted. "You're with them when I can't be. I can't do it alone."

"Listen, Bryse," Melissa replied, trying to remain calm, "Jessica trusts me. She opens up to me and talks about her feelings concerning many things. I can do more good for her by remaining neutral than by going against her for the sake of backing you up. You handled it just fine."

"And what exactly do you tell her in your little chats? She didn't learn to talk that way from her mother."

Melissa's eyes widened as she realized what he was implying. "Are you trying to tell me that I'm doing something to encourage Jessica's disrespect?"

"Well, that *sassy* tone she uses does sound familiar."

Melissa couldn't believe it. How quickly she recalled her reasons for disliking him before they'd embarked on this journey together. She'd overheard him speaking to Ilene this way a number of times, but she'd begun to believe he'd grown beyond it. She had to bite her tongue to keep from calling him an arrogant, ungrateful jerk. Instead she said firmly, "You don't have any idea what you're talking about, Bryson Davis. And, so you don't make an even bigger fool of yourself, I'm going to explain it to you."

He folded his arms indignantly. "Why don't you do that!"

"First of all, it's no secret that you and I have never gotten along very well. But I have never—not once—shown any disrespect toward you in front of the children. Whether you were present or not, I have encouraged them to respect and obey you, even when I didn't agree with the way you were handling something. And, just because Ilene was too sweet to tell you what she really thought doesn't mean you don't need to hear it once in a while."

She could see the anger rising in his eyes but didn't give him a chance to break in before she got to her point. "And last of all, what Jessica is exhibiting is normal for any fourteen-year-old girl. She didn't have to learn that sassy tone of voice from anybody. It comes naturally to any number of human beings with out-of-control hormones."

That word *hormones* caught Bryson off guard. It was the first time he'd ever heard it in reference to one of his children. "What do you mean by that?" he asked cautiously, suddenly more concerned than angry.

Melissa sighed and reminded herself they were two mature adults. "It's that time of the month, Bryse," she stated. He glared at her, and she realized he'd misunderstood. "Not mine—hers!"

Bryson sat down. His mind raced through all that had been happening the past several months, and the realization hit him that he had missed something important—something that he wouldn't have known how to deal with even if he had seen it coming.

"That's right," Melissa said in response to his dumbfounded silence, "she's not a little girl anymore. She's a teenager, well on her way to becoming a woman. And the tension between the two of you is likely to get a lot worse before it gets better."

"When did all this start?" he asked, trying not to be embarrassed.

Melissa glanced down and said, "Just before Ilene died."

Bryson sighed, trying to comprehend what it might be like to be fourteen, going through drastic emotional and physical changes, and having your mother on her deathbed.

"Of course she knew what was happening," Melissa continued, hoping to ease his obvious concern. "Ilene had explained everything to her long before then. But she came to me for some help, and I answered her questions. No big deal—at least not for me."

Bryson glanced up at Melissa, wanting to tell her that he appreciated her being there. But he remembered that he'd been trying to blame all these problems on her a few minutes ago. He didn't know how to say anything without making an even bigger fool of himself, as she'd so quaintly put it. He nodded absently and was relieved when she left the room.

Melissa found herself so angry she could hardly tolerate being in the same room with Bryson. She wondered how Ilene had managed to accept his attitudes so meekly all those years. But then, Ilene had always been gifted with patience and tolerance. Melissa figured she could probably use a little *more* tolerance, but perhaps Ilene could have been a little more outspoken.

When Melissa thought about how he'd tried to blame his argument with Jessica on her, she just wanted to hit him. Knowing there was nothing to do without causing more strain, she prayed to be free of these feelings and remember that she was here for the children. But clearly, she'd have to think about moving on in the near future. She wasn't sure how much longer she could stay under the same roof with Bryson Davis, and sooner or later he'd have to learn to manage without her—one way or another.

* * * * *

Bryson came home from work on a windy day and found total chaos. "Where's Melissa?" he asked Jessica, once he turned off the T.V. and got her attention.

"She's in bed," Jessica reported blandly. "She was lying on the couch when I got home, then she told me to watch the kids and went downstairs."

"Is this what you call watching the kids?" he asked, indicating the disarray and havoc surrounding them.

Jessica glared at him. "I had a bad day at school. Don't be such a dweeb."

Bryson let her comment roll off him and instead bellowed, "Okay, guys, get this mess cleaned up. Nobody's getting any dinner until it is." He left them to do it and went to his room to remove his tie and jacket before he went downstairs to investigate the problem with Melissa. His knock at her door was answered by an indiscernible groan. "Are you sick?" he asked, sticking his head in the door.

Without opening her eyes, she reported, "I think it's just a bad cold, but I ache all over. Are the kids—"

"The kids are fine," he reported. "Can I get you anything?"

Melissa found his offer admirable, but there was a subtle terseness in his voice that only heightened the anger she'd been trying to subdue. Proudly she said, "No, thank you. I can take care of myself. I'm just worried about the kids and—"

"I told you I'd manage. Just get some rest. I'll send down some dinner," he added, wondering what they'd eat.

"Thank you," she said, but he was already gone.

Bryson ordered pizza to be delivered, then followed the kids around until they got the house cleaned up. He sent Jessica to take Melissa some dinner when it arrived, and told her to ask if she needed anything else. The rest of the evening was spent with homework and getting the kids to bed without any major fights.

Bryson went to bed exhausted, hoping Melissa would be feeling better by morning. He went to her room just as soon as he got up. She claimed to feel a little better, but he called Sister Broadbent anyway, asking if she knew of anyone who could watch Jamie for the day. He explained the situation and told her he was able and willing to pay for the day care, but he didn't have much time. She called back before he was finished with breakfast, telling him where to take Jamie, declaring this woman was in need of some extra money and she was delighted with the opportunity.

With that taken care of, Bryson gave the children careful instructions to look out for each other after school and keep the house in order. He checked on Melissa before he left, but she was asleep.

That evening Melissa seemed a little better, and he hoped she would be back to normal by tomorrow. He couldn't deny the added stress, though he wasn't sure he wanted to admit to it. Things had been tense between them since that last argument, and he had no desire to broach anything at all with her at the moment. So he just tried to be considerate, hoping this wouldn't last.

Melissa came to the family room to watch T.V. for a while, but she didn't eat much of the Tuna Helper Bryson had made. After the kids had gone to bed, she said, "Bryson, I think I'm sick."

"No kidding," he replied with subtle sarcasm.

"I mean . . . I keep expecting this ache to go away, but it always comes back, a little worse each time."

"Have you had a fever?" he asked, briefly pressing the back of his hand to her forehead as if she were one of his children.

"A little, I think. I keep feeling hot and then cold. But this ache . . ."

"Do you have a sore throat?" he asked.

"No, but it feels . . . weird."

"Weird?" he repeated dubiously. "Here, let me look at it," he offered. "But don't breathe on me." She opened her mouth but he said, "I need a flashlight. Just a minute." He returned to shine it down her throat and said, "Oh, boy. I think you're sick."

"No kidding." She mimicked him, but he wasn't amused.

Bryson made some phone calls, then came back to find Melissa sprawled out on the couch, looking as if she would rather be comatose. "I've made arrangements to have Jamie watched as long as necessary. I think you'd better see the doctor tomorrow and get a throat culture." He added with anything but compassion, "Can I get you something before I go to bed?"

"No," she groaned, "I'll be fine."

The next morning, Bryson went down to check on Melissa before he left for work. He met her on the stairs and followed her back up, noticing that she could hardly walk.

"Are you going to be all right?" he asked, feeling his subtle resentments melt into concern. He reminded himself of all that Melissa had done for him and the children.

"It's just this ache," she admitted, leaning momentarily against the wall to catch her breath. "I don't think I've ever hurt so bad in my life."

"Have you taken something for it?"

"I've taken the maximum I can take, over an hour ago. But the medicine hardly touches it. Nothing seems to help."

While Melissa was in the bathroom, Bryson called the doctor and made her an appointment, then he called the office and told them he wouldn't be in until after lunch.

"You have an appointment at ten-thirty," he announced, following her back downstairs.

"Oh, thank you," she said.

"And I'm staying home to take you," he added.

"I can drive myself to the doctor, Bryson."

"You can barely walk," he retorted. "So try to act gracious and stop arguing with me."

Melissa turned to look at him in astonishment, but he was smiling and she realized he was teasing her. "Okay," she said. "Wake me twenty minutes before we have to go . . . as if I could sleep," she added under her breath.

Melissa was declared to have a strong case of strep throat. She was given a shot that she claimed hurt so bad it put the body aches in perspective. Bryson made certain she had everything she needed before he went to work, but he didn't like the feeling that consumed him as he drove. How many days had he left home, wondering if Ilene would be okay, worried about the children? This vulnerability was all too familiar, and he hated it.

Melissa got worse before she got better. When her body aches had prevented her from sleeping for more than two days, she requested a priesthood blessing and slept through the night, waking up free of any aching. But her throat gradually became raw before it healed, and she hardly ate anything for three days because it simply hurt too much to swallow.

Bryson adjusted to managing without Melissa, but he wasn't terribly fond of the situation, even though it brought some startling realizations to light. He began to wonder what it might be like at this point without her, and the reality frightened him. But Amber put the whole thing into perspective when she crawled onto his lap one evening, asking with huge tears in her eyes, "Is Aunt Melissa going to die, too?"

After Bryson recovered from the shock, he pulled Amber close to him and assured her, "No, Aunt Melissa is not going to die. She's going to be better in just a few days, and everything will be fine."

Amber was easily convinced, but Bryson's mind stayed with the incident. He wondered what kind of attachment his children had developed with Melissa to cause such a fear in Amber. Then he realized that in a different way, he had the same problem. Hadn't her illness proven to him how difficult life was without her? He'd struggled on his own through much of Ilene's illness before Melissa arrived, but he'd quickly gotten used to having her there, and had obviously lost perspective on just how much of his stress she alleviated.

Bryson thought guiltily of the argument they'd had over Jessica. He knew he hadn't been fair with her, but he'd been too proud to apologize. He would much prefer to just put it behind him and pretend it hadn't happened, but something in him wondered what Ilene would think if she could see what was happening. And maybe she could. He wanted to be a man of integrity, for her if for no other reason. He wondered how many years he'd been rationalizing his integrity for reasons of pride or convenience, without consciously acknowledging it.

Tired of wrestling with his conscience, Bryson ventured to Melissa's room and found her sitting in bed with a book. "How you feeling?" he asked, leaning against the door frame, his hands deep in his pockets.

"My throat's a little better," she said, but she still grimaced when she swallowed. "How are the kids? I've been worried sick that they would get this, and—"

"The kids are fine," he assured her. "The doctor said at the first hint of symptoms he'd prescribe an antibiotic. But so far, they're okay."

"Good, I hope it stays that way."

"Is there anything I can get you?" he asked when the purpose of his visit seemed to be slow in coming out.

"You want the truth?" she asked and he nodded. "I want a chocolate malt."

Bryson smiled. "Okay, once I get the kids settled, I'll go get you one."

"Really?"

"Is that such a surprise?"

"Well, I am just a sassy little brat," she said a little too seriously.

"Actually," he drawled, knowing he'd not get a better opportunity than this, "I've been wanting to say something to you."

"Go on," she urged.

"About what I said concerning Jessica." He looked at the floor and fidgeted slightly. "I wasn't fair to you, and I'm sorry. I want you to know that I'm grateful you're here, and I don't know what I'd do without you."

Melissa was momentarily stunned. "Well, thank you, Bryse. I accept your apology. I hope to be back on my feet soon and be worth something again."

"You take your time," he insisted. "If nothing else, this has made me realize just how much you do."

Melissa met his eyes and felt her respect for him deepening. She believed Ilene's death had humbled and refined him. But she also realized what Ilene had told her long ago—that Bryson Davis was a good man. He always had been; perhaps he was just a little rough around the edges.

"You know," he went on, "we have actually been very blessed. I mean . . . I certainly wouldn't choose to give up my wife to cancer, but we're making it financially, and we've had you, and . . . well, I know it could be much worse."

"Yes, that's true," she agreed. "I remember when my mother died. Dad worked long hours, and Ilene and I were on our own most of the time. I remember being lonely and scared a lot. I guess there are many kids out there who have to get by with one parent for a number of reasons. But all in all, you're right, Bryse. Your children have been blessed."

Bryson looked momentarily embarrassed. "I'll get them to bed and—"

"Bryson," she stopped him as he turned to leave, "thanks for taking care of me."

"I haven't done much," he chuckled.

"Well, it was nice to know you were there, and . . . actually, you have. After living alone for so long, it's been nice to just have somebody around who knows whether or not I'm alive."

Bryson nodded and turned to leave, but he felt compelled to say something more that had occurred to him recently. "You know, Lissa, I think I'm beginning to understand why you and Ilene were so close. And in a way, I almost feel like you're my sister, too. I guess I should have felt that way years ago, but . . . well, I just wanted you to know that."

Melissa nodded, suddenly feeling too emotional to speak.

"I'll get you that malt," he said with a smile and left the room, wondering what he would ever do when Melissa decided she had to go back to California. He almost hoped she would stay indefinitely. Perhaps she would meet someone from the area, get married, and live close by. Or maybe she could get a job in Utah and . . . Bryson stopped his speculating when he realized such things were not up to him. Melissa had her own life to live, and it was inevitable that he'd eventually have to face his life without her. He only hoped that day wouldn't come too soon.

CHAPTER TEN

Ilene had been gone a little over three months when Melissa first noticed the change. It didn't happen with a thunderbolt or a flash of light. And the very fact that the change occurred within made her wonder how long it had been coming on. Had it been so gradual that she hadn't noticed its evolution?

She first noticed it when Bryson was leaning over the tub to wash Jamie's hair. Melissa had seen him do it countless times, and he was good at it. While she picked bath toys up off the floor and mopped up the water, she happened to notice the way his shirt stretched over the muscles of his back. The first surprise was that she'd notice something like that to begin with. But beyond that, she wasn't prepared for the tingling that erupted somewhere inside her. She heard him laugh as if he were miles away, then he reached out a hand for the towel she'd told him she'd get.

"Hey," he nudged her, "where are you? I need a towel."

Melissa forced herself back to the moment and handed it to him. He caught her eye, seeming to sense something unusual. She could almost feel her face becoming flushed, as if he could read her thoughts.

"Are you okay?" he asked as he pulled a dripping Jamie into the towel.

"I'm fine," she said tensely, hoping he couldn't sense the shame and guilt that suddenly seized her.

Bryson looked distracted but said nothing as he hurried out of the bathroom to get Jamie ready for bed.

Day after day, Melissa prayed to be free of these feelings, certain they were not proper. What was wrong with her, that she would find some bizarre attraction to her sister's husband? Or perhaps it wasn't an attraction at all, she rationalized. Maybe she had simply grown close to him through their shared grief and struggles, and she felt somehow dependent on him. She'd just about convinced herself of this when she saw him lying on the family room floor, tickling Amber. She found herself staring as if she'd never seen him before. When Amber finally escaped and Bryson lay back with an exhausted sigh, he glanced toward her. It took Melissa a moment to realize that he'd caught her watching him, and he was staring back, some kind of strange intrigue sparkling in his eyes.

"What are you looking at?" He smirked as if he'd caught her at mischief.

"Nothing," she snapped. "I was just . . . thinking about Ilene."

Melissa turned away abruptly, hoping the reminder of Ilene's part in this family would shock them both back to reality. Was it possible to assume, from the way he was looking at her, that Bryson was feeling this way, too? He was twelve years older than her, for crying out loud! *He was her sister's husband!* She had no business feeling this way, and she knew she had to do something fast.

Continually praying that she might be free of these feelings, Melissa stayed close to the scriptures and felt sure the attraction would go away. While Bryson was at work, she distracted herself with other thoughts and became convinced she had the problem mastered. But when he walked through the door with a vibrant, "Dad's home and I want somebody to tickle!" Melissa felt her knees go weak.

Feeling somehow wicked for not being able to overcome this odd attraction, Melissa convinced herself that there was only one option. By the following evening she had a plan worked out. It felt logical, and she approached Bryson right after dinner when the kids had all dispersed to play or do homework.

"Bryson, I've been thinking that . . ."

"What?" he urged when she hesitated, absently clearing the table at the same time.

"Maybe it's time I went back to California."

He stopped and looked up abruptly with a glare in his eyes that nearly burned through her. "What on earth for?"

Melissa couldn't look at him. Suddenly, the thought of being away from him was terrifying. "I can't . . . stay here forever . . . under the circumstances, Bryse. I mean . . . I should be working. You could afford a housekeeper who could look after the kids while you're at work. Why, Sister Hoover—she's looking for that kind of work. She could be right here. She'd be wonderful."

Bryson nearly dropped the stack of plates onto the table, startling Melissa. He wondered why he felt so angry. "My kids don't need a housekeeper, Lissa. They need *you*. You're family."

"I'm not their mother, Bryse. I could never replace her."

"You're a lot closer than some . . . hired help."

Melissa turned away from him, wondering if she were fighting him or herself. "I just . . . need to get away. I . . . have my own life to live, Bryse."

Bryson's anger melted into fear. He hurried around the table, feeling suddenly desperate without fully understanding why. "Listen to me," his voice turned husky, "tell me what you need and we'll get it. I can pay you more. I could. I could work it out somehow. The kids need you, Lissa. Please . . . don't do this."

Melissa frantically tried to think what to do. She didn't *want* to leave, but she feared any other course would be disastrous. She had to get away from these feelings.

"Well," she said quietly, "maybe I could get a place close by. If you could pay me enough to—"

Bryson shook his head before she even finished. "It's not good enough. You have to be *here*."

Something in his tone forced Melissa to look at him directly. "Why, Bryson?" she asked in a voice that chilled him. "Why do I need to be here?"

"The kids need you."

"I can take care of the kids and live elsewhere. But I can't stay here under the circumstances."

"What circumstances?" he asked. When she didn't answer, he guessed, "If you mean what people might think, I don't care if—"

"You know I don't care what people think."

"Then . . . what? Don't make me beg it out of you!"

"Because I can't live here with you!" she shouted, then immediately regretted it when his eyes widened in disbelief.

Bryson watched her closely, trying to figure what she meant. Before he had a chance to think about it, she hurried downstairs and he heard the door to her room slam closed. He stood in the kitchen for several minutes with his hands in the pockets of his jeans, wondering what he might do if Melissa left. The fear that seized him was almost tangibly painful, and he hated the thought of having become so dependent on her that he would feel this way. He nearly convinced himself that his concern was on behalf of the children; and of course, that was legitimate. But there was more, and he knew it. And yet, she had just told him she couldn't live here with him. Was he so obnoxious? Was she implying that she found being with him so distasteful that she couldn't bear it anymore?

When he couldn't come up with any answers, Bryson found Jessica and reminded her that she should be washing the dishes. After putting in a load of laundry, he was tempted to just try and forget about what Melissa had said, but something deep within told him if he didn't face it head on, he could very well lose her. So he took a deep breath and knocked at her bedroom door.

"Who is it?" she called after a long pause.

"It's me . . . Bryse," he admitted hoarsely.

Following an even longer pause, Melissa slowly opened the door.

"That's not like you to walk away from a good argument," he said facetiously.

"It's not like you to come looking for one," she retorted.

Bryson chuckled uncomfortably and glanced down. Melissa didn't even crack a smile. Their eyes met, and he knew he had to get to the point.

"Listen, I . . ." He cleared his throat and folded his arms. "Apparently the situation here is not . . . working for you. But I . . ." He rubbed a hand over his face. "Well, let's talk about it. Surely we can work something out."

Melissa sat down on the edge of her bed with a sigh. Bryson leaned a shoulder against the door frame and watched her closely.

"Bryson, I understand that you've come to depend on me to help with the house and the kids. And I know they need someone here who loves them and . . . well, the bottom line is, you should get married again. You can't raise them alone. And I don't think you'll do anything about it as long as you have your sister-in-law living under your roof. As for me, well, I'm not getting any younger. Being here has made me realize that I need to settle down and have a family of my own. I need to get out and do something about that."

Bryson tried to remain expressionless as everything she said struck him as totally preposterous and unthinkable. On the surface he could see her logic, but his spirit seemed to balk at the very idea. Was his heart still so bound to Ilene that the thought of actually dating another woman seemed downright nauseating? Trying to be sensitive to Melissa's circumstances, he offered an objective point of view. "There's no reason why you can't live here and . . . well, date." Her eyes widened, and he wondered what he'd said wrong. "There are some single men around here, you know."

Melissa's eyes penetrated him so fiercely that he felt sure she would stand up and start packing immediately.

"The kids need you," he said again, as if it was his only defense.

Melissa felt suddenly frustrated and uttered a silent prayer to be able to handle this. She thought of the children, and realized it would be selfish of her to desert them because of her own fears. While she watched Bryson fidgeting nervously, her pulse raced without restraint. Needing time to think, she temporarily dismissed the conversation with a simple, "I need to pray about it, Bryson. If this is where the Lord wants me to be, I'll stay."

Bryson sighed with visible relief, while Melissa felt sure the Lord would not want her to stay here and be subject to these feelings that could only cause problems. "We can talk about it tomorrow," she said tersely, just wanting him to leave so she could think clearly.

Bryson nodded and stepped into the hall.

"Maybe you ought to pray about it, too," she said.

Bryson nodded again and walked away. Melissa kicked her door shut, wondering how her sister had survived that many years with a man who wouldn't talk.

Melissa didn't come out of her room until it was time for family prayer, then she quickly returned. She prayed more fervently than ever before in her life, intermittently studying the scriptures far into the night. She somehow convinced herself that this attraction for her sister's husband had withdrawn the Spirit from her, and she was going to have to work very hard to get it back in order to know what she should do. She fell asleep without coming to any definite conclusions

The following day, everything seemed to go wrong. What she expected to get better became worse, until she was so confused and frustrated she wanted to scream. Long after the children had gone to bed, Bryson returned from home teaching to find her washing dishes as if she had no motivation at all.

"How did you get stuck with this?" he asked as he rolled up his sleeves.

"The kids had homework," she answered dryly, wishing her heart wouldn't pound this way when he walked into a room—which was the very reason she sounded so distressed as she added, "What are you doing?"

Bryson looked up in surprise as he stuck his hands into the sink, probing for the dishrag. "I thought I'd help you. It's late. You look tired. You should get some sleep."

Melissa was about to protest when his hand brushed against hers somewhere in the suds. While part of her wanted to run away and somehow hide from these feelings, part of her suddenly wanted to be standing here. She wanted to be close to him, to breathe in the scent of his shaving lotion.

"I'll wash," he said, nudging her over a little with his shoulder. "You rinse," he added. "One day, we might get that stupid dishwasher fixed."

"Then we wouldn't have anywhere to store the extra glasses," she replied blandly. "Besides, it's helping the kids learn the work ethic."

"Good point," he chuckled softly. She wondered if it was her imagination that his voice was becoming a little raspy. She watched his hands as he washed a plate and passed it to her. She rinsed it and set it in the drainer. He washed a bowl, and their fingers touched for a moment. Melissa wondered if she was going insane as she became intimately aware of his every movement, every detail of him and the way he did what he did. As they carried out the menial task with no conversation, she felt her chest rise and fall with every breath she took, and wondered how he could possibly *not* notice the effect he was having on her. She wished she could tell him how she really felt. The thought of actually exploring these feelings was enticing, but it seemed so wrong. She felt so afraid.

Meanwhile, Bryson was surprised at the thought that popped into his head. He started paying too much attention to Melissa's hands as she rinsed the dishes and set them aside. He scolded himself inwardly and tried to think of something else, but he only became aware of her in a way he never had before. Of course he'd grown to care for Melissa, and lately he'd found that he was actually quite fond of her. But she was Ilene's sister. Was he so lonely and deprived that he would lower himself to looking at her in a way that simply wasn't appropriate?

Bryson was both relieved and disappointed when the dishes were finished. Melissa dried her hands and passed him the towel without a word spoken. The transaction stopped midway as their eyes met, and something nameless seemed to freeze around them. He tried to figure what she was thinking, but unlike with Ilene, he found it impossible to read Melissa's emotions. As he looked deeper into her eyes, perhaps searching for the reasons she wanted to leave, Melissa took a step back, her expression turning momentarily to obvious fear. Before he could question it she hurried away, leaving him to wonder if her desire to get away from him had something to do with these feelings. Did she sense that his thoughts of her were out of line? Had they simply been together too much?

The questions evoked a sudden rush of emotion. Bryson sat down unsteadily and tried futilely to make sense of all this. An hour later he crawled wearily into bed, no closer to understanding than before. He only knew he was tired of being alone, but he feared what that loneliness might do to him. True, Ilene had only been dead for three and a half months. But it was long before that when she had ceased sleeping in this bed with him. At moments like this, he missed her so much he wondered if he could bear it. Certain he couldn't, he rolled his face into her pillow and cried himself into oblivion.

For Melissa, the following day was longer and harder than the day before. Bryson hardly said a word to her. Their eyes never met. The very fact that their agreement to pray about this decision was not brought up made her certain that he had come to no better conclusions than she had. She was only more confused and distraught. By the time she went to bed, she felt as if she would go over the edge. Idly she thumbed through the pages of her scriptures, searching for something that might bring her peace. She read in Ecclesiastes the well-known words, *To every thing there is a season, and a time to every purpose under the heaven.* It was easy to relate the concept to her life and the death she had been close to; but as she tried to apply it to her present dilemma, it seemed incredibly trite. Melissa felt sure she was trying to read her own desires into it, so she continued to search and peruse. Looking in the *Topical Guide* to cross reference *time* and *season*, she came across some verses in section eighty-eight of the Doctrine and Covenants. She knew the Spirit often worked by leading one to the proper verse of scripture, where an answer might lie. It had happened to her before. But it wasn't until warm tears welled into her eyes that Melissa had to admit the Spirit was not absent from her at all. In truth, it had been trying to tell her something for several days, and she had been too stubborn in her mind-set to see it.

Once she had absorbed her initial reaction, Melissa blinked away the mist in her eyes and read from verse forty-four again: *And they give light to each other in their times and in their seasons . . . and the sun giveth his light by day, and the moon giveth her light by night, and the stars also give their light, as they roll upon their wings in their glory, in the midst of the power of God.*

The thought appearing in Melissa's mind seemed so outlandish that she wanted to protest the very idea. But she couldn't deny the warmth she felt. Instantaneously, everything changed; but it took over an hour of staring at the ceiling to come to terms with it. The symbolism she'd found in the scriptures was vague, but what she had learned from it was plain and clear. She understood now. She had never found the right man because the time had not been right. She recalled conversations with Ilene that made Melissa almost believe her sister had known, even then, that this would happen. The thought was so poignant that Melissa turned her face into her pillow and cried.

The clock on her dresser read 3:38 a.m. when she pulled on her robe and headed upstairs to take something for a headache. She thought of the day ahead and wondered how she would make it through on so little sleep. But there was a new peace inside that calmed her. Though she couldn't help being afraid of what it might take to face up to these feelings, Melissa knew it was right to be here. Her prayers had been answered.

She turned on the kitchen light and dug quietly into the upper cabinet for the Tylenol. In the process of swallowing them, Bryson's voice startled her. "Couldn't sleep?" he said, and she nearly choked. Bryson slapped her on the back when she couldn't stop coughing. When she finally gained control and realized the pills had made it down, her eyes focused on the wedding band on his finger. The answer to her prayers rushed to her mind, while thoughts of Ilene tore at her heart. She looked up to meet Bryson's eyes and felt something shift inside of her. All these years she had barely tolerated him—and now she was wondering what it might be like to have him kiss her, to hold him close, to share his life in every way.

"Are you okay?" he chuckled, shocking her into the realization that she'd been staring at him again.

"Just tired," she replied in a squeaky voice and hurried away.

Bryson stood for a full minute wondering why the look in Melissa's eyes had affected him so strongly. He finally got the drink of water he'd come for and shuffled back to bed, even less prone to fall asleep than he had been before. While he had prayed and pondered the situation, he began to feel sure that Melissa wanted to leave because she sensed the change in his feelings. He wondered if the Lord was trying to tell him he needed to learn to make it on his own before his loneliness got any more out of hand. What other explanation could there be for the way his mind wandered when he thought of Melissa? She was his wife's sister, for heaven's sake! He felt sure the lonely ache he was feeling had completely squelched his scruples as he wondered what it might be like to hold her in his arms and taste her sassy little mouth.

Bryson penitently forced his thoughts back to Ilene, and tears burned into his eyes. He felt ashamed and guilty as he wondered if she could read his mind from where she was now. How would she feel, knowing that her husband was attracted to her little sister?

Bryson squeezed his eyes shut in an effort to block out Melissa's image. He prayed with all the strength of his spirit to be able to deal with this, and realized that he was idly toying with his wedding ring.

Bryson felt a sharp contrast of emotions as a thought appeared in his mind. *You're not married anymore, Bryson. She's gone, and it's time to get on with your life.* Sadness enveloped him as he could almost hear Ilene's sweet voice putting life to those words. She *was* gone. And it was a long life ahead that he was facing without her. But at the same moment, an intense ray of hope seemed to filter through the darkness. He *did* have a long life ahead, and he knew Ilene would want him to live it fully—for himself as well as for the children.

With peaceful resolution, Bryson slipped the ring off his finger and set it on the bedside table. Then he rolled over and went to sleep.

Melissa got out of bed twenty minutes before the alarm was set to go off. Without a moment's sleep behind her, she decided it would be well to get as much done as she could before she collapsed from exhaustion. With a prayer that she would make it through the day, she dressed and went to the kitchen to start breakfast. The morning quickly became hectic, and it wasn't until Bryson had left for work that she felt the frustration rise inside her. He hadn't spoken a single word to her, and she wondered how he expected her to stay when he wasn't even willing to acknowledge her existence. She could see now what the real problem was. And she knew overcoming it would not be easy.

While Jamie played contentedly with Legos, Melissa hurried through the household routine, working with a vigor that was spurred on by her rising anger. The more she thought about Bryson and his unwillingness to communicate, the more angry she became. She wondered again how Ilene had tolerated it all those years, then she almost convinced herself that maybe the idea of considering a life with him was preposterous. She wasn't sure she could do it—not unless he learned to talk.

Melissa took out a degree of her frustration on Bryson's pillows as she punched and fluffed them and tucked them into his freshly made bed. She might not have noticed the ring on the bedside table if the phone hadn't rung. It was only a wrong number, but as she set the receiver back down, her eye caught the gold band sitting there idly.

She sat on the edge of the bed and picked it up. She examined it carefully, contemplating all it stood for. A never-ending gold circle—the symbol of eternal marriage. Ilene's marriage. Recalling that Bryson had been wearing the ring last night in the kitchen, Melissa wondered what had made him take it off and set it aside in the hours before he'd gone to work.

Suddenly, all the anger and frustration melted into a warm compassion. She thought of the years he had shared with Ilene, and wondered how he must be feeling to realize she was gone. As much as Melissa loved and missed her sister, she couldn't comprehend the love she had shared with her husband. Of course, Bryson knew he and Ilene would be together again, and there was peace in that understanding. But a lifetime was a long time to be alone in the mortal perspective. Melissa knew then that the Lord intended for them to share that lifetime, and it was up to her to see that he was not alone. If only she could reach him!

When the children were all in bed that evening, Melissa had to acknowledge that she had been blessed with the stamina to make it through the day. Even now she didn't feel especially tired, though it was tempting to slip off to bed rather than opening what she knew would be a difficult conversation with Bryson. But it had to be done. They had to start somewhere.

Knowing from experience that only desperation would make him talk, she resigned herself to the only plausible approach. She found him sitting at the dining-room table, staring at the wall in a way that had become familiar.

"So," she said, startling him, "have you come up with anyone you can hire to replace me?"

Bryson swallowed hard and forced a calm response that disguised his panic. "I thought you were going to pray about it."

"I did," she stated. Then, hoping to evade a question about the answer she'd received, she added, "Did you?"

"Yes," he said, hoping she wouldn't press this too far. He had no desire to voice where his real feelings were, or to admit that he'd found no definite answers to his prayers—only a bizarre sense of confusion.

"And what conclusion have you come to?" she asked, sitting

down next to him.

"The kids need you," he stated.

Melissa willed her anger to settle and decided to get to the heart of the problem. *"I need more,"* she insisted, unprepared for the tears that seeped into her eyes.

Bryson leaned his elbows on the table and pressed his face into his hands with a heavy sigh. He thought of what she'd said about wanting to get married and have a life of her own. Was it right for him to selfishly want her to stay to satisfy his own feelings? Perhaps the Lord was trying to tell him that he needed to get on with his life as well, and Melissa's leaving would force him to do it, however painful it might be.

"Bryson," she continued when he said nothing, "I'm trying to have a conversation here, but I can't do it alone."

He sighed. "I know you need more, Melissa. And I . . . I suppose I do, too."

"Well, now we're getting somewhere."

"What's that supposed to mean?" he snapped.

"It's no secret that you're a man of few words and prefer to keep your emotions to yourself. Ilene was an expert at coaxing your thoughts and feelings out of you, or at least knowing you well enough to know where you were coming from. But I can't do that, Bryse. You're never going to be able to get on with your life if you don't start talking. So, forget about the kids, Bryson. What do *you* need? If you want me to stay, I've got to know why."

He just stared at her blankly, and she wanted to slap him.

"I had a life before all of this, you know," she rambled, if only to ease the unbearable lengths of silence. "I had an apartment, friends; I still have a storage unit in California with my life in it." She paused and almost convinced herself not to say the next thought that popped into her mind. When it persisted, she just let it out. "If there is a reason you think I should stay, Bryson, then convince me. Otherwise, you're going to have to find someone else to raise your children."

Bryson's heart pounded into his ears. He'd hadn't felt any more afraid than this the night Ilene died. It was pure desperation that forced him to admit, "I . . . I need you."

"For what?" she asked intently.

"Isn't it obvious?" he asked curtly.

"I'm afraid it is. Unless you tell me otherwise, I have to assume that you need me for cheap labor. I am your housekeeper, your cook, your baby-sitter, your—"

"I get the idea," he snarled.

Melissa pushed her chair back and came abruptly to her feet. "If that's all I am to you, Bryson, then I *have* to leave, because I can't stay here and—"

"I *need* you," he interrupted. She looked briefly stunned. Bryson took hold of her arm and stood beside her. "I need *you*. Do you hear what I'm saying?"

"I hear you saying that you need me," she said, trying to keep her voice from trembling, "but you haven't told me why."

"Can't you see it?" he asked, his face so close to hers she could feel his breath. "Can't you *feel* it?"

Melissa's heart quickened. She didn't have to wonder what he was talking about, but by all she held dear, she was not going to say it for him.

Their eyes met with something electric passing between them. "Talk to me, Bryson," she whispered in a husky voice.

"How can I explain it to you, when I don't understand it myself? I only know that I need you here."

"That's not good enough."

The desperation rose in Bryson, and he almost shook her. "Listen to me, Melissa. I'm sick and tired of feeling like my life is hanging in the balance. Since the day I found out Ilene was going to die, I've been terrified to think of anything beyond living one day at a time. I'm not sure I have the strength to think of getting on with my life, but if you're determined to get on with yours then I just might have to accept it. If you want me to tell you I appreciate all you've done for me, I'll say it. If you want me to say that I never could have made it without you, fine, I will. But don't expect me to open up my heart to you and let it bleed all over the place, when you've made it perfectly clear that just living under the same roof with me is intolerable."

Melissa was so surprised she couldn't help the sharp tone of her voice. "When did I say that?"

"Just the other day!" he retorted. "You told me that under the circumstances, you couldn't live here with me."

"Well, it's true," she said in a quiet voice that got his attention. "Under the present circumstances, I *can't* stay. Something's got to change."

"What?" he said, the desperation in his voice all too evident. "Tell me what, and I'll change it."

Melissa looked into his eyes and was so stunned she couldn't speak. She sensed something that she didn't dare hope for, but at the same time, something she feared.

Bryson searched her eyes as if he could find her thoughts in there somewhere. Was it possible that she truly detested him? There was a time when he would have believed that. But something in all of this contradicted the very idea. He narrowed his eyes and tried to search deeper, praying inwardly that he could find a way to make her stay. He needed her. "Tell me, Melissa," he uttered softly. "I'll do anything."

While his willingness was touching, Melissa knew it wasn't enough. "Bryson." She took his hands into hers to ease them away from her arms. "Don't promise me something you can't keep, and don't tell me things you don't mean. I will not stay here under false pretenses. If it's not from the heart, I don't want to hear it."

She drew her hands from his and took a step back. "There is only one thing I need, Bryson. I need to know why you want me here. But it's like you said a minute ago; you can't explain it to me if you don't understand it yourself. So, maybe you'd better take some time to figure it out, and when you do, let me know. In the meantime, I'm going to get reservations for a flight to L.A."

"What for?" he asked, hating the edge of panic in his voice.

"One way or another," she said, "I've got a storage unit to clean out."

Bryson watched her walk away, hating this helplessness he felt that seemed all too familiar. He had been helpless to save Ilene or to spare her any of the pain. He had become accustomed to living his life at the mercy of those willing to help him with the children and keep his life going—most especially Melissa. And now he felt helpless to keep her here.

It wasn't until the middle of the night that it occurred to him he wasn't helpless at all. Ilene was gone, yes. But he was adjusting. His financial circumstances were secure, and he had learned a lot about being both the mother and the father. If Melissa felt she had to go, he could somehow manage. And yet, the thought of her leaving threatened to tear him apart inside. Why? There was only one answer. And if that answer was what she needed to hear him say, then surely he was man enough to say it.

As Bryson guided his mind through every avenue of the situation, he dusted away the cobwebs of guilt and regret, and brushed away the outdated conception that he was a married man with no business wanting to ease this lonely ache. He could see then that what he wanted and what he needed were the same. And in that moment, he knew Ilene would not only approve, she would feel joy in the possibility. He recalled the way Ilene had often told him she had never had to wonder how he felt about her. And yet, he'd always found it difficult to express his feelings. He could almost wonder if she had been blessed with the ability to read his mind. Or maybe he'd never been afraid or inhibited with Ilene, and words hadn't been necessary for her to know. Well, he wasn't so stupid that he couldn't see he was afraid and inhibited with Melissa. And why shouldn't he be? She was Ilene's sister, for crying out loud. When he had been married and having children, Melissa had been little more than a child. But she was not a child now, and Bryson felt a rush of joy at the thought of pursuing these feelings. He could only pray that she would listen.

In spite of his lack of sleep, Bryson felt unusually chipper as he got out of the shower and dressed for work the next morning. He noticed his wedding ring sitting on the bedside table where he'd left it, and picked it up. For a moment he fingered it, contemplating the memories it represented. A wave of emotion struck him, but it in no way contradicted his hope for the future. With a sense of peace, he put the ring safely into a drawer and headed to the kitchen. He paused in the doorway when he saw Melissa standing at the counter, shredding cheese for omelettes. A rush of butterflies compelled him to move closer, and he smiled to himself when he realized that she was unaware of his presence.

Melissa gasped in surprise when Bryson's arms appeared on either side of her. He set his palms on the counter, trapping her where she stood. She held her breath, wishing she could see his face.

"I need you, Melissa," he whispered behind her ear. "I need you because you are the only thing that keeps my life stable. I need you because you are strong and capable and so willing to give. I need you because what you give to me, no one else could. I need the light and laughter you bring into my home. I need the love you give my children—the things you do for them that I could never do. I need you because you've made me realize that I am capable of living without Ilene; because you have made me feel something that I believed I would never feel again. Please don't leave me, Melissa. Without you I would be lost."

In the silence following Bryson's impassioned speech, Melissa could hear herself breathing. Bryson heard his own vulnerability pounding in time with his heart. While he waited for a reaction, he took a step back and pushed his hands into his pockets. She turned so abruptly that it startled him. The emotion in her eyes gave him the courage to go on.

"I don't know if that's what you've been trying to get me to say; or maybe it's the last thing you wanted to hear. But it really doesn't matter, because what I said came from the heart. I guess it's up to you to decide whether or not you can live with it."

Melissa was so stunned she could neither speak nor move. The sincerity in his eyes was so touching that she absently put a hand to her heart. As the silence lingered, she could see vulnerability showing in his expression. She knew such an effort had not been easy for him, and she was determined to let him know how much it meant to her. If only she knew where to begin. "Bryson, you know I . . . well, I . . ."

Greg and Amber bounded into the kitchen, screaming back and forth with the usual morning television dispute. Bryson managed an abrupt chuckle and rubbed a hand over his face. "It's time for breakfast anyway," he scolded. "So go turn off the T.V. and wash up." He halted any further protests by lifting a stern finger. They sulked away, and his eyes caught Melissa's. While he was waiting for her to go on, Jamie started to cry in the distance.

"I'll get her," Melissa said eagerly. The tension was so thick she feared it would overwhelm her if she didn't have some time to think.

Through breakfast Melissa avoided Bryson's eyes, perhaps fearing he could read the truth of her feelings before she had a chance to explain. While he supervised the tooth-brushing and last-minute off-to-school routine, Melissa dressed Jamie and went to work hastily in the kitchen. Perhaps if she stayed busy until he left for work, she could have the time and space to absorb everything he'd said. Filling the sink with sudsy water, she had a brief memory of the way their hands had touched as they'd washed dishes together. Then she recalled his words, so close to her ear, *"You have made me feel something that I believed I would never feel again."*

She tried to ignore the tremor that started down her spine and ended somewhere in her stomach. Glancing at the clock, she expected to hear Bryson leave any minute. Instead she heard him talking on the phone, though she couldn't tell what he was saying. A moment later he was standing a few feet away, his hands deep in his pockets. His expression made it clear he was not leaving their conversation unfinished. "I told them I'd be late," he said. "I think we need to talk."

Melissa chuckled tensely and tried to concentrate on clearing off the counter. "I . . . I don't know what to say."

Bryson couldn't recall Melissa's ever being at a loss for words. Why now? He felt as if his life were hanging in the balance again. And he *hated* it. Trying to remain calm, he simply asked, "Will you be staying or not? If I need to find someone to replace you, I'd like to know."

Melissa turned to him abruptly, wondering at his terseness. But the vulnerability in his eyes explained everything. She felt a sudden rush of emotion that made her voice crack as she answered, "Of course I'll be staying. I need you, too, Bryson."

Bryson squeezed his eyes shut and uttered a silent, *Thank you, Lord.*

The intense emotion became too much to bear, and Melissa turned away, pressing a hand to her mouth as if she could keep it from him. She was suddenly overcome with weakness from her recent lack of sleep. And while she fleetingly wished Ilene were here to pour her heart out to, the ironies bombarded her in a rush of tears.

Bryson opened his eyes to see Melissa's shoulders tremble. He heard a vague whimper, and ignored everything but his instincts as he took those delicate shoulders in his hands and turned her to face him.

"Why are you crying?" he asked, wiping at her tears with his fingertips. The gesture warmed Melissa, but only deepened the irony. Unable to hold back any longer, she took hold of his arms as if he could save her from drowning. With no thought of anything but releasing these emotions, she pressed her face to his shoulder and cried like she hadn't since the week Ilene died. She was vaguely aware of his arms coming around her, and she couldn't deny the comfort she felt from his nearness. But she was completely unaware of the silent tears he cried as he held her.

They had cried together many times before. They had shared the sorrow of pain and death. Grief had been their common bond through these months as they had worked to sustain each other. But now it was different. There was something intangible about the way he held her. And there was no mistaking the way his lips brushed idly through her hair. Or the gentle way he smoothed it back from her face as she wept. And while Melissa was absorbed in her emotion, Bryson deftly lifted her into his arms and carried her to the couch. For a long while after her crying had ceased, she kept her head against his shoulder, wondering how she had ended up sitting here beside him, her legs draped over his lap. But she felt secure here, almost cradled against him. She marveled at the way his fingers toyed idly in her hair. A quiver erupted somewhere inside her when his lips made subtle contact with her brow.

Just when she began to think the silence would go on indefinitely, Bryson spoke in a low voice, "Did I say something to upset you?"

Melissa shook her head and nuzzled instinctively closer to his shoulder.

"Talk to me, Lissa," he whispered. "We've been through a lot together, and you've always managed to tell me what I needed to hear, in spite of myself. Don't shut down on me now."

"I'm sorry," she said quietly. "It's just . . . hard to know what to say." She sighed, and his arm tightened around her. "I . . . it's hard to understand how I can miss Ilene so much, and at the same time . . ." She drew the courage to lift her face and look at him. But the emotion she read in his eyes made it difficult to finish.

"At the same time what?" he urged.

"Admit to the way I'm feeling."

Bryson sighed. He almost smiled. "You've told me yourself that I'm a man who needs things clearly spelled out. I'm afraid you're going to have to be a little more specific."

Melissa felt somehow put on the spot, but she recalled the things he'd said to her earlier in the kitchen, and knew he was not expecting her to admit to something that he wasn't already feeling. It was a difficult bridge to cross, but at least they were crossing it together.

Gingerly she reached up a hand to touch his face. "I never wanted to feel this way about you, Bryse. The last man I expected to fall in love with was my sister's husband. I can only hope she understands."

Melissa held her breath as she realized what she had just admitted. But everything seemed to fall into place as he said, "We can only hope together."

Bryson had forgotten there was a two-year-old in the house until he heard toys being dumped in the family room.

"Oh, dear," Melissa said and tried to stand up, "I wonder what kind of mess she's making while I—"

"I'll take care of it," Bryson insisted without giving her a chance to protest before he hurried down the stairs. Melissa took a moment to gather her wits and take a deep breath. She was stunned at the realization of how life could change in a matter of days. Even since she'd gotten out of bed this morning, so much had changed. Admitting her feelings aloud had already spurred them on, and she hurried after Bryson, if only to be in the same room with him. She came to the top of the stairs to find him at the bottom, heading up.

"It's all right," he chuckled. "She actually picked up the animals before she dumped out the Legos." His expression sobered slightly. "She must have known we needed some time alone."

Melissa nodded tensely and looked at the floor.

"I suppose I should get to work, but . . ." The way Melissa's eyes met his, blatantly telling him she didn't want him to leave, took him momentarily off guard and he just stared at her, wondering what he had ever done to deserve such a blessing. He'd believed that he would never be able to love another woman, and felt sure that even if he could, he would never find one to compare to Ilene. But here she was. And she had been here all along. He only wished he knew how to tell her that without gushing all over the place.

"But?" she urged, and he shook his head slightly.

"I . . . just want you to know that I . . . well, I'm glad you're staying. I know I'm not easy to live with . . . but I do need you."

"Maybe we could . . . talk more . . . later."

Bryson nodded and hurried to the bedroom to finish getting ready. He was about to leave when he stopped and turned back to say, "Don't bother reserving a flight to L.A. We'll drive there— together. We'll take the kids to Disneyland and the beach, and we'll sort all of your life out together. We'll rent a U-Haul and bring it back here. There's no need to go out and look for your life, Melissa. Your life is right here."

CHAPTER ELEVEN

A different kind of tension hovered about the house through the evening. Melissa's heart skipped a beat nearly every time she looked at Bryson. And if he so much as smiled in her direction, she felt a giddy rush somewhere inside. The kitchen was cleaned up earlier than usual, and Bryson offered to get the children to bed. Melissa put on a sweater and followed her urge to go outside and enjoy the pleasant breeze. She sat on the back porch swing and watched the stars, trying to comprehend the turn her life was taking. When she had come here in December, she would never have considered staying indefinitely. She had grown accustomed to caring for this home and these children, but it was almost frightening to think of taking it on officially. Then she thought of Bryson, and that recently familiar sensation erupted inside her. She wrapped an arm around her middle in an effort to calm it, but as her thoughts deepened, so did that quivering inside. She wondered if she was being presumptuous to think this was the beginning of a lifetime with him. He'd admitted that he cared for her, that he felt something for her, but that didn't necessarily mean he intended to marry her. Or did it?

The question stuck in her mind when she heard the screen door squeak open, then slam shut. She looked up to see Bryson in the light that filtered through the screen. She would never have thought a man could look so good in a sweatshirt and a pair of faded jeans.

"Mind if I join you?" he asked.

Melissa slid over to make room for him. "Please do."

Bryson sat beside her and leaned his forearms on his thighs. "You know," he said after several moments of silence, "I was thinking earlier about the first time I saw Ilene. I don't suppose you'd remember that."

"Why would I?" she laughed slightly.

"Because you were there."

"I was?"

"You were playing basketball with your Young Women's team." He chuckled. "All I remember of you then is this skinny kid with stringy, short-cropped hair and freckles." His eyes shifted momentarily to her face. "You've changed a little since then."

Melissa said nothing, wondering what he was getting to.

"Anyway," he went on, "I remember looking across the gymnasium and seeing Ilene. The last thing I had expected that night was to walk in that building without a care in the world, and to walk out a changed man."

"Changed?" she questioned when he became thoughtful.

"Just seeing her made something inside me shift. I had never felt any desire to be committed. Beyond having a testimony of the gospel, I believed I didn't need anything or anyone. Then I saw her—and of course I had to talk to her. Nothing was ever the same after that. Everything I did, I wanted her to do it with me. I wanted her by my side everywhere I went. Just looking at her made me realize why man was not meant to be alone."

Melissa heard emotion creep into his voice, and for a full minute he said nothing. She might have expected discussing Ilene to have become somehow uncomfortable, in light of the way things were changing. But it was as it always had been. She was their common bond. They both loved her, and they both missed her. She would forever be a part of their lives.

"Are you all right?" she asked when he still didn't speak.

"Yeah," he said with a shaky laugh. He cleared his throat and continued toward his point. "When I learned that Ilene was going to die, I realized I had taken her for granted during much of our married life. She was always there, always capable, and she always loved me unconditionally. I thought a lot about how strongly she had affected my life, and I believed with all my heart and soul that I could never feel that way again." Melissa's heart quickened as he turned to look at her and added firmly, "I was wrong."

Bryson lifted his arm onto the back of the swing behind her, and spoke close to her face. "She was an incredible woman, Melissa, and I will always love her. But she was no more incredible than you. To try and compare the two of you is impossible—and pointless. It would be like comparing a lily to a rose. No one could question that each is beautiful and unique. But is one possibly better than the other?"

Bryson felt suddenly uncomfortable as the words flowing out of him seemed far too eloquent for his nature. He wondered if the Spirit assisted in times such as this.

"Melissa," his voice lowered and his arm tightened around her shoulders, "what I'm trying to say is that I . . . I never wanted to love you; I didn't try to make this happen. I'm not sitting here saying these things to you because it's easier than venturing into the world in search of companionship. Or because the children love you and depend on you. As I see it, there is only one reason this is happening at all. It was *meant* to. I could never understand why someone like you wouldn't have a dozen men beating down your door, begging you to marry them. But you can't imagine how grateful I am now that you've waited—that you're here."

Melissa was speechless. They watched each other in contemplative silence, but she didn't feel the tension she had felt in the past. She took a sharp breath when she realized he was going to kiss her. Something almost magical happened when his lips meekly made contact with hers. She opened her eyes to find him watching her. She smiled timidly and closed her eyes when he did. As he kissed her again, his arm tightened around her. He brought his other hand to her face, tentatively rubbing a thumb over her cheek as if she were fragile and precious. Something vaguely passionate seeped through the timidity of his kiss, and Melissa never wanted it to end. Just as she abandoned herself to accept his affection without reservation, he drew back and cleared his throat with a breathy chuckle.

"What's the matter?" she asked, fearing she'd done something wrong.

He looked at her and chuckled again as he pressed a kiss to her brow. "I think I need to be careful." The question in her eyes deepened and he clarified, "I think I've been alone too long."

Melissa was tempted to feel embarrassed at his implication, but there was something about his attitude that put her at ease. They had shared so much of the harsh reality of life that discussing the down-to-earth truth of their attraction seemed appropriate, and perhaps necessary. She felt warmed to realize that she had such an effect on him. She would hate to think that she was alone in her feelings.

"You know," he said, concentrating briefly on the starlit sky before he turned to her again, "there are moments when I am tempted to feel guilty for wanting you the way I do, but . . ." He paused when Melissa's eyes grew large. "Well," he justified, "you wanted me to talk. I have to tell you how I feel."

"It's all right, Bryse," she assured him. "It's just going to take some getting used to."

"Boy, you can say that again." He chuckled and kissed her quickly on the mouth. Then he laughed as if he couldn't hold back the joy. "Where was I?"

"You were talking about feeling guilty."

"Oh, yes." His expression sobered. "Whenever I am tempted to feel guilty, I remember Ilene telling me that she wanted me to get on with my life. She told me in no uncertain terms that she believed I would learn to love someone sooner than I expected, and it would be someone I already knew, and . . ." Bryson stopped abruptly as those words came back to him. She had sounded so sure, as if she had seen some kind of vision. At the time he had disregarded it, unable to think of anything but losing Ilene. But now he realized something that made a chill rush down his spine. He looked at Melissa as if he had never seen her before.

"What?" she questioned.

"She knew." He came abruptly to his feet as the reality struck him deeply. "I don't know how, but I'm absolutely sure that she knew it would be you."

A sudden warmth confirmed to Bryson the truth of what he'd just said. He turned to look at Melissa and knew, without asking, the reason tears were streaming down her face.

"Did she say something to you?" he demanded gently.

"Nothing specific, but . . . looking back, I know you're right."

For several moments they watched each other, mutually trying to comprehend the realization that they had somehow come upon their destiny. Something beyond the bonds they shared, beyond this physical attraction, drew their spirits together as if they had no choice. Melissa came to her feet in the same moment that he took a step forward. In one agile movement, Bryson drew her into his arms and pressed his mouth over hers. Melissa clung to him and resisted the urge to cry from the pure joy she felt. How many times had she wondered if she would ever know what it was like to be held this way, to share such affection? She thought it funny that she would recall the coy smile that had come to Ilene's face when she had said that Bryson was a passionate man. Feeling no desire for self-control, she was relieved when Bryson pulled back and took a deep breath. She could almost literally feel him putting his passion in check as he pressed her face to his shoulder and held her there.

"I love you, Melissa," he said, rummaging his lips through her hair.

Melissa sighed—a long, breathy sigh, as if she'd been holding her breath for years, searching for her place in life. And now she had found it. She looked up into his face and saw nothing but raw sincerity. "I love you, too, Bryson Davis," she said, and moisture rose into her eyes. She put her face back to his shoulder, wishing she could just stand here all night. Never had she felt so secure, so unafraid.

"Bryson," she said at last, and he responded with a pleasurable noise. "Do you remember when Bishop Hodges talked to us about the children and the way they might perceive our relationship?"

Bryson drew back to look at her, concern showing in his eyes. "I remember," he said, wondering what she was getting at.

"If something has changed between us, Bryse, we must let the children know. We have to help them understand that it hasn't been this way all along—especially the younger ones."

"You're right," he said. "I'm glad you think of these things. I'm sure I would be lost without you." She smiled and pressed a hand to his face. "Tomorrow is Saturday," he said. "We'll tell them right after breakfast." Melissa nodded and Bryson kissed her again, taking care to not get carried away. They reluctantly said good night in the hall and went their separate ways. At three o'clock, Bryson was still staring, wide-eyed, at the ceiling. He felt suddenly more lonely than he had since Ilene's death. He was awed by the full reality of his feelings for Melissa, and the knowledge that she was here, living in his home, already a part of their lives. Since Melissa had come here, she had gradually taken over as the mother in the home. The little ones were already calling her that. And in nearly every respect, she was already existing as his wife. She made his bed, cleaned his house, prepared his meals, even washed and pressed his clothes. She straightened his tie if it was crooked, and mended his socks and underwear. With the declaration of their feelings, there was only one thing missing from their lives. And in that moment, Bryson felt a physical ache to just hold Melissa in his arms and let these feelings take their course. While his spirit battled silently with his mortal desires, Bryson contemplated the situation and knew there was only one possible course for their lives now; and the sooner they set their feet on that course, the better for all of them. If only Melissa would agree.

Bryson glanced at the clock, then decided to ignore it. He would never be able to sleep until he knew for sure. Hastily he pulled on his jeans and a sweatshirt. He quietly went down to Melissa's room and found the door ajar. He slipped inside and felt his way to the lamp on the bedside table. She was sleeping soundly and made no response to the light falling over her face. Bryson knelt carefully by the bed, and for several minutes he just watched her. She seemed so young—perhaps because she was. He wondered briefly if their age difference should concern him, but recalling the feelings that had sent him here in the middle of the night, Bryson knew he had no choice but to make her a part of his life—completely.

"Melissa," he said, gently nudging her shoulder. She moaned but remained asleep. "Melissa," he said louder, nudging her a little harder. "Wake up, sleeping beauty, I need to talk to you."

Melissa thought she was dreaming until she felt something against her lips. Her eyes flew open, and she realized Bryson was kissing her. "What are you doing?" She pulled back, startled.

Bryson chuckled. "I'm sorry. I didn't mean to scare you. I just . . ." His expression sobered. "I have to talk to you, and it can't wait."

"All right." She sat up, wearing a baggy T-shirt that showed above the covers. She yawned and tried to hold her eyes open. "So, let's talk."

Bryson took both her hands into his and looked at her intently. "Melissa, I want to marry you."

She suddenly found it easy to hold her eyes wide open.

"With the way I feel about you, there is no other option. You know that, don't you?"

"Yes," she admitted, "I suppose I do."

"Does that mean you'll marry me?" he asked so intently she wanted to cry.

"Only if you ask me. I've waited a long time for the right proposal. I expect it to be a good one."

Bryson chuckled, and couldn't resist giving her a quick kiss. "I'm already on my knees," he said. "Will you marry me, Melissa?"

Melissa swallowed hard and tried not to cry. "Yes," she barely whispered, "of course I'll marry you."

Bryson sighed audibly and pressed both her hands to his lips. "We mustn't wait," he insisted. "With you living here like this . . . we've got to be so careful. I fear if we wait too long, I'll . . ." Melissa actually saw him blush. He glanced down briefly, then looked up with fortitude. "What I'm trying to say is that I'm going to take you to the temple, Melissa, and I don't want anything to happen that will keep either of us from getting there. We're going to do this right. Do you understand what I'm saying?"

Melissa couldn't hold the tears back any longer. "I'd say you're learning to speak your feelings rather well, Mr. Davis."

He laughed and hugged her. "We have to hurry and get everything arranged. We'll tell the children in the morning. I want you to have a nice wedding, Lissa, with lots of flowers, and—"

Melissa drew back to look at him. "That's not necessary, Bryson. As long as we're married, the rest doesn't matter. I don't care if—"

"It *does* matter," he insisted. "This is the only wedding you'll ever have, and it's going to be memorable. We can afford it. We'll just have to work fast. I was thinking that maybe if we got the children involved with our plans, they might feel better about the whole thing."

Melissa tried to catch her breath as she absorbed what he was saying. It was all so fast that she could hardly believe it. But she couldn't deny the warmth she felt in knowing beyond any doubt that this was right.

"I . . . I don't know what to say," she finally responded in a breathy voice. "It's all so . . . incredible . . . so wonderful."

"Yes, I know." He smiled and his eyes sparkled. Melissa looked into those eyes and tried to comprehend the man who had picked her up at the airport less than a year ago. If she had known then, what might she have thought?

"I should let you get some sleep," he said, thinking more that he'd do well to separate himself from her before he followed his urge to kiss her good and hard.

"You wake me up in the middle of the night, propose marriage on your knees, and expect me to go back to sleep?"

He chuckled. "I doubt either of us will be able to sleep. But whatever we do, we'd best do it in separate bedrooms."

Melissa smiled timidly and he kissed her brow. "Good night, my love," he whispered and reluctantly came to his feet. "I'll see you at breakfast."

"Good night," she replied and watched him back out of the door. He waved comically and disappeared. Melissa fell back onto her pillow with a sigh, overwhelmed and overjoyed. She didn't know how long it took for her to finally drift back to sleep, but she was awakened by a knock at her open door. She squinted at the sunlight streaming across her bed, then focused her eyes on Jessica and Brandon, who were standing in the doorway with a breakfast tray and a cup of hot chocolate.

"Good morning," Jessica said. "Dad told us to bring you this."

"He did?" she asked through a yawn as she leaned against the headboard and Jessica set the tray over her lap.

"Yeah," Brandon grinned, "he said you work too hard and we should all treat you better."

Melissa chuckled. "I can assure you I get treated just fine. But I won't complain. Oooh, it smells good. Did your dad cook it?"

"He did most of it," Jessica said. "He was up real early."

Melissa smiled as she took a careful sip of her hot chocolate. She wondered if he had gotten any sleep at all, and felt a rush of butterflies to recall him proposing to her last night. It was too incredible to believe.

Jessica and Brandon slipped away, and Melissa enjoyed her breakfast almost as much as she enjoyed thinking about what the next few weeks would bring. She was almost finished when Bryson appeared in the door. He leaned his shoulder against the frame and folded his arms, smiling complacently.

"Good morning," she said.

"Good morning."

"You're really not a bad cook, Bryse. But it's kind of lonely eating here all by myself."

"You'd better enjoy it. With five kids, you'll find little time to be lonely."

"I've spent too many years being lonely to ever want it any other way."

Bryson smiled, then his expression sobered. Their eyes met in one of those time-stopping moments. "I love you," he said, his voice husky.

"I love you, too," she replied, then she cleared her throat and tried to calm the pace of her heart. "How did you sleep?"

"Not at all, actually," he said. "But I've lost sleep for lesser things."

"Good point," she smiled.

"If you're finished, I'll take that upstairs and you can get dressed."

"Okay," she said. "Time for the big family meeting, eh?"

Bryson took hold of the tray and leaned over to give her a quick kiss. "We'd better make it public before we get caught at mischief and get into trouble."

"I'll be there in five minutes."

But after Bryson left, it took Melissa almost that long just to stop daydreaming and get out of bed. She dressed quickly, brushed her teeth and hair, and went upstairs to find all of the children sitting in the front room, looking impatient.

"Dad! She's here!" Greg hollered toward the kitchen. "Can we have the meeting now?"

Bryson came from the kitchen to find Melissa sitting on the floor, leaning back against the couch. Jamie quite naturally moved to sit on her lap, and Amber sat right beside her. She smiled at him as he sat on the edge of the big chair where he could see the whole family.

"You know, of course," he began, "that Melissa has been with us for a long time, and she's done a lot to help us get through these past several months. I think we've all gotten comfortable with having her here, and she takes good care of us. But I want all of you to know that time often changes circumstances. Melissa and I have talked about it, and we both feel that it's time to make some changes. I feel that—"

"You're going to leave, aren't you?" Jessica blurted out with so much distress in her voice that Bryson was startled. He saw the concern rise into Melissa's eyes as Jessica stared at her defiantly. Before Melissa had a chance to respond, Jessica came to her feet. "I knew you would leave. I knew it was—"

"Jessica," Bryson said, putting a gentle hand on her arm and urging her back to her seat, "there is no need to be upset. If you'll let me finish, we can all have a chance to express our feelings. All right?"

Jessica nodded firmly, but he saw her chin quiver as she sat down carefully. This was suddenly difficult, and he wasn't sure why. Bryson met Melissa's eyes, silently pleading for support, and not surprised to find it. He took a deep breath and continued. "I'm sure you were all aware that when Melissa first came, she and I had many differences. But she has taught me a great deal, and she has been a great blessing to our family. I know it's been hard for all of us to learn to live without your mother, and we all miss her. But we know that she is happy, and we know we'll all be with her again someday."

Bryson drew a deep breath and looked again at Melissa. She was almost smirking, and he could imagine her wanting to say, *"Get on with it, Bryse."* He cleared his throat and said, "In the past few weeks, I have grown to care for Melissa very much, and . . . well, she's almost become like a sister to me, just as she was to your mother. But, well . . . feelings can change, and . . ."

Bryson felt the older children become more focused on him, as if they sensed this was not what they'd expected.

"What I'm trying to say is . . . well, Melissa is not leaving—not ever. I've asked her to stay with us always." By the reactions on the children's faces, only Jessica seemed to realize that this could not be accomplished without some changes. He met Melissa's eyes and it was easy to say, "Melissa and I are going to be married."

"Awesome!" Brandon said with a grin.

Jessica's eyes shot to Melissa, then back to Bryson. It was difficult to tell what she was thinking.

"That's real awesome," Greg added.

Amber looked up at Melissa and asked, "Are you going to get married to my dad like Ariel married Prince Eric in *The Little Mermaid?*"

Melissa chuckled. "Something like that."

Bryson quickly surmised that all of the children were okay with this except Jessica, and he didn't have a clue whether she was pleased or not. When he apparently wasn't going to get any reaction out of her, he cleared his throat again and went on. "So, we're going to be busy the next couple of weeks, preparing for a wedding. We want all of you to help us plan it, and—"

"Are you getting married in the temple?" Greg asked.

"Yes, of course," Bryson said. "But we want to have an open house or something, and—"

"Will it be the Salt Lake Temple?" Brandon asked.

"Well, I . . ." Bryson met Melissa's eyes and she nodded subtly. "I guess it will. It *is* the closest and—"

"The most beautiful," Melissa said. "Forty years of pioneer handiwork make it a nice place to get married."

Bryson smiled. Then his eyes shifted to Jessica. "You haven't said anything, angel. What do you think of all this?"

"I'm glad she's staying," Jessica said tonelessly. Then after a long pause she added, "If you get married in the temple, won't you be sealed for eternity?"

"That's right," Bryson said, already suspecting what was coming.

"But aren't you already sealed to Mom for eternity?"

Bryson sighed and studied his hands as he pressed them together carefully. Then he looked back at Jessica. "I believe there are a lot of things about eternity that we could never comprehend from our point of view here on earth. But I know that our Heavenly Father loves us, and he will make it possible for us to be happy through eternity, if we live for that blessing. Since the veil has been drawn, and we can't remember anything from our former life, God has given us instructions through the scriptures and prophets, so that we can do things the way they should be done. And even though some of those things might not make sense to us, we have to believe that God knows what he is doing."

Jessica seemed to contemplate this while Bryson checked Melissa's expression and felt some relief to see approval in her eyes.

"So you're saying it's all right to have more than one wife in eternity, even though it's not all right now?" Jessica asked.

"It would seem to be that way," Bryson replied.

Jessica nodded as if she accepted his explanation, but Bryson still felt uneasy. He knew something was bothering her, and he'd give a lot to know what. But he reminded himself that she was at an impressionable age, and she'd been very close to the pain and suffering of her mother's death. He shouldn't expect this to be easy for her.

"Will we have cake at the wedding, Dad?" Amber asked. "You know, one of those big cakes with all the pretty flowers and stuff on? Will it be chocolate, Dad?"

Bryson chuckled, and Melissa reached around Amber with a big hug. "Yes, yes, and I certainly hope so," he answered.

Amber screwed up her nose in question.

"Yes, there will be cake. Yes, it will be big with lots of pretty flowers, if that's what Melissa wants. And I certainly hope it will be chocolate."

"Can you imagine me having any other flavor?" Melissa asked.

The conversation lightened as plans were discussed. Melissa asked Jessica to get a notebook and write some things down. She complied easily, but it was still difficult to know what she thought of all this.

Bryson suggested they have an open house in the backyard, since all of the flowers were in bloom. Since the Hansen family in the ward ran a catering business, he said they would talk to them about doing refreshments and providing tables, chairs, and simple decorations. They decided to talk to the bishop tomorrow at church, and then call about a marriage license on Monday before setting a date. But they tentatively set it for two weeks.

"How come so soon?" Jessica asked.

"Under the circumstances," Bryson said, "we both feel it would be better to not wait. Since Melissa is already living here, we need to get married right away."

Jessica nodded, and Bryson felt sure that with her knowledge of the facts of life, she was well aware of what he meant. The discussion went on, but he noticed the way Jessica glanced back and forth between himself and Melissa, as if she were trying to comprehend them having the intimate relationship that she had known he shared with her mother. Bryson watched Melissa and found himself contemplating the same thing. A quivering in his stomach caught him off guard, and it took him several moments to recall what they'd been talking about.

Melissa insisted that renting a tuxedo would be a waste of money when Bryson looked so handsome in his suit. It seemed ironic, but somehow fitting, that the children would wear the suits and nice dresses that had been new for the funeral. Melissa would see about getting some simple announcements printed in a hurry, once they decided on a date. Then she asked Jessica if she would be willing to go with her to pick out a wedding dress. Jessica looked up from her notebook in surprise.

"I need a mature, feminine opinion," Melissa said. "I always assumed that when I got married, my sister would be there to help me with such things, but . . ."

Bryson saw the emotional gaze that passed between Jessica and Melissa. He almost wanted to cry from the irony, but he felt sure that if anyone could help Jessica accept this situation, Melissa could. She was too good to be true.

With the list made and a plan settled, Bryson suggested that it might be a good day to go to the zoo. The children all cheered.

The day was a success. The kids didn't seem to have a problem with Bryson holding Melissa's hand and putting his arm around her as they walked through the zoo. Even Jessica began to relax more as the day wore on, and they were all laughing and singing on the way home. Bryson reached over and took Melissa's hand and pressed it to his lips while he drove. He felt sure that life could get no better than this.

The children were exhausted and went to bed without much protest. Melissa went to the family room and put on a quiet CD so she could unwind a little before bed. Bryson found her there, feet up on the coffee table, her eyes closed. He stood and watched her until he couldn't stand not touching her any longer.

"Would you like to dance?" he asked, and her eyes came open in surprise.

"Do you *do* that?" she asked skeptically.

He chuckled. "It was something Ilene insisted upon every once in a while. After a while I learned to accept that it was a worthwhile endeavor."

Melissa came to her feet and held out her hand. "You make it sound so romantic," she said with light sarcasm.

Bryson took her hand in his and placed his other at the small of her back, leading her easily into a slow, steady rhythm. Melissa set her hand on his shoulder and looked up into his eyes, wondering how he managed to make her feel this way with just his touch.

"If I'm romantic at all, you can blame it on Ilene. She claimed that it took years to *train* me."

"Then I'm a very lucky woman," Melissa smiled, "to be getting a husband who's been well trained by someone with impeccable taste."

"I always told Ilene she had impeccable taste." He smirked. "I mean, look who she married."

Melissa chuckled softly. "Then my taste isn't so bad, either. But I don't think the James sisters could ever measure up to *your* good taste. Imagine a man with sense enough to fall in love with two such incredible women."

"I won't argue with that," he said seriously.

Bryson moved his arm a little further around her waist to draw her closer. The song ended and another began, but he kept dancing through the brief silence in between. Melissa held his eyes intently and moved her hand from his shoulder to the back of his neck, where she toyed idly with his hair.

While they danced, Melissa rested her head on his shoulder, and Bryson's mind wandered to the events of the day, ending with his concern for Jessica's questions of that morning. In a quiet voice he asked, "How do you feel about what Jessica said earlier—about the sealings?"

Melissa lifted her head to look at him. "I think you handled it well."

"Thank you, but . . . I guess what I want to know is . . . well, I know that some people have a problem with this plural marriage stuff. Ilene told me that many women she knew balked at the very idea of sharing their husbands with another woman—even in the next life."

"And you want to know how *I* feel?"

"Yes, I do."

"I think that God gave the commandment of plural marriage in the early days of the Church to show the members that it was part of the eternal plan, but also perhaps to illustrate that it takes a higher law to live it properly. He took it away because in this mortal state, it's impossible for most people to live that law without greed or jealousy. It would take a man with no pride or arrogance about having more than one wife, who was wholly committed to his patriarchal responsibilities. And it would take women who were not insecure or prone to jealousy, who could trust each other completely. On a personal level, I've never thought too much about it—until the last few weeks."

Bryson smiled and looked almost embarrassed.

"If you must know, the prospect of living through eternity with my sister, in such a complete and perfect sisterhood, brings me a great deal of peace. I'm sure that when we reach the other side, we will understand many things that are beyond our comprehension now. But I believe that the three of us were likely together long before we came to this earth, and we knew it would be this way."

Bryson kissed her hand as they continued to dance. He marveled at her strength and wisdom, but the only words he could think to say were, "You are an incredible woman."

Melissa smiled. "Do you think you're man enough to handle both of us?"

He chuckled. "Maybe I could use a little more training in the years ahead."

"I think I can handle that. You're learning how to talk a lot more than you used to."

"Maybe too much," he said.

"No," she shook her head and her eyes sparkled, "you could never talk too much. I love to listen to you talk. Especially when you tell

188 *ANITA STANSFIELD*

me how much you love me, and how you can't wait to marry me, and . . ." She lowered her voice to a whisper. "And how you're afraid to get too close to me, or you might compromise my virtue."

She giggled like a child, and Bryson couldn't help laughing. "It's true, you know," he said. "I wouldn't say it if I didn't mean it."

Melissa's tone sobered. "I know. That's why I like it."

Their eyes met and Bryson said, "We've got to stay real busy the next couple of weeks, Lissa. This isn't going to be easy for me."

"Not for me, either," she replied, and his heart skipped a beat.

He pressed his lips to her brow, as if he could have more control if he didn't look at her. "I was never very good at self-control," he said. "I had to take chaperones on nearly every date with Ilene."

"Ilene told me more than once that she was married to a passionate man." He drew back quickly to look at her, surprised that she was serious. "She used to get this little smile on her face, and her eyes would grow kind of distant, but she never said any more than that."

He put his lips again to her brow and was thoughtful for a long moment. "I never considered myself passionate. I just thought I had a problem with self-control."

"For a man with little self-control, you have a lot of wisdom."

"Maybe. Or maybe I'm just scared to death of doing something that might hurt you. I was taught very clearly in my youth that some things are simply meant to be shared in marriage, and any other way can only bring misery."

"That must have been your father."

"Of course."

Bryson drew back to look at her again, and she was amazed at how he continued to dance without breaking the rhythm. She felt his arm tighten around her, as if to prove the need for his next statement. "You must keep me in line, Melissa. After being married so many years, I know all too well how quickly it can happen when two people want it badly enough."

Melissa pressed her face to his shoulder, not wanting him to see the sudden rush of guilt that seized her. She had been praying these past couple of days to know whether or not it was necessary to share with him a segment of her past that was better forgotten. All of this had happened so quickly that she'd hardly had time to contemplate it. She recalled being told that it was not necessary to tell anyone in her future what had happened, but something inside told her that she must. For reasons she didn't understand, she could feel the Spirit prompting her to tell him. But it wasn't an easy thing to broach. Thinking of his last statement, she answered him with a quiet, "Yes, I know."

It took Bryson a minute to figure how her reply connected to what he'd said. When it sank in, he stopped dancing immediately, and the music surrounding them seemed suddenly too poignant. He lifted Melissa's chin with his finger so that he could see her eyes. "What are you saying?" he asked gently.

Melissa swallowed and gathered courage. "I'm saying that I know how quickly it can happen when two people want it badly enough."

Bryson absorbed this for a moment, then he took an abrupt step backward. He stared at her with no expression, and Melissa's heart began to pound as she wondered if this was a mistake. Bryson felt suddenly a little weak and sat carefully on the edge of the couch. He waited expectantly for her to explain. When she didn't, he said, "I'm listening."

Melissa took a deep breath and slid the rocking chair over so she could sit down and face him directly. "I don't know what to say," she admitted. Her voice trembled as she added, "What do you want to know?"

"Whatever you feel you should tell me," he said tonelessly. "I assume you wanted me to know, or you wouldn't have said anything."

Melissa looked at her hands, fidgeting tensely in her lap. "I felt I should tell you, though I'm not sure why. I suppose I didn't want you to marry me and then figure it out."

Bryson glanced away and stifled a cough. His eyes returned to hers, more intense than before, and Melissa knew she had to just tell him everything and get it over with. She prayed inwardly for help and resigned herself to it.

"It's difficult to admit that being raised with the gospel, and being a returned missionary, wasn't enough to keep me from getting caught up in things that I knew weren't right. I can't tell you where it started exactly; I only remember the day I came to the conclusion that living the gospel had not given me what I wanted in life. You know how much I cared for Sean, and it seemed that when things didn't work out with him, my life just went downhill. I was nearly a quarter of a century old, and felt sure I was the only virgin woman in the state of California. The people I enjoyed being with were not LDS. I had two good friends who had live-in boyfriends, and another who was married. The only single LDS people I had any contact with were . . . well, to put it mildly, they were losers. I had plenty of marriage proposals to choose from. Oh, there was the man who swore to me that he had been shown in a dream that he and I were meant to be together, and I should trust him, as a priesthood holder, to know that this was best for me. When I told him I didn't get the same answer, he insisted that women were not created for such privileges. And then there was the one who had a two-year supply of food and fuel, drove a car that barely managed to function, and dressed in clothes his brother had handed down to him in high school. He talked about nothing but the end of the world, and how blessed I should feel to be taken care of by a man who was well prepared for it. And then there was the man who almost had me convinced he was a decent human being, but when he dropped our plans—three times—because his mother needed him, I knew this was not a good sign. There were a few others with equally interesting theories on life.

"So," Melissa sighed deeply, "I woke up one day and decided there wasn't a Mormon man worth having, and if living righteously had left me with such options, then I'd had enough of it. I started spending more time with my *other* friends, many of whom I worked with. I met a man who was dignified, successful, and who respected me. He was younger than I was, but he, too, had never been involved. Looking back, I know I cared for him, but I can't say that I loved him. I let nature take its course, and I almost convinced myself that it was enough to make me happy. But I realized all too quickly that I wasn't really happy at all. I left him. I know I hurt him. I went back to church and straight to the bishop's office."

Melissa wasn't surprised at her emotion, but she wasn't sure if her tears were from regret, or the reminder of what she'd gone through to find her way back. Or, most likely, the fear she was feeling that this would somehow come between her and Bryson. She looked down as the tears spilled, then she wiped her face and continued.

"I was excommunicated." She met Bryson's eyes and said with conviction, "I've never lived through anything so difficult in my life. I have never felt so alone. I told Ilene, and she was very supportive—as much as she could be with the miles between us. I never would have made it through without her. But I wouldn't trade what I learned during that time for anything that might have kept me from going through it."

Melissa felt more peace as she progressed to the bright side of the story. "I always believed the Church was true, Bryson. I never had trouble with it. But it wasn't until then that I was truly converted. I had to come to terms with it; I had to *know* for myself. Otherwise, I never could have made it through. I felt the Spirit closer to me, as I emerged from all of that, than I ever had in my life."

Melissa wiped away the continuing tears and said more quietly, "I was rebaptized the same month Ilene had her mastectomy. I had wanted her to be with me, but I think we were together in spirit, somehow. I had all of my temple blessings restored before I came here last year, and I have been told that it's truly as if it never happened. I believe that's true in the sense of my standing with God. But I am a product of my own experiences, and it was a significant part of my life and the things that have shaped who and what I am now. I can't spend the rest of my life with you and try to pretend that it didn't happen. I hope you can understand that, Bryson."

The ensuing silence became unbearable to Melissa as she felt her life somehow hanging in the balance. His reaction could have so much bearing on the future they would share. She couldn't imagine his being the kind of man to hold something like that against her, not when she'd worked so hard to make restitution. But she still had much to discover about him, and she couldn't help being afraid.

When it went a moment too long, Melissa came abruptly to her feet and hurried toward the stairs. If he wasn't going to talk, she would rather be alone. She made it up three steps before he grabbed her around the waist to stop her. The fear caught in her throat, and she tried to choke back a sob as he forced her to face him. She ended up sitting on the middle stair, her wrists in his hands as he knelt on the step below her.

"Don't walk out on me," he said with quiet vehemence. "You and I have carried each other through too much to turn back now."

"Then *say* something to me," she cried. "Don't sit there while I turn my heart inside out at your feet, and leave me wondering if I should have said anything at all."

"I'm glad you told me," he insisted. "You're right. You shouldn't have to spend the rest of your life pretending it didn't happen. I don't want either of us to ever have to keep anything from each other. I always envied the way you and Ilene could sit together and talk and giggle like a couple of kids. I asked her once why she couldn't be that way with me. She told me she found it difficult to be silly with me. I don't know what I did to make her feel that way, but I love the way you're not afraid to be just plain ridiculous with me. We can laugh together. We can talk. Maybe it's because we became brother and sister before we fell in love. I don't know. But I know I don't ever want that to change. So don't walk away from me now when there is so much I want to say, but being the bumbling idiot that I am, it takes me a while to put the right words together."

Melissa felt so much relief that she nearly collapsed against him. As she pressed her face to his shoulder and felt his arms come around her, she thought she might melt from the joy of his acceptance. Bryson shifted to sit on the stair beside her with his arm around her shoulders. He lifted her face to his view and wiped at her tears.

"First of all, let me say that when I married Ilene, she and I started on equal ground. And I was glad, because with all my lack of self-control, or passion, or whatever it was, I was truly awkward. But a part of me was a little frightened at the thought of marrying someone now who had no idea of what to expect. Maybe this puts us a little more on equal ground. And secondly, I have to say that I was praying you would tell me, because I didn't know how to tell you that I already knew."

Melissa's eyes widened and her breathing became sharp. Before she could think of a response, he said, "I hope you won't feel that Ilene betrayed your confidence. I know you asked her not to tell anyone, and it never went past the two of us. But I could see that something was troubling her deeply. She told me I just needed to trust her and let it rest. I knew it had something to do with you, and I was concerned. Finally one day she just let it out. She said if she didn't tell somebody, she thought she would die inside."

Bryson felt Melissa's emotion gaining momentum, and it was difficult for him to finish without sharing it. "There were many times, Melissa, when I watched you crying for Ilene's pain, and I thought of the way she had cried when she knew you were hurting. I believe the two of you share a bond that many people could never comprehend. And while I think a part of me envied it, I couldn't help but admire it."

Melissa pressed her face to his shoulder and cried. She understood now what had prompted her to tell him, and she felt incredibly relieved to have it all out, to know that it was all right. Her heart was so full that it almost seemed trite to simply say, "I love you, Bryson."

"I love you, too," he whispered, then he just held her until she cried herself into exhaustion. She was barely this side of sleep when he lifted her into his arms and carried her to her bed. Like Ilene, she was light and delicate. He kissed her briefly as her head met the pillow, but with a hint of all he felt for her. He hoped she understood just how wonderful their life together would be.

CHAPTER TWELVE

Melissa couldn't resist the urge to call Sean. She phoned his office and expected to get the machine, but he answered himself.

"Guess what?" she said after the usual greetings and inquiries about the children.

"What?" he repeated histrionically, and she giggled.

"I'm getting married."

Sean laughed. "I knew there was some lucky man out there, just waiting for the right time to come along."

"I guess you could say that."

"Well, do we get to meet him?"

"Actually, I was hoping we could all go out to dinner or something. Are you and Tara busy Friday? It'll be our treat."

"I think we're open. I won't turn down an offer like that."

"Good, why don't we meet at our house about seven. Bring the baby. Jessica loves babies. She can watch her, if that's all right with Tara."

"If there's a problem, I'll let you know."

"We'll be looking forward to it." She almost laughed, wondering how he would react when he realized who she was marrying.

"Hey, Lissa," he said before she hung up, "I can't tell you how happy I am for you. I knew it would happen."

"Thank you, Sean. And I want you to know how grateful I am that it worked out this way. I never dreamed I could be so happy. I hope you understand when I say that it kind of makes what you and I had seem . . . well, perhaps trite."

Sean laughed softly. "I know *exactly* how you feel."

"I suspected you did. Oh, by the way, I'd like you to come to the wedding. It'll be in the Salt Lake Temple. I'll give you an announcement when I see you."

"That sounds great. We'll see you Friday."

Sean and Tara arrived Friday evening a few minutes after seven. Brandon answered the door and hollered, "Aunt Melissa! Your friends are here!"

Melissa hurried to the front room and greeted Sean with a quick embrace.

"You remember Tara," he said.

"Of course," Melissa warmly took her hand, "it's so good to see you again. It's been a long time."

"I was sorry to hear about your sister," Tara said. "She was very sweet."

"Yes, she was," Melissa agreed, then her attention turned to the baby. "Oh, she's adorable. May I hold her?"

Tara turned the baby over to Melissa. "She looks like you, Sean," Melissa declared, laughing at the baby's silly grin.

"Yeah," he replied sheepishly. "With any luck, she'll grow out of it."

"What's her name, again?"

"Melanie," he reported proudly.

Melissa finally relinquished the baby and left Jessica to receive instructions from Tara while she finished getting ready. Bryson and Melissa returned to the front room together a few minutes later.

"Hello, Bryse." Sean came to his feet and extended a hand.

"Good to see you, Sean," he replied.

"You remember my wife, Tara."

"Hello, Tara," Bryson smiled. "It's good to see you again."

A brief silence ensued, and Melissa had to fight to keep from laughing. It was apparent that Sean was waiting for some kind of explanation concerning her fiancé. She was looking for the right words to say it when Bryson put his arm around her and said, "Are you ready to go, love?"

She nodded, more preoccupied with Sean's widening eyes. "But first I'd better introduce my fiancé, don't you think?"

"Good idea," Bryson said with a smirk.

"Sean, Tara, I'd like you to meet the man I'm going to marry." She put her arm around Bryson and he grinned like a child.

"I can't believe it," Sean laughed. "I mean . . . it's wonderful. It's just that . . ." He laughed again, and they all joined him.

"Funny how things work out, isn't it?" Bryson said, momentarily lost in Melissa's eyes.

"Well, congratulations," Tara said. "This is great."

"When's the big day?" Scan asked.

"A week from tomorrow," Melissa reported.

"Well," Bryson chuckled, responding to their astonishment, "since she's already living here, we thought we'd better hurry."

"Very wise," Sean said with a chuckle, but Melissa caught a brief glance from him that told her more than words could. They had once been very close, and she knew now that he understood the significance of how things had come together—for both of them.

The evening was so enjoyable that Melissa hoped they could all be good friends through the years to come. She could easily see why Sean loved Tara so much. And while she observed their obvious affection for each other, she felt no envy or sadness—only complete peace as she turned to Bryson and drew the same affection from his eyes.

* * * * *

The wedding plans fell together so easily that Melissa hardly had a moment to worry about being alone with Bryson. The time they had when the children were asleep was spent addressing announcements and working on a thorough cleaning project in preparation for the wedding. Occasionally they would stop what they were doing and just hold hands and talk, speculating on the future, sharing their views and opinions, their hopes and dreams, for this world and beyond. The chaste kiss they exchanged several times a day was the closest Bryson would bring himself to his carefully-guarded passion. But Melissa remembered well the way he'd held her on the back porch the evening he had first confessed his feelings for her. And she felt a keen anticipation as the time seemed to fly.

As the day drew closer, Bryson and Melissa progressively slept less, and their late evenings became more prone to laughter. The more Melissa made him laugh, the closer Bryson came to being free of those twinges of pain and emptiness he felt at Ilene's absence. The peace of having Melissa a part of his life made the reality of losing Ilene fit comfortably into the puzzle of their lives with the knowledge that God's hand was in all of this. And that could only bring more peace.

The children seemed eager for the wedding, and chattered much of the time about the planned events. While Jessica became caught up in the excitement, it was still difficult to know where she stood. Two days prior to the wedding, Bryson reluctantly kissed Melissa good night on the stairs and went to his room, silently figuring how many hours he had left to be alone. He turned on the light in his bedroom and found Jessica asleep on his bed. He was about to just leave her and go to her bed to sleep, but it occurred to him that she wouldn't have been there if she hadn't wanted to talk to him.

Carefully he nudged her. "Hey, angel," he said, "I think you're in the wrong room. Come on," he lifted her into his arms, "I'll take you to bed." He was hoping she'd be awake enough to remember what she might have wanted to say before he got to her room.

"Dad," she said as he was about to lay her down. Instead, he sat on the bed and left her on his lap. He looked at her sweet face in the lamplight and thought how strongly she resembled Ilene.

"What is it, angel?"

"Why are you going to marry Melissa?"

"Why?" He chuckled uncomfortably, wondering how to answer such a question. "There are a lot of reasons."

"I mean," her voice became serious, "is it because you just miss Mom and you don't want Melissa to leave, or—"

"Listen, Jess. I *do* miss Mom. I love your mother more than words could ever explain. And I *don't* want Melissa to leave. I think we would all be lost without her. But before I ever asked her to marry me, I thought it through very carefully, and I asked Heavenly Father to help me understand. In spite of everything, there is only one reason I'm marrying her. It's because I love her."

"As much as Mom?" she asked in a childlike way that he hadn't seen in her for many years.

Bryson sighed and searched for the most honest words to answer her. "Your mother and Melissa are two very different women in many ways. In some ways they're alike. I told Melissa that trying to compare them would be like comparing a lily to a rose. They're both flowers. They're both beautiful. But one is not better than the other. And it's only a matter of opinion, or maybe timing, that might make someone prefer the beauty or the aroma of one over the other. In a way, I think I love your mother more because I spent so many years with her, and love grows with time. But I have feelings for Melissa that are very much like what I felt for your mother. I believe that with time, I will love Melissa every bit as much. I don't believe I have to divide my love. In these circumstances, my love only grows. I didn't have to love you less when your brothers and sisters were born; I only came to love them as much as I loved you. Am I making any sense?"

"I think so," she said quietly.

"Did I tell you what you wanted to know?"

"Yeah," she said through a yawn.

"Now, why don't you tell me something, Jessica. Is there a reason you think I shouldn't marry Melissa?"

Jessica looked surprised. "No. I'm glad you're going to marry her. I was afraid she was going to leave and you were going to start going on dates with women we'd never even seen before. I just didn't want you to marry her because you thought us kids needed her. I wanted you to really love her and be happy, the way you were with Mom."

Bryson was so touched that his voice broke as he touched her face and said, "You're so much like your mother. It only makes me love you all the more."

"I love you, too, Dad," she said.

He tucked her into bed and kissed her, thinking how it seemed she had been Amber's size not so long ago. In his mind he could clearly see the day they'd brought her home from the hospital, as if it had only been last year.

As Bryson returned to his bedroom and attempted to sleep, the memories continued to roll through his head. He tried to distract himself with the reality that he was getting married the day after tomorrow. But thoughts of Ilene kept creeping in, bringing with them the poignancy of her death, and the irony of his second marriage. In his heart, he knew he was doing the right thing. He felt peace over Ilene's death, and he believed that time would heal the wounds even further. But in the dark, still vacuum of the night, he couldn't keep his mind from drifting onto paths that provoked pain. How could he prepare for this wedding without recalling his marriage to Ilene? He thought of their happiness, and his belief that they would grow old together. Then he wondered if he could bear it if something happened to Melissa.

Feeling as if the darkness would swallow him up, Bryson pulled on a pair of jeans and abandoned the eerie stillness of his bedroom. Wandering the house, he hoped to get tired by walking the floor, but he only ended up on the family room couch, staring at the wall, contemplating the final weeks of Ilene's life that she'd spent here. He managed to hold the emotion back until he allowed his thoughts to dwell a moment too long on the morning she'd died. The tears came slowly at first, then he was grateful to be alone as he sobbed into his hands. He wondered if he had truly been dealing with her death as he should have, or if he'd just buried it all inside. Whatever the reason, he only hoped he could get control of himself before morning came and he had to face Melissa.

* * * * *

Melissa found it difficult to sleep as anticipation of her wedding day mingled with the ironies of the situation. But she hadn't expected to hear footsteps moving around upstairs—undoubtedly Bryson's. She wondered if something was wrong with one of the children, but she heard no activity near their rooms. She wondered if he was restless, too, but the sounds stopped and she assumed he'd gone back to bed.

A long while later, she was still wide awake and went quietly upstairs for a drink of water and some Tylenol. Just before she turned on the light, she heard a muffled cry and hesitated. It took only a moment to realize that Bryson was in the family room, crying alone in the dark. Filled with compassion, she felt her way down the stairs, barely able to see his shadow, sitting on the floor, leaning against the couch.

"Bryson," she said gently and his head shot up, startled. "What's wrong?" she asked when he said nothing.

Bryson felt embarrassed and uncertain, as if he'd been caught at mischief. He wiped his tears and swallowed hard as Melissa moved toward him.

"Bryson? Are you all right?"

He nearly told her he was, but he couldn't bring himself to lie. "Not really," he admitted.

Melissa sat on the floor beside him, expecting him to explain, but he said nothing more.

"You're not talking much, Bryse."

"I don't know what to say."

"You can either say what you're feeling, or you can tell me to go away and leave you alone."

Despite his embarrassment, one thing was clear. Now that she was here, he didn't want to be alone. He put his arm around her and drew her closer, somehow feeling better already. "What are you doing up, anyway?" he asked.

"I couldn't sleep." She paused then added, "Maybe I knew you needed me."

"Maybe."

"You do need me, don't you, Bryse?"

"Yes," he admitted humbly and pressed his lips into her hair. "I do."

"Then maybe you need to tell me what's wrong." Bryson hesitated and she nudged him in the ribs with her elbow. "Talk to me, Bryse. I refuse to marry a man who won't talk to me."

"Maybe it's not something you want to hear."

"Try me."

Bryson took a deep breath and reminded himself this woman was going to be his wife, and they'd been through too much together for him to believe he couldn't say this. "Isn't it somehow wrong for me to admit that we're getting married soon, and I'm sitting here crying over Ilene? Shouldn't I feel guilty or something to . . ."

His voice broke with emotion and Melissa touched a hand to his face. "Bryson," she whispered with empathy, "I don't expect you to stop feeling anything for her just because we're getting married. I love her and miss her. And I know you do, too."

"Yes, but . . . it's all so . . . tragic. And yet, if it hadn't been, you and I wouldn't be where we are now, and . . ."

"I can see why that could be confusing at times. But we know this is right, Bryson, and—"

"I know that, Lissa. I do. I'm not having doubts or anything. I guess things just get blown out of proportion in the middle of the night, and I just . . ."

"Do you think we're moving too fast?" she asked, even though she didn't want to.

Bryson looked into her face, wishing he could see more than shadows in the darkness. "No," he said firmly. "As long as I can be honest with you about my feelings, then we can put it behind us together. I need you, Melissa. It's this incessant loneliness that gets to me." He pressed a kiss to her brow. "I don't know what I would do without you." She sighed and nuzzled closer. He lifted her chin with his finger and pressed his mouth over hers. In an instant, Bryson felt all of his loneliness and grief rush into her and back again. He could almost literally feel the way she buffered the pain in his life, making it bearable, giving him hope for a bright future—a future that he had believed would be bleak since the day he realized Ilene was going to leave him.

"I love you, Melissa," he murmured against her face, then he kissed her again. She clutched his shoulders, and a whimper of longing escaped her. She pressed a hand into his hair and another to the back of his neck. Bryson eased her closer and kissed her harder, wishing away the hours until they were married. A momentary vision popped into his head of kneeling at a temple altar with her, and it was easy to draw back and take a deep breath.

"I shouldn't kiss you like that," he whispered close to her ear.

"On the contrary," Melissa replied softly, toying idly with his hair, "after tomorrow, you should kiss me like that *frequently*."

"I don't think that will be a problem," he chuckled and kissed her once more, briefly. She settled her head onto his shoulder and he felt compelled to say, "Did I ever tell you that Ilene came to me once . . . after she died?"

Melissa looked up abruptly, wishing she could see his eyes. "No, you didn't."

"It was one of those moments when I just hit rock bottom. I was worried about the kids, and I felt so alone. I was sitting here in this room, and I felt her there. It was just like the times she used to sneak up on me. And then I felt her arms around me, and I knew everything would be all right."

Bryson knew Melissa was crying before he touched the tears on her face. But he knew they were tears of peace. And he couldn't deny the tranquility he felt within himself, a sharp contrast to the anguish he'd felt just a while ago. He knew now, just as he'd known then, that everything would be all right.

Bryson went reluctantly back to bed. He fell asleep quickly and was glad he'd taken the next day off to get ready for the wedding. He woke up late morning, immediately feeling a sense of peace and anticipation that made his emotions the night before seem like a dream. Even so, he didn't doubt it had likely been good for him to cry it all out and come a little closer to putting it all behind him.

Robert and Lindy arrived late afternoon, and the reality began to settle in. Everyone was too busy to talk much, but the excitement was evident. Occasionally Bryson would catch Melissa's eye, and he'd recall how it had felt to kiss her last night in the darkness. He felt almost like a kid again as butterflies rushed through him, making him wonder how he had ever lived without her.

* * * * *

Melissa reached over and smacked her alarm clock, feeling as if she'd only been asleep a few minutes. Then she realized it was her wedding day and bolted upright in the dark. She was barely out of bed when she heard footsteps upstairs and knew Bryson was up. A familiar quiver erupted inside her, and she hurried to make her bed and get dressed. She sneaked into the kitchen when she knew he was in the bathroom, and grabbed a piece of toast and some juice to take back to her room. She kept glancing at the clock while she did her hair and makeup. Three minutes before they were supposed to leave, she turned off her light and headed up the stairs, her temple suitcase in one hand and a dress bag draped over her other arm. She came into the front room to find Bryson waiting with the keys in his hand. For a long moment they just stared at each other, then they smiled in unison.

"Good morning, Miss James. That is the last time anyone is ever going to call you that."

"Good morning. Do you have the license?"

"I have the license."

"Your temple recommend?"

"Yes, dear."

"The ring?"

He grinned. "I have the ring. Do you have *yours?*" he asked.

"I have everything. I promise."

"Then let's go. I already told Jess we were leaving. She knows what to do. I called Dad at the motel. They'll meet us there. I called Wendy, and she'll be over to help the kids in a while."

Melissa took a deep breath and led the way out the door. In the car, Bryson said, "You know, Melissa, I was thinking, if you don't have anything special in mind for the rest of your life, maybe we could get married. I mean, I know it's probably a shock to your system, the idea of actually *living* with me and *getting along* with me. But maybe we could make it work. What do you think?"

"It sounds like a good idea to me," she answered in the same serious tone.

"How about today? Are you busy? Do you think you could fit it in to your schedule?"

Melissa chuckled and squeezed his hand. "I think I could manage, but I'd better check my planner."

Together they laughed, and Melissa was surprised that they had arrived at Temple Square already. Bryson parked the car and helped her out, then they walked hand in hand across the street in silence. The reality settled in through a flurry of emotions, as everything in the temple took on a whole new meaning at the prospect of being married. She had never been so grateful to be alive as Bryson held her hand in the celestial room, and escorted her across the hall to one of the many sealing rooms.

Bryson's brothers and their wives had come from out of state.

Lynette and Keith were there, and of course, Bob and Lindy. Sean and Tara also came, as well as a few close ward members. The sealing room was full, and Melissa felt warmed by the love and support of those around them. As she and Bryson knelt across the altar, Melissa had a brief sensation that made her wonder if Ilene was there in spirit. At the same moment, she saw Bryson's focus shift slightly, as if he were momentarily looking for something he couldn't see. The sensation passed and his eyes returned to hers, sparkling as a serene smile touched his lips. Vows were exchanged, then rings, and then Bryson kissed her and she realized she was his wife—forever.

A short while later, they stepped outside together to take pictures. The children were all waiting with Wendy, and Bryson laughed when he saw them. "Look at that," he said, "their faces are all clean at the same time."

"Just don't expect it to last," Melissa said.

He laughed again and kissed her. In between pictures, he pulled her close and pressed his lips in front of her ear, whispering in a warm voice, "I'll meet you in my bedroom after lunch. No one will ever miss us. And if they do, they'll get over it."

Melissa giggled like a schoolgirl being asked to her first dance. Then she met his eyes and realized he was serious. Her pulse raced, and she heard a clear memory of Ilene telling her that Bryson was a passionate man.

When they returned to the house, Bryson insisted on carrying her over the threshold. She was seized with a flutter of anticipation, but it was soon lost in the flurry of the buffet lunch that was set out in the yard for all those who had attended the ceremony. When their guests finally departed for the afternoon, Melissa got the kids out of their dress clothes and sponged out a few spots so they would be ready for the open house. Bryson helped the Hansens load some things in their van, and they promised to be back at five to set up before the photographer came.

Bryson went inside and found all five kids playing Legos on the family room floor. There were thousands of the little things spread over a sheet on the carpet, but they were all being quiet and coopera-tive. He was amazed.

"Where's Melissa?" he asked Jessica.

"She said she was going to take a nap and asked me to watch the kids." She smiled up at him and added, "Maybe you ought to take a nap, too, Dad. I bet you didn't sleep very good last night."

By the way she almost snickered, Bryson was about to tell her that teenagers these days knew too much for their own good. But he only smiled at her and feigned an exaggerated yawn.

Bryson wondered if Melissa would have actually gone to her room and gone to sleep. But he felt a giddy rush when he pushed open his bedroom door to find her standing at the window, looking at the closed curtains as if she could see something beyond. He closed the door and locked it for the first time in months. At the sound of the latch, she turned to look at him. In the same moment they both started across the room, and stopped when they were face to face.

"Do you see this, Bryson?" she asked, holding up her hand to indicate the wedding band she now wore. He nodded. "Do you know what it means?" she asked. He nodded again, and she moved a step closer.

In one agile movement, Bryson pushed an arm around her waist, pulling her against him. And he pressed his mouth over hers with a kiss that said more than words ever could. They were married now. She was his. He was hers. The waiting was over. Melissa could almost feel him aching to become a part of her. She urged him on, oblivious to anything but these feelings he roused in her. She had never imagined that anything in this worldly sphere could be so incredible. While she felt herself reaching for something akin to heaven, she believed she had lived her entire life for this moment.

They held each other in silence long afterward, surrounded by a formless magical spell that words would only break. Melissa looked into Bryson's eyes and touched her lips to his. He met her gaze boldly, pressing his fingers over her face like a blind man wanting to absorb every detail of her features. Melissa kissed him again, knowing that her sister had been right. Bryson *was* a passionate man.

* * * * *

Following the open house, Bryson took Melissa to one of the nicer hotels in downtown Salt Lake City for their wedding night. He kissed her hungrily in the elevator, grateful they were alone, and carried her over the threshold of their room. The next morning they went to Park City, where they stayed three days, oblivious to anything beyond being together—except for an occasional chuckle as they wondered how Bob and Lindy were doing with the kids.

The children greeted them with laughter and excitement when they returned from their honeymoon, bringing along souvenirs for everyone.

"How did Grandma and Grandpa do?" Bryson asked as he embraced Lindy.

"We had the time of our lives," she insisted, and Bryson's father agreed.

Two days later, Bob and Lindy returned to St. George, and the next morning Bryson and Melissa loaded the kids into the van and headed for Disneyland. At moments it was difficult for Bryson to recall that he'd taken this same trip last summer with Ilene. But he found so much happiness in his relationship with Melissa that the memories were gradually enveloped by feelings of peace.

Before returning home, they took a couple of days to clean out Melissa's storage unit. She gave many of her things away to friends or charity, and they loaded the rest into a U-Haul to take home. She then finished up some business, including the final transaction on selling her BMW, which had been parked in a friend's backyard.

Somewhere in Nevada, while the children were being unusually quiet, Bryson took Melissa's hand and said softly, "Do you ever wish you could go back to your life in California?"

He was surprised at her seriousness as she said, "Not even a little. I can honestly say there is nothing I miss. When I went out there originally, I knew it was right. But that time is over. *You* are what's right for me now, Bryson Davis."

Bryson pressed her hand to his lips, keeping his eyes on the road. "You can't imagine how happy that makes me." He glanced quickly toward her and added, "Melissa Davis."

She smiled and lifted her eyebrows in a gesture of comical mischief. "How much longer till we get to a motel?"

"Tired?"

"No."

Bryson chuckled. "Well, when you take five kids on your honeymoon, you ought to be tired. And when you have to share a room with them, sleep is all you're going to get."

Melissa laughed and leaned over to kiss his cheek. Then she blew in his ear and he laughed with her. She never dreamed life could be so good.

CHAPTER THIRTEEN

Being married to Melissa changed Bryson's life very little in most respects. Their routine of working together to care for the home and children continued in much the same way. But Melissa gradually became more relaxed, as if knowing she wasn't ever leaving made her settle into her life. She became more involved with the ward and the neighborhood, and she was able to make some friends.

As Melissa settled in, the children also seemed more relaxed. They couldn't help but sense the peace and security she radiated, and soon even the older children were calling her *Mom*. Gradually the house began to take on a subtly different look as Melissa's personality influenced the arrangements and decor. But she managed to do it in a way that allowed Ilene's spirit to remain in the home, and Bryson had to admit he liked it.

As Bryson observed the changes, a deep contentment settled into him that he'd never felt before. Looking back, he realized that he had never been the man he believed in his heart he should have been. It wasn't anything big. He simply knew that he felt better inside knowing he was not subconsciously trying to prove his male supremacy with some kind of abstract arrogance. He was tempted to regret that he had not been more open and helpful with Ilene, but he knew that regret was pointless. Ilene died knowing he loved her, and she would have forgiven him long before now. Still, he found that the more he gave to his home and family—and Melissa—the more at peace he became. His job went better, his church work was easier, and he was grateful for all he had learned.

Above and beyond all of that, the biggest change in Bryson's life was the private relationship he shared with Melissa. When he thought of how indignant he'd been toward her when she'd first arrived, it was difficult to comprehend the love he felt for her now. He only had to look at her to be reminded of how blessed he was.

As the months passed and holidays came and went, there was always a twinge of sadness at Ilene's absence in recalling how it had been in years past. But they talked about it openly and became more and more at peace in knowing they could never have shared the joy they had now without first enduring the tragedy of Ilene's death. The irony at times was a struggle, but the peace of the gospel put it all into an eternal perspective.

Bryson was even amazed at how little they argued. If a disagreement came up, Melissa had a way of facing it with maturity, helping him to communicate with her, and coming to an agreeable conclusion. She even taught him that it was okay to agree that they disagreed on certain issues.

Bryson expected Christmas to be difficult, and there were moments when tears were shed. They couldn't help recalling last Christmas, when Ilene had been so close to the end of her time on earth. But on the twenty-third of December, Melissa found out she was pregnant and the family had great cause to celebrate.

In January, Bryson was called to be a counselor in the bishopric; two months later, Melissa was made the Young Women's secretary. Jessica enjoyed having Melissa involved in the program, and their relationship was good.

In September Steven was born, strong and healthy. Melissa recovered quickly, and the family drew closer together as the children all hovered around the baby. Bryson's newest pastime was to watch Melissa nurse their new little son. Together, mother and child created such a beautiful scene that he wished he could somehow capture the mood of it to save forever.

A month after Steven's second birthday, Melissa gave birth to a tiny little girl—Heather Ilene. She was born early and weighed barely five pounds, but she was healthy and grew quickly. Melissa felt sure that seven children was a good family. Bryson liked the way she treated the first five as if they were her own. They agreed to fast and pray about it, and they both knew in their hearts that it was time to stop having babies and raise the family they had.

On their fifth wedding anniversary, they left the children with Jessica for three days to enjoy a second honeymoon. They reminisced, looked at the life they shared, and admitted without reservation that they had much to be grateful for. Jessica was well on her way to becoming a legal secretary, Brandon was a junior in high school, and Greg had just been ordained a teacher. Amber was about to go into Young Women, and Jamie had recently been baptized. Steven was three and a half, and Heather was eighteen months—old enough to go in the nursery at church.

Bryson marveled at the blessings in his life as they drove home together. Melissa sat close to him, dozing with her head on his shoulder. She was so much younger than him that he found it easy to ignore his graying temples and the deepening lines around his eyes. She made him feel ten years younger. When many men his age were going through some kind of mid-life crisis, he was happier at forty-five than he had ever been.

The thought stayed with him through the next several weeks. The family went to Disneyland and the beach, and he felt sure no family on earth could be so close. Of course the children had their bad moments, but for the most part they were good kids, and he gave much of the credit to the women in his life—Ilene for teaching them right from the start and laying a firm foundation, and Melissa for building upon it and following through during the more difficult years.

He was lying in bed on a summer night with a pleasant breeze floating through the window, wondering why he should be so lucky. Melissa came in quietly from reading in the other room, and slipped beneath the sheet next to him.

"It must be a good one," he said.

"I didn't mean to wake you."

"You didn't wake me," he replied and rolled over to put his hand on her shoulder. She made a pleasurable noise as he rubbed a tight spot at the base of her neck and down the center of her back. "How was your day?" he asked, leaning up on one elbow to kiss the side of her face.

"Besides Steven trying to make his own lunch, you mean?"

He chuckled. "You did say the peanut butter added a nice touch to the centerpiece."

"What else could I say?" She laughed with him and rolled onto her side. "Oh, it wasn't such a bad day," she added, and Bryson pressed his chest to her back.

"I love you, Lissa," he whispered, relaxing his head on the pillow just behind hers.

"I love you, too," she replied, lifting a hand behind her to touch his face, then play gently in his hair. Bryson moved his hand up and down her ribs, occasionally tickling her a little, which brought out a noise somewhere between a growl and a giggle. He tickled her beneath the arm, and she lightly kicked his shin.

"You beast," she teased and tried to relax again. She was trying to decide if he was intent on continuing this tickling game, or trying to provoke some intimacy.

She decided he was too tired to make up his mind when his hand would stop for a long moment, then persist a little, then stop again. She had almost given in to sleep when he startled her with a harsh, "What on earth is that?"

"What?" she responded, barely coherent.

"This!" he snapped.

While Melissa tried to figure out what he was talking about, she felt his fingers probing in the fleshy tissue just beneath her arm. It took her another moment to consciously realize what he meant. "What are you talking about, Bryse?" she asked.

"There is a lump, right here."

"I think you're paranoid," she insisted.

"You're damn right I am," he snarled.

"Bryson!" She turned toward him and pushed his hand away. "That's no reason to swear at me. How can you possibly feel a lump through two layers of fabric?"

With a determination that put her on edge, Bryson turned on the lamp and pushed his hand beneath her nightgown and underclothing. "Lift up your arm," he said, and she did it with a patronizing sigh. "There!" he said immediately, when she'd not expected him to find anything at all. "Feel that."

Bryson guided her fingers to the spot and pressed them beneath his. "Now," he said in a husky whisper that betrayed an emotion she'd not seen in a long time, "you tell me what that is."

Melissa was not expecting to feel something so utterly impossible to ignore. She met Bryson's eyes and had to admit, "I don't know."

There was no change in his expression, but Melissa saw the fear and doubt creep into his eyes. Instinctively wanting to ease his anxiety, she said soothingly, "I'm sure it's nothing, Bryson. There could be all kinds of reasons for something to be there."

Bryson couldn't find any words to respond. The memories came back so vividly that he almost felt a tangible pain inside. In an effort to quell it, he pressed a hand to his chest and realized his heart was pounding.

"Bryson," Melissa said gently, "you can't possibly believe that this is anything like what happened to Ilene."

"It's *exactly* what happened to Ilene. It felt just like that."

"Where was it?" she asked quietly.

Bryson pressed his fingers on the opposite breast, lower down. "It was right there," he said. The spot was emblazoned in his memory.

"How did she find it?" Melissa asked, trying to be empathetic.

Bryson's gaze became distant as the memories deepened. "She didn't find it. I did."

"Bryson," she touched his face gently, "I'm sure it's nothing to worry about. I—"

"That's exactly what Ilene said."

"I'll get it checked out, Bryse. Soon."

"Not soon." His mind came abruptly back to the present. "Tomorrow, Melissa. You're going to get it checked tomorrow, and I'm going with you."

"All right," she agreed. "I'll call first thing in the morning. In the meantime, why don't we both get some sleep."

Bryson turned off the light and lay down beside her. But Melissa didn't sleep for hours, and she was well aware that Bryson didn't, either.

Melissa had to be insistent to get an appointment, but the receptionist finally agreed to fit her in when Melissa told her firmly, "Listen. My husband lost his first wife to breast cancer, and I have a significant lump in my breast. He is not going to eat or sleep until I do something about this. Now, what time can I come in?"

They sat in the waiting room for over an hour. Melissa thumbed idly through magazines but couldn't concentrate long enough to read anything. Bryson tapped his fingers and recrossed his legs every few minutes. They waited in the exam room for another fifteen minutes, then the doctor finally appeared. He listened as Melissa explained what they had discovered. The doctor probed and made contemplative noises, then he concluded firmly, "There is definitely something there. We'll see if we can get you scheduled for a mammogram next week, and—"

"No." Bryson shot to his feet so fast that Melissa was almost as startled as the doctor. "Not next week. I want it *today*. If I have to bribe some technician to miss their lunch hour or stay until midnight, we will have a mammogram today. And I want a CAT scan, and a biopsy, and whatever it takes to know *exactly* what that is."

"Bryson," Melissa said gently, "please sit down. I'm sure they will get us in as quickly as possible."

Bryson looked at Melissa and just wanted to bawl like a baby. How could he forget Ilene reminding him that it was not the doctor's fault when he told them she was going to die? He swallowed hard and sat down. The doctor did the same.

"Your first wife died of breast cancer," he said as it apparently came together in his mind.

"Yes, she did," Bryson said spitefully. "And you're the man who told me that it was too bad they couldn't have moved faster, because it might have saved her life. I'm not going to live through that again, Doctor. And I shouldn't need to tell you that I will not allow my children to live through it again, either."

The doctor nodded and turned to Melissa. "Do you have any history of cancer in your family?"

Melissa glanced at Bryson, then back to the doctor. "Only my sister." She paused and sighed. "She was Bryson's first wife."

"I see," he said, his compassion seeming to deepen. "What about your mother, aunts, grandmother; is there any history of breast cancer prior to your sister's?"

"My mother was killed in a car accident. She had no sisters. I know nothing about my mother's mother. We were raised by our father's second wife."

"Well," he came to his feet, "I will go make a call personally, and see if we can get you in today. Wait here."

"Thank you, Doctor," Bryson said humbly.

The doctor nodded and walked out, closing the door behind him.

"I'm sorry about that, Melissa," Bryson said.

"I understand," she said, and her voice broke. "Really, I do." Their eyes met, and Bryson saw her chin quiver at the same time he felt his do the same. "I'm scared, Bryson," she admitted.

He put his arms around her. "I know. So am I."

At the hospital, the tests were conducted so smoothly that Bryson wondered what the doctor had told them. Little was said about it through the following week as they waited for the results. The only thing they knew for certain was that more than one tumor had been discovered in the same breast. The morning the results were expected, Bryson dreaded going to work. "You call me when you find out," he said as he kissed Melissa good-bye.

She nodded and watched him go, knowing she couldn't tell him one way or another over the phone. When he came home at the usual time, the house was quiet and he found Melissa sitting at the table, drinking a glass of lemonade. There was another glass waiting for him. He kissed Melissa and sat down. "Where are the kids?"

"Jessica took them out to dinner."

Bryson emptied the glass with little effort, then tapped it lightly on the table. Melissa knew he wanted to ask but didn't dare. She knew she should tell him but didn't want to. Unable to meet his eyes, she looked away and said, "I told her we needed some time alone."

Bryson felt his heart pound into his throat as he saw the tears pool in her eyes. He tapped the glass in his hand at a faster pace. He had almost built up the nerve to ask when she said in a quiet voice, "The tumors are malignant. It is cancer." The tapping ceased.

Melissa gathered the courage to look at him, and wasn't surprised at the hardness in his eyes. She could see his chest rise and fall, then with no warning he threw the glass across the room, where it hit the wall and shattered. Melissa whimpered and pressed a hand over her mouth. Bryson stood up so fast his chair fell over. He pushed both hands brutally through his hair and groaned from deep in his chest. Then he kicked the chair and it slid across the floor.

"Bryson!" Melissa shouted. "Calm down."

He turned his back to her and tugged at his hair. She saw his shoulders heaving, heard his labored breathing. But she couldn't begin to think what to say. While her heart filled with compassion for what he must be feeling, she was struggling with the reality of what lay ahead for her. Trying not to think about that, she put a gentle hand to his arm.

"Bryson, I understand how you feel, but—"

"Oh, no you do not!" He turned on her like a cornered animal, and she stepped back abruptly. "You have no idea how I feel, so don't try to tell me!"

Melissa subdued her anger and tried to have empathy. "Why don't you tell me how you feel, Bryson. Let's talk about it."

"I don't *want* to talk about it," he growled. "And I don't have the strength to go through this again. *I can't do it!*" He pointed a finger at her. "Do you have any idea what it was like for me?"

"Yes, Bryson, I do."

Bryson shook his head, so frustrated and angry and scared that he couldn't even begin to sort it all out. He suddenly felt as if the walls were going to close in on him, and he rushed for the door.

Melissa panicked at the thought of being alone to face this. She'd been waiting for him to come home. She needed his support. Not until he was out the door did she realize he was actually intending to leave. She ran out after him and grabbed his arm just as he was opening the car door. In an effort to avoid a scene in front of the neighbors, she said in a quiet, firm voice that caught his attention, "Don't you *dare* walk out on me, Bryson Davis. And don't you think for one minute that you can wallow in self-pity and believe that I don't know what you went through."

She could see that hardness still glazing his eyes, but she ignored it and went on. "*I* was there. I saw the pain. I held her while she cried. I held *you* while *you* cried. I did most of my crying alone in my room because I figured she didn't need to see it, and neither did you.

You're not the only one who loved her, Bryson. She was my sister long before she was your wife. So, the bottom line is this: We both went through it. We're both scared to face it again. But you took vows with me, and by heaven and earth, you are *not* going to walk out on me when I am more scared than I have ever been in my life."

Melissa sensed him softening, if only a little. She lowered her voice. "I often wondered how it all felt from Ilene's point of view. Well, let me tell you something, in the last hour I've begun to get an idea." Her voice quivered with emotion. "It's *me* they're going to cut apart, Bryson." He squeezed his eyes shut as if he could block it out. "It's *me* who has to face the months of treatment," she continued. "It's *my* hair that's going to fall out. But I'll tell you something, Bryson." She took hold of his other arm and shook him gently to make him look at her. *"I'm not going to die!"* She relaxed slightly and glanced down. "Not yet, at least. I am going to take care of you when you're eighty. I am going to be alive and well to see every one of these children baptized. I am going to send them on their missions, and I'm going to be there when they come home. I am going to be there at every wedding, and I am going to see every one of my grandchildren blessed. I won't die until that's done. *I won't!*" she finished through clenched teeth.

"How can you possibly know?" he asked, his voice edged with bitterness.

"I just know," she said with so much confidence that he almost believed her. He *wanted* to believe her. He was just so scared.

When Bryson just stood and stared at her, Melissa closed the car door and put both arms around his neck. "I'm scheduled for a mastectomy the day after tomorrow. I need to spend some time with you."

Bryson tried to comprehend what she was saying. But he felt numb. It was all like a bad dream—one that he'd dreamt before. Mechanically he put his arm around her and walked into the house. Melissa closed the door and sat on the couch, urging him to sit beside her. He knew he should say something to console her. He should apologize for the way he'd behaved. But he felt as if he had turned to stone. Something between his mind and his heart had just died.

Melissa watched Bryson as he stared at the wall. At one time it had been common for him to get lost in these deep thoughts as he'd dealt with losing Ilene. But since they had married, she'd not seen him so somber.

"Talk to me, Bryson," she insisted gently. "I need you."

"I . . . I don't know what to say."

"Say what you're feeling. If you're angry, fine. But tell me about it. Don't start throwing things and acting like a child. Just tell me about it."

Bryson met her eyes and forced his most prominent thought into words. "I can't believe God would do this to us—again."

"God is bound by natural laws, Bryson. This is not some kind of punishment. These things just happen."

"Okay, they happen," he growled, but at least he was talking. "But not twice to the same family. I hope you know how I'm supposed to tell those kids that you've got the same thing that killed their mother. Because I don't think I can do it."

"I'm not going to die, Bryson."

He shot to his feet. "How can you know that?"

"I just know it. Ilene knew it was going to kill her. She told me she knew from the start. It was her time to go." Melissa stood up to face him. "It's not my time, and I know it."

"Well, I'm not sure I believe you," he said so bitterly that she couldn't hold back the tears. "I'm not sure I can sit back and just watch it happen all over again. When she was lying there dying, I swore I would never allow myself to feel so helpless again in my life. Well, I *do*! And I *hate* it!"

"As I see it," Melissa stifled a sob, "you've got two choices. You can either face up to what is happening here and help me through it, or you can leave." His eyes widened in disbelief. "I guess you've got your choice, Bryson Davis. As for me, I don't have one. Either I go into surgery and start treatments, or I *will* die."

She might as well have slapped him for the stunned look on his face. He took a step back, then sat down carefully. Melissa watched him through her tears and felt angry as the hard lines in his face deepened. How clearly she remembered his hardness toward the emotion Ilene was feeling, and Ilene's sorrow over his unwillingness to feel it. She was debating whether to hit him or throw something at him, at the risk of lowering herself to the childishness he had displayed earlier. Deciding she could do neither, she was about to get down on her knees and just beg him to stay with her, to cry with her, to help her through this.

Car doors slammed outside, and seconds later the kids came bounding through the door. Melissa turned her back and tried to gain her composure. The younger ones didn't seem to notice, but she turned to see Brandon and Jessica staring at her with obvious concern.

"Is something wrong?" Jessica asked.

Melissa glanced at Bryson, then back to Jessica. She couldn't speak without falling apart all over again, so she hurried down the hall to the bedroom where she could cry it all out.

"Dad?" Brandon drawled carefully, as if to emphasize Jessica's unanswered question.

"Yes," Bryson snapped, "something is terribly wrong. And I don't know what the hell to do about it."

Brandon and Jessica exchanged a wary glance. Their father didn't cuss unless it was *really* bad.

"Do you want me to take the kids to the mall or—"

"Just keep an eye on them, would you?" Bryson asked, coming to his feet. "And could one of you clean up the broken glass in the kitchen?" He set a hand on each of their shoulders. "I'm going to try to talk to her, and then I think we're going to need a little family meeting."

"Okay," Jessica said tensely.

Bryson found the bedroom door locked, and what little control he'd gained over his anger quickly fled. "Open the door, Lissa," he shouted. She didn't respond. He went through the bathroom, but it too was locked. "Open this door and talk to me!" he demanded.

"Why should I talk to you?" she called back. "Give me one good reason!"

All the hurt and the fear and the anger washed over him in a violent torrent. Bryson knew he could find something to spring the lock, and he knew his emotions were out of control. But he didn't think twice before he took hold of the door frame for leverage, lifted one foot, and broke the lock beneath his boot. Melissa gasped and recoiled toward the headboard as he bounded into the room and almost hurled himself toward her.

"You want one good reason?" he snarled. Kneeling in front of her, he took hold of her arms and almost shook her. "I'm your husband, and like it or not, we're in this together. You should know me better than to think I could possibly turn my back and walk away from this. But I *don't* have to like it."

"Nobody said you had to like it, Bryson. But that doesn't give you the right to treat me as if I've done something to hurt you. I didn't ask for this. I don't know why it happened, and I don't know how. But I'm terrified. And I will not spend the next several months of my life feeling guilty because you don't want to face this again. When I exchanged vows with you, there were no clauses in the agreement. It's forever, and it's for everything. *Even this!* So be scared. I'm scared, too. Be hurt and afraid and sad. But don't think for one moment that you're the only one hurting. We're struggling for the same reasons, Bryson. We're in it together. I need you. But I don't need you to retreat into your shell and put up that hard, cold look. Ilene *hated* that. She was too sweet to tell you, but she told *me*." Bryson's expression softened, along with his grip on her arms. "One of the last coherent things she said to me was, 'Why does he never cry?' She couldn't understand how you could be so close to all of it and never allow yourself to *feel* it. Well, I didn't understand it either. I am absolutely certain that I am going to do a lot of crying in the next few months, Bryson Davis. But I'm not going to cry alone. So either cry with me, or go wallow somewhere by yourself, because I'm not going to live with that hard, cold man you were before I married you. The Bryson Davis I fell in love with is a man who is willing to admit he has feelings and show them. So, show them or leave me in peace!"

Bryson let go of her and sat back on the bed. He felt suddenly weak as he realized she was right. Why did she always have to be so blasted right? As the memories mingled with his fears, he felt as if his head might burst. He wrapped his arms up over it and groaned. He felt the emotion welling up and realized that the old feelings had brought with them the old habits, telling him to force the pain back down where he wouldn't feel it. He felt Melissa's hands on his shoulders, and willed the knot in his throat to come forward before he was tempted to swallow it. He choked out a stilted sob, and Melissa pulled him close.

"It's okay," she said gently. "Just let it out."

As if her permission was all he needed to break the final barrier, the tears sprang forth. Bryson grabbed onto Melissa and held her as if he might never be able to again. She lay back on the bed and he curled up beside her, crying like he hadn't since Ilene died. He lost track of the time that he held her, oblivious to anything but his emotion. A desperation crept into his sobs and he held her tighter. When crying alone just wasn't enough, he pressed his mouth over hers and kissed her as if he could somehow feed his life into her and prevent this horrible thing from happening. A helpless passion quickly consumed him, but it didn't counteract the emotion even slightly. His tears fell over her face, mingling with hers as he kissed her harder, fumbling awkwardly between his desire and the pain.

"I won't let you die," he uttered as they became one. "I won't. I won't!"

Melissa sobbed and pulled him closer, knowing in her heart that a part of him believed she would die, in spite of anything he could do to stop it.

The emotion and the passion subsided together into a stillness that was almost eerie—like the calm that followed a tremor of the earth, but preceded the threatening quake.

"I'm sorry, Melissa," Bryson whispered when the room had become completely dark. "I thought I had dealt with all those memories. I thought I had grown above it. I was wrong—again. Whatever comes of this, I *will* be there. I *will!*"

"I know," she whispered, pressing her lips to his brow.

"It's getting late. I told Jess and Brandon we needed to talk to the kids. I think we'd better do it."

Melissa reluctantly moved from his side and reached for the lamp. While she looked around for her clothes, she caught Bryson watching her. The sadness in his eyes left little doubt that he was thinking how this surgery would change her. She wished then that she could somehow talk to Ilene. She had so many questions, so many things she wanted to know. How had Bryson reacted after the surgery? What kind of changes would this bring into their relationship?

"You'd better get dressed," she said, turning her back to do the same. Trying not to think too much about any of this, Melissa concentrated on the beauty of what they had just shared, hoping it would be that way again—someday.

Bryson emerged first from the bedroom. He found Jessica and Brandon sitting at opposite ends of the couch in the family room, obviously distressed. Greg and Amber were on the floor, playing war with a deck of Uno cards. Jamie was reading. All eyes turned toward their father as he descended the stairs but hesitated at the bottom, holding onto the railing as if it might save him.

"We put Steven and Heather to bed," Jessica said. "They're a little young to care about such things, anyway."

"Thank heaven for that," Bryson said to himself, then more loudly, "Thanks for your help—both of you."

"No problem," Brandon said, and Bryson knew they sensed something was terribly wrong. Brandon was rarely so willing to help.

Melissa took hold of Bryson's arm before he realized she was there. He met her eyes and wished they could just turn around and go back to the bedroom, that they could hide in their love for each other and just forget about facing this. But he knew it had to be done, and if nothing else, her presence gave him courage.

As Melissa and Bryson sat on the other couch, Brandon nudged Greg with his foot. He passed it along, and all five children turned their attention to their parents. Bryson didn't realize his hands were trembling until Melissa took them both into hers and they became still.

"Uh . . ." he began, then nothing more came out.

"Do you want me to tell them?" Melissa asked quietly, but he shook his head.

"Uh . . . your mother has . . ." He hesitated again at the irony. Melissa was not their real mother. They were all aware of the fact, but it had never seemed to matter; they had called her mother for many years. While he was trying to think how to explain this, he didn't know how to distinguish between Melissa and Ilene.

Bryson pushed a hand through his hair and chuckled to avoid

crying. "You know that Melissa has been a mother to you ever since your real mother died. That's why what I have to tell you is not going to be easy for any of us." He chuckled again. "Least of all, me. As you can see, I'm not handling this very well at all."

Bryson glanced around at the children. Jessica already had tears in her eyes. Of all the kids, she had been closest to Ilene, and she was closest to Melissa.

"Well . . ." he tried again, "your mother—Melissa—has got to have surgery the day after tomorrow."

"What kind of surgery?" Jessica demanded.

Bryson met Melissa's eyes and knew that she would tell them if he wanted her to. But he was the patriarch of this family. It was his place to tell them. "Well, Jess," he said directly to her, "she has breast cancer."

Jessica shook her head slowly and clamped a hand over her mouth.

"What's that?" Jamie asked, and Bryson couldn't hold back the tears. Jamie barely remembered her mother, but the ordeal had still left deep impressions on her young mind.

"It's what Mom died of," Brandon said tonelessly.

After a length of silence, Amber asked, "Are you going to die, too?"

"No," Melissa said firmly, "I'm not."

Bryson turned to her, a hint of hardness seeping back into his eyes. "Don't make them promises you can't keep." Before Melissa had a chance to explain her feelings to the children, Bryson turned to them and said in a shaky voice, "We don't know yet how bad it is. We're just going to have to work together to get through it, and pray that she'll be all right."

Bryson's emotion gained momentum and he felt briefly embarrassed to be crying like this in front of his children, until he realized they were all crying, too. Even Brandon, sixteen and taller than his father, was wiping helplessly at his tears.

Trying to remain somewhat rational, Bryson went over the changes that would have to be made while Melissa recovered from surgery and underwent chemotherapy. Brandon, Jessica, and Greg worked out a schedule where they could each take shifts watching the little ones and helping around the house. If nothing else, Bryson felt some peace in realizing how capable and willing his children were.

Jessica suggested that they fast together on Melissa's behalf, and on the day of the surgery she would make arrangements to be with her father so he wouldn't be waiting alone. Brandon volunteered to stay with the kids through the day, declaring he wasn't about to try concentrating in school under the circumstances.

"We have a wonderful family," Melissa said to Bryson, squeezing his hand tightly.

He nodded in agreement, but couldn't speak. He was wondering if he could bear seeing his family torn apart all over again.

CHAPTER FOURTEEN

While Melissa spent some time with each of the children individually before they went to sleep, Bryson called his father. With Lindy on the extension, Bryson told them what was happening. He talked and cried for nearly an hour, and eagerly accepted their offer to come the following day and offer support in person.

It was nearly midnight before Bryson finally crawled into bed. He found Melissa crying silent tears, and wished he could think of something to say that might offer comfort or hope—for himself as much as for her. But he could only cry with her. They held each other and wept until the tears gradually dissipated into a numb, silent shock.

Melissa finally broke the stillness. "There are so many things I wish I could ask Ilene—things I wish I would have asked when she was alive."

Bryson said nothing, and she wondered if he was asleep. But she only moved slightly and he pressed his lips to her face with a kiss that mingled love and desperation.

"Bryson," she said, and he made a noise to indicate he was listening, "before the surgery, I need you to give me a blessing." Bryson sat up so abruptly it startled her. "What's wrong?" she questioned gently, sitting beside him.

Bryson pressed a hand to his chest, trying to gain control over the tangible pain pounding there. How could he explain the fear that assaulted him at the very thought of giving her a blessing under these circumstances?

"Bryson, what is it?" she pressed when his only response was labored breathing.

"I . . . I don't know if I can," he replied hoarsely. Melissa was so stunned that she didn't know what to say. She was grateful when he went on to clarify his feelings. "There were several times through Ilene's ordeal that she asked for priesthood blessings." His voice broke and he rubbed a hand over his face. "Every time I put my hands on her head, trying with everything I had to feel the Spirit and say what God wanted me to say, I . . . I . . ."

Bryson's emotion overcame him and Melissa urged his head to her shoulder, stroking her fingers through his hair. "It's okay to cry, Bryse. Go ahead and cry."

With some of the emotion released, Bryson drew a deep breath and attempted to explain. "I wanted with all my heart and soul to tell her that she would be healed, that she would live, but . . ." He pulled Melissa closer and choked back a sob. "But the words just wouldn't come. I knew it was her time to go. The scriptures tell us if someone is appointed to death, they cannot be healed. But it was just so hard to accept it, to face it, and I . . ." He took Melissa by the shoulders and looked into her face. In spite of the darkness, he could see her emotion. "I'm scared, Melissa. What if the words that come to me are . . ." He couldn't finish, but he felt sure Melissa knew what he meant.

"We have to accept the Lord's will, Bryson, whatever it may be."

"That's what scares me," he admitted. "If the Lord's will is to take you away from us, I'm not certain I can bear it."

"You can bear whatever you have to, Bryson." She eased him closer and kissed his face. "I believe you're a lot stronger than you think you are."

Bryson only shook his head and cried. He felt anything but strong. To his very core, he felt nothing but just plain scared.

Nothing more was said about the blessing before Bryson went to work. He didn't want to go, but he had some things that required his attention, and he had to tell George he needed some time off to be with Melissa. That thought alone gave him chills. It was all like reliving a bad dream. A nightmare.

While Bryson tried to concentrate and get his work in order as much as possible, he had to stop occasionally and just choke back the emotion. Late morning it finally got the better of him, and that just had to be the same minute that George Reese walked into his office. Bryson wiped a hand discreetly over his face and turned away, but he knew it was futile trying to hide the fact that he was sitting there crying like a baby.

George quietly closed the door and leaned against it. "Forgive me," he said gently. "I didn't mean to—"

"It's okay." Bryson tried to chuckle. "Better you than Stanley. He's a nice guy, but . . ."

"Is there anything you want to tell me about, Bryson?"

"Actually," Bryson took a deep breath, "you could save me the trouble of coming to tell you that I need a few days off." He swallowed hard and added, "My wife is going in for surgery tomorrow."

George's eyes narrowed, and Bryson knew he was remembering Ilene. "What kind of surgery?" he asked firmly, as if to say he wasn't going to allow Bryson to keep his problems to himself this time. And after all George had done to help Bryson, he had a right to know.

Bryson pressed his hands over his eyes but the tears leaked out anyway. "She has breast cancer."

Following a long silence, George muttered, "I can't believe it." He paused and asked, "Isn't she your first wife's sister?"

Bryson nodded but kept his face in his hands. He wished George would just leave him in peace and let him cry, but George made himself comfortable and urged him to talk. An hour later, Bryson had to admit he was grateful for George's support, and for the time he'd taken to give him a chance to vent feelings he couldn't express to Melissa.

Bryson left work in mid-afternoon with the assurance that he could take all the time he needed. He drove around for nearly an hour, trying to come to terms with this enough to give Melissa the support he knew she needed. Feeling doubtful that he could, he finally headed home, wanting only to be with her every moment possible.

* * * * *

Lynette came by early to pick up Steven and Heather for the day, giving Melissa some time to get things done and adjust to this turn in her life. But the quiet of the house became oppressive. She tried to keep herself busy, putting everything in order, but something in the back of her mind wondered how long it would be before she'd feel good enough to do any more housework at all. The aggressiveness with which she tackled her chores wouldn't squelch the memories and worries accumulating in her head. She began to wonder if her confidence in telling Bryson that she wouldn't die had been just the expression of a subconscious hope. Had she imagined those feelings? Was she simply unable to face up to the possibility of dying?

Melissa ached for Ilene. She wanted to hold her hand and talk to her endlessly of all she had been through. She envied Ilene's faith and courage, and wondered if she could handle cancer with the same dignity. Somewhere in the middle of scrubbing the kitchen floor, Melissa just sat down and cried. Then she left the job half finished and hurried to the basement, searching for a particular storage box. "Oh, Ilene," she muttered aloud as she pulled off the lid and reverently touched the scarves and hats—keepsakes she had saved because they somehow represented all that Ilene had been through, and the way she had handled it. She never would have imagined being grateful to have them for practical purposes, and she wondered how long it would be before her own hair fell out, making such things a necessity.

Feeling suddenly close to Ilene, Melissa fingered the silk scarves, talking aloud and crying to her sister for nearly an hour. She finally put the box away and went back upstairs, grateful to have the children gone so she could have this time to collect herself. She felt somehow better, instinctively knowing that Ilene was aware of her fears and would be there beside her. Still, she couldn't get rid of the little nagging doubts. She was scared, plain and simple, and prayed that Bryson would be able to get home early. She needed him.

While she finished cleaning the kitchen floor, her mind wandered to what the doctor had said. If she and Ilene both had breast cancer, then it was likely the result of something hereditary. She wished she knew more about her mother's background. Realizing such thoughts were pointless, Melissa tried to push them away. But they hovered with her until she felt certain she should call her stepmother, on the chance that she might know something—perhaps about her grandmother—that Melissa didn't know.

With determination Melissa looked up the number and dialed, half hoping there would be no answer. But her stepmother spoke a cheerful "Hello?" after the second ring.

"Hi," she replied, "this is Melissa."

"Oh, Melissa," Thelma James said sweetly, "how are you?" Melissa hurried to explain the situation before she could get too upset about it. Thelma was sympathetic and kind. But that wasn't the reason she'd called. She mentioned the doctor's questions concerning their family medical history, and asked Thelma if she knew anything at all about her grandmother.

"Well," Thelma said thoughtfully, "I believe your father told me that . . . now, let me think. Am I getting the story right? Yes, I remember now. Your mother's mother died when your mother was seven or eight, I believe. But, you know, they lived out in the middle of nowhere on a farm. She just got sick and died. Nobody ever knew why."

"Then it could have been cancer," Melissa said with a degree of confidence.

"I suppose it could have been," Thelma replied. "It's too bad there weren't any journals or records. But your mother came from a terribly poor family, and they didn't go to church or anything. Her circumstances were not good."

"I suppose I'd heard some of that," Melissa said sadly. "Actually, I hardly remember my mother."

"Her death was tragic," Thelma said. "It took your father years to get over it."

"Yes, I know," Melissa said distantly while her mind was still absorbed with curiosity over her grandmother's death. "But then, accidents happen, and—" She stopped when she heard a breathy gasp from the other end of the phone. "What's wrong?" she asked, wondering if Thelma had spilled something or hurt herself.

"I just assumed that you knew," she said with a guilty edge to her voice.

"Knew what?" Melissa asked, her heart pounding.

"It wasn't an accident, Melissa. But I was sure your father had told you and Ilene, and—"

"Told us *what?*" she asked, trying not to sound sharp.

"Your father didn't believe it was an accident, Melissa. The timing was just too coincidental."

"I don't understand."

"Two days before her *accident*, your mother was diagnosed with widespread cancer. There was nothing they could do."

Melissa groped weakly for a chair and sat down. She was so stunned she couldn't speak. She wondered briefly if it might have made a difference to Ilene—or to her—if they had known there was a family history of cancer. Would they have been more aware, more on guard? Then that same old irony came back. If Ilene had lived, Melissa would never have found happiness in her life with Bryson and the children. It didn't take much thought to realize that things happened the way they did for a reason. All of this was in God's hands, and she had to remember that. Still, the news was hard to take.

"Melissa?" Thelma said gently. "Are you all right?"

"Just . . . surprised," she finally admitted. "Like I said, I hardly remember my mother. But it helps me understand why Dad had such a hard time getting over her death."

"I think it bothered him most that she chose to take her own life and deny them even a little more time together. But on the other hand," Thelma said with empathy, "you can't blame her."

"No," Melissa said, recalling all too clearly Ilene's suffering, "you can't."

"Are you going to be okay?" Thelma asked. "Is there anything we can do?"

"No, thank you," Melissa said easily. "I'm sure I'll be fine. We'll keep you posted."

"We'll be praying for you," she said gently.

"That's what we need most," Melissa admitted.

For several minutes after she hung up the phone, Melissa stared at the wall, trying to comprehend the reality. She was almost grateful for the numbness that seemed to be shrouding her emotions. Facing up to cancer herself made it difficult to feel the full impact of what she'd just learned about her mother. Still, she was glad to know, for reasons she didn't fully understand.

When Bryson walked in, she looked up to meet his eyes. For a long moment they said nothing. Melissa felt tears welling up again and reached out a hand. Bryson took it and fell to his knees beside her, burying his face in her lap. They held each other and cried. Melissa told him the things Thelma had revealed, and he told her of George's kindness at work.

Bryson's father and Lindy arrived soon after the children got home from school. They were able to talk some feelings out as a family, and Melissa thought they had come a long way since the time they had needed Sean to help them. Yet she was glad to know that they could call on him if they needed to. Bryson's emotion was so intense that Melissa nearly felt afraid. When this had happened to Ilene, he'd been unable to cry. Now he could hardly stop. She felt it was better that he be willing to feel his emotions as opposed to burying them, but she was deeply concerned for him in a way that seemed to intensify her own fears.

When everything had calmed down somewhat, Lindy suggested that Bryson and Melissa go out to dinner. At first Bryson was reluctant, but he finally agreed that it might be good for them to get out and be alone for a while. They were about to leave when the doorbell rang. Bryson opened the door and wondered if life could get any worse.

"Hello, Mother," he said tonelessly. "Your timing is impeccable." The last time he'd seen her was soon after Heather had been born prematurely and the family was in general chaos. She had stayed only a few hours and said very little. At the moment, he was wondering how he could deal with her along with everything else.

"It's nice to see you, too, son," she said and walked in without his permission. Marie froze as Bryson closed the door. It was evident that she had not expected her ex-husband and his wife to be here. And if that weren't uncomfortable enough, it had to be obvious that something was wrong by the glum countenances worn by everyone in the room.

Melissa broke the silence with a kind, "Hello, Marie. Come in and sit down."

"Is something wrong?" Marie asked, sitting gingerly on the edge of the couch. Silence followed for several moments.

"Melissa has cancer," Bryson's father finally reported. "She's going in for a mastectomy tomorrow."

"Thank you, Robert." Marie gave him a phony smile. "You were always so good to keep me informed." She turned to Melissa and added, "I do hope it's being caught sooner than your sister's cancer was."

"We all hope the same," Melissa stated, feeling suddenly more unnerved than she had all day.

"We'll know more after the surgery," Bryson stated. "But I doubt you'll be around that long."

Marie looked offended. "I will if you'll have me," she insisted. "Surely there's something I can do to help."

Bryson cast a wary glance toward Melissa, wondering what would happen with his mother and father under the same roof—not to mention Lindy. He was relieved when Lindy said with complete acceptance, "I'm certain they could use all the support they can get, Marie. We should all be able to get along for the sake of Bryson and Melissa."

"Of course we can," Marie agreed with a smile.

Bryson felt compelled to add, "We've got all the stress we can handle, Mother. You're welcome to stay, but please don't be—"

"Don't you worry about me," Marie insisted. "I'll just help out and mind my business."

"Fine," Bryson said tersely. "Right now, Melissa and I are going out. Lynette should be bringing the little ones back soon. I trust that you can all behave and see that my children are taken care of."

"Have a good time," Lindy insisted. "And don't worry about a thing."

Bryson was glad to leave, but he couldn't help wondering what might transpire in their absence. His father and mother had never been on good terms, and it had been years since they'd even seen each other.

Melissa enjoyed their evening out, as much as it was possible under the circumstances. But she dreaded going home, knowing that she would be checked into the hospital first thing in the morning. Bryson was mostly quiet, but she couldn't deny the emotion in his eyes. It seemed that their entire relationship had been tinged with irony; and, added to the present poignancy, it seemed almost unbearable.

After sharing a nice dinner, they took a long drive. Melissa felt it was the best opportunity to bring up something she'd been thinking about. "When this is all over," she said, "I want to have reconstructive surgery."

It took Bryson a minute to figure what she meant. "What difference does it make?" he asked, as if the very idea was somehow an insult to him.

"It makes a lot of difference," she insisted.

"Not to me, it doesn't. Whatever changes you might go through, my love for you will not change."

"I'm glad to know that, Bryson. I really am. But it makes a difference to *me*. With the medical technology available, I don't have to spend the rest of my life feeling like half a woman."

Bryson had never been prone to compare Melissa and Ilene, but he couldn't keep himself from saying, "Ilene didn't feel such a thing was necessary."

"Ilene knew she was going to die."

Bryson gave her the cold glare that was becoming all too familiar. "Are you so sure you're not?" he asked.

Melissa said nothing. She only turned to look out the window, wondering if her doubts were trying to tell her something, or if they were only Satan's attempts to distract and confuse her. It wouldn't be the first time he had used her emotions against her in subtle ways that were difficult to recognize.

Bryson pushed a hand through his hair and swallowed the emotion rising in his throat. He wanted to believe she would live through this, but he didn't dare hope. He was just plain scared. Trying to distract himself with the present issue, he stated blandly, "If you want reconstructive surgery done, I will support you in it. We'll cross that bridge when we come to it."

"Thank you," she replied. "That was all I wanted to know."

The drive continued in silence, but Bryson held Melissa's hand with an unspoken desperation that made her ache. They finally returned home to find the younger children sleeping, and the older ones visiting with their grandparents. There was a definite cloud hanging over the household, but Marie seemed to be getting along well enough.

"So, now what?" Robert bellowed as they sat down in the family room with the others.

Melissa hesitated only a moment before she said, "I was hoping that you would help Bryson give me a blessing." Bryson shot his gaze to Melissa, fear showing blatantly in his eyes.

"I don't think I can do it," he said, and those blasted tears burned into his eyes again. Would they never stop?

"We understand why this is hard for you, Bryson," Lindy said gently. "After losing Ilene the way you did, it's so . . ."

She didn't finish, but Robert piped in. "Is there a problem with giving your wife a blessing, son?"

Bryson couldn't answer through his emotion. Melissa felt frustrated but didn't know how to vent it. She knew this was difficult for Bryson, and she understood why. But she needed him. She needed his strength to sustain her, and wondered how she could possibly reach him. Surely men had faced worse things and dealt with them, and she knew he could survive losing her if he had to. But at the moment she was too caught up in her own emotions to know how to confront his.

"Bryson," Melissa said gently, "I need you to help me through this. I can't do it without—"

"Oh, for crying out loud," Marie interrupted, and everyone turned toward her in astonishment. She pointed a finger at Bryson and looked directly at him. "Do you think you're the first person to live through heartache more than once in your life? My fourth husband lost three wives in twelve years—two to cancer, and one in an accident. Now, I know for a fact that your father didn't raise his sons to be wimps. Cry and hurt, fine. But stop blubbering like a baby and act like a man. Your wife needs a man to lean on, not another little boy to worry about and take care of. You're never going to find happiness sobbing about your hard luck. It was your sweet wife who told me that. She also told me that cancer is not some punishment; it's just one of those things that happens. And she told me that in spite of losing Ilene, you had a lot to be grateful for. She's still alive, Bryson Davis, so get hold of yourself and enjoy the life you've got."

Bryson was so stunned he could hardly breathe. He glanced help-lessly at the blank expressions of everyone in the room, then he stood up and walked to the bedroom. With a groan of anguish he fell to his knees beside the bed, praying with all the strength of his soul to be able to cope with this. He wanted to be embarrassed or humiliated by his mother's outburst. But the truth of it was simple: she was right. For over thirty years she had been a thorn in his side; but now, just when he needed it most, she was the one with the courage and insight to slap some sense into him.

Bryson wondered how he could be such a fool. Whether he cried all the time or not at all, it was obvious he hadn't learned the most important lesson of all. If he could trust in the Lord and endure his struggles with faith and courage, he would surely be more at peace. He thought of Ilene, the example she'd set for him, and wondered why he hadn't learned that lesson from her long before she ever became ill.

With new humility and fresh courage, Bryson begged forgiveness of the Lord and asked for the strength he needed to face this chal-lenge and help Melissa and the children through it. Not with denial and anger, as he had before, but with faith and maturity.

Bryson returned to the family room, calm and composed. He was met with a variety of concerned expressions. Refusing to let any issue so petty as his pride mar the moment, he swallowed hard and said to Marie, "Thank you, Mother. I think I needed that. I can honestly say that I'm glad you're here."

For the first time in thirty years, Bryson saw tears in his mother's eyes. He wondered what might have happened in her life to bring about this softening. But he knew it didn't matter; he was only grateful to have her with them now. His gaze shifted to Melissa and he said softly, "I'm ready to give you that blessing."

Melissa stood and moved into his embrace. He held her tightly, whispering close to her ear, "I love you, Lissa. Forgive me for—"

"It's okay," she replied close to his face, tears of gratitude brim-ming in her eyes. "I understand."

He nodded, then urged her to the chair that his father provided. Robert did the anointing, then Bryson took a deep breath and placed his hands on Melissa's head. Trying to block out everything but a desire to feel the Spirit and speak on the Lord's behalf, he said nothing for at least a minute. Then he stepped back and lifted his hands away abruptly. Melissa turned and glanced at him, concerned and uncertain. He nodded firmly, indicating that he just needed some time. A minute later, he again placed his hands on her head and cleared his throat.

As Bryson began to speak, a subtle calm settled over him. It was nothing spectacular, but undeniable nevertheless. He felt prompted to tell Melissa that her surgery would go well and she would come through without difficulty. He told her that her children, including those she had mothered since her sister's death, would be made stronger through this ordeal, but they would all come through it well. He blessed her with faith and courage, telling her that the months ahead would be difficult, but that once she had passed through the treatments she would—

Bryson stopped when the thought that appeared in his mind came as a surprise. He might have believed it was the product of his own desires, except that he'd been so absorbed in the blessing that it had been the furthest thing from his mind. He tried not to say it, wondering if his own fears were reading something into this that the Lord didn't intend to be there. But the words came again with such strength that Bryson knew he had no choice but to say them. And he was not ashamed of the tears that fell with them.

"I promise you," he continued, "that you will be healed completely of this disease, and you will live to enjoy the full maturity of your life."

Calm tears trickled down Melissa's face as the promise struck her deeply. The Spirit confirmed that what had just been said came from the Lord, and there was no doubting its truth. The blessing continued as Bryson told her that their daughters would be spared from this disease as they cared for their bodies and took appropriate precautions. She was promised that modern science and medicine would successfully see her through this, until it was in the past and she would wonder if it had ever occurred.

When the blessing was finished, Bryson embraced Melissa and they laughed and cried together, holding each other's faces, kissing each other over and over. The family shared tearful hugs all around, and Bryson couldn't believe the joy and peace he felt in contrast to his earlier feelings. How grateful he was to know that God lived and answered prayers, and life was eternal.

By the glow of several candles, Bryson made love to Melissa, feeling none of the desperation and urgency he might have expected. He knew in his heart that what lay ahead would not be easy, but they would make it through. And they had a whole lifetime before them.

Melissa marveled at the peace she felt in Bryson's arms, and wondered why she should be so blessed. They had yet to know the medical results of her surgery, but she knew that the promises in that blessing would be fulfilled. She felt it with such intensity there was no denying it. Melissa knew everything would be okay.

The surgery went smoothly, and Bryson was there when Melissa emerged from the anesthetic. He looked into her eyes and smiled, saying with conviction, "You are the most beautiful woman in the world, Melissa Davis, and I'm going to be right there, holding your hand, when you're eighty."

She smiled back and touched his face. "I love you, Bryse. Maybe I always did. Maybe that's why I didn't like to be around you all those years."

"Maybe," he smiled.

Melissa's hospital room nearly overflowed with flowers. The kids went in on a huge bouquet of spring blossoms. Robert and Lindy brought an arrangement with mums and carnations. Marie brought daisies. Some people in the ward sent a beautiful plant with pink flowers. And Bryson's company sent a large basket with a variety of plants. But they were all overshadowed by Bryson's offering as he walked into the room and handed her a bouquet of red roses, white calla lilies, and baby's breath.

As their eyes met, Melissa realized she had learned to nearly read his thoughts at times. She understood now why Ilene had been able to understand him even when he kept his feelings to himself. She held the flowers close to her face and inhaled the intriguing combination of their fragrances. How could she not remember the same flowers on Ilene's casket? And she knew he remembered, too. But he didn't have to tell her that he was giving them to her now as a declaration that such flowers would not be needed for her death, because she was going to live.

"Thank you, Bryson," she said. "They're beautiful."

"I love you, Melissa." He touched her face. "I'm grateful beyond words to know that we have a long life ahead—together. But it's still nice to know we have forever, in spite of what might happen."

"Yes," she agreed, "it's nice."

The doctor informed them that of the several lymph nodes removed, only one had microscopic evidence of cancer. Chemotherapy and radiation were recommended, but there was a great deal of hope that the disease would never come back.

"Your wife is going to be just fine, Mr. Davis," the doctor said with a grin.

"Yes," Bryson said, squeezing Melissa's hand. "I know."

Photo by Nathan Barney

About the Author

Anita Stansfield is an imaginative and prolific writer whose stories of love and romance have captivated the LDS market. *A Promise of Forever* is her fifth novel to be published by Covenant; her other best-selling titles include *First Love and Forever* (winner of the 1994-1995 Best Fiction Award from the Independent LDS Booksellers), *First Love, Second Chances, Now and Forever,* and *By Love and Grace.*

Anita has been writing since she was in high school, and her work has appeared in *Cosmopolitan* and other publications. She is an active member of the League of Utah Writers.

Anita and her husband, Vince, live with their four children in Orem, Utah.

The author enjoys hearing from her readers. You can write to her at:
P.O. Box 50795
Provo, UT 84605-0795